Also by J.McDonald

"Upon Reflection" from *The Book of Demons*
"Pis Aller" from *The Last Horizon*
"A Wake" from *The Book of the Dead*

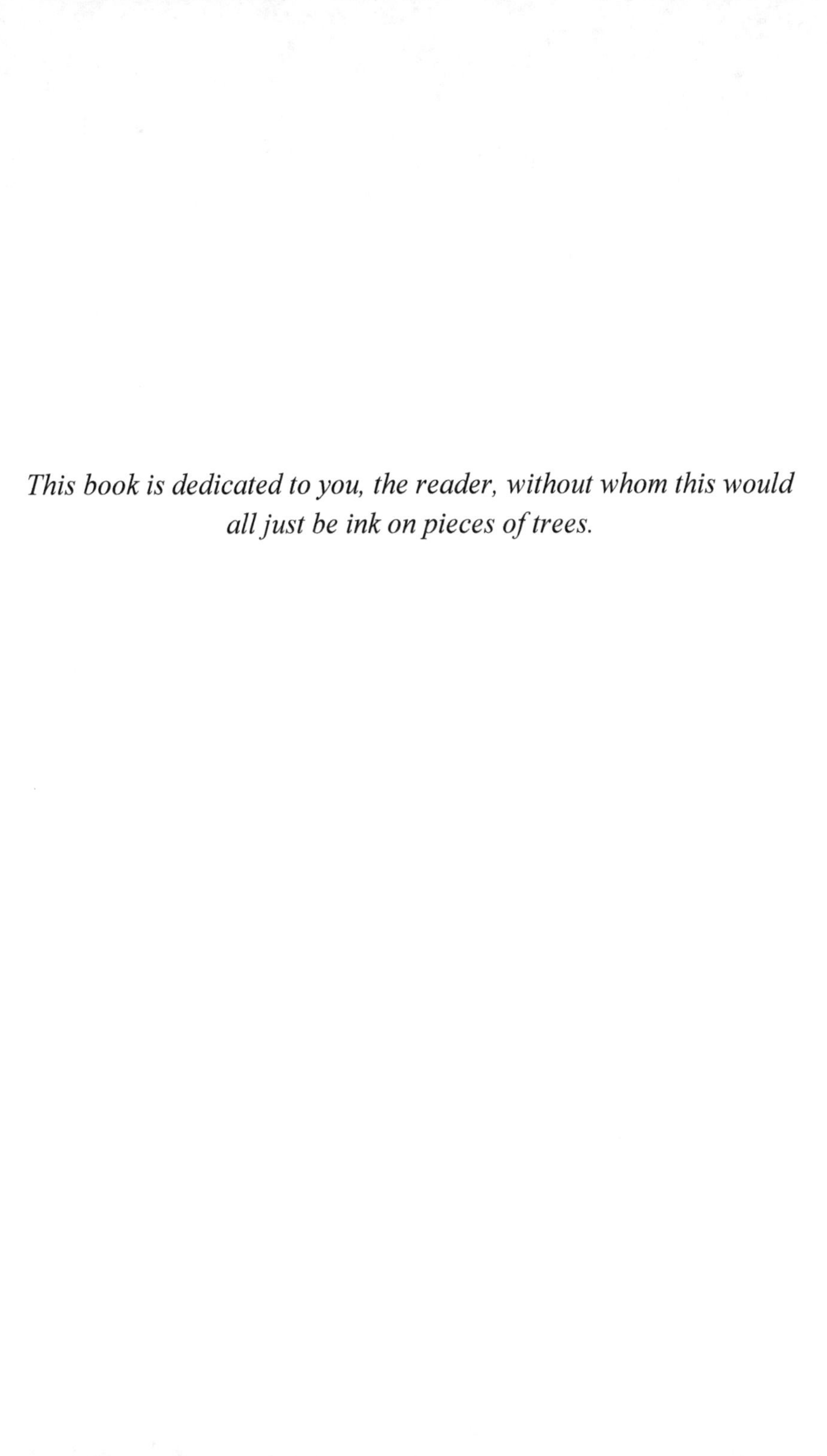

This book is dedicated to you, the reader, without whom this would all just be ink on pieces of trees.

The Pale

Diary of the Dead

J.McDonald

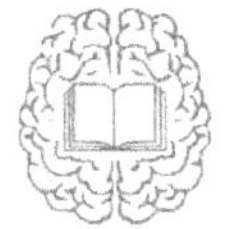

Cover design by J.McDonald
ISBN-13 (hardcover): 978-1-7381810-1-8
ISBN-13 (paperback): 978-1-7381810-0-1
ISBN-13 (ebook): 978-1-7381810-2-5

Prologue

I awoke to a dense fog. The night was dark, but I could make out some graffiti on the brick wall across from me, lit by the flickering beam of a security light above a thick metal door. Everything else was dull and misty but I seemed to be in an alleyway. I slowly stood and looked to my right in the hopes of getting my bearings. My eyes were struggling to adjust. Glancing down, my heart nearly stopped. I struggled to make sense of what I was looking at. There, at my feet, was a shadow-version of myself. Its translucent form slumped against the wall. Sweater soaked in blood. A knife buried deep in "my" stomach.

My hand trembled as I reached out to touch the shoulder of my motionless body, but my fingers passed right through it. The only sensation I felt was an almost imperceptible, dampness — like when you let your hand drift outside a car window on an early spring morning. I gasped as I jumped back, my mind struggling to process what the hell was happening. Out of habit, I ran my fingers through my hair and was relieved to discover that at least I – the me that wasn't passed out – was solid.

This wasn't the first time I'd been huddled somewhere, left battered and bleeding, but the ghostly copy of myself was a disconcerting first. As a sense of panic at the precariousness of my situation began to set in, I looked around for other people, but the alley was dark, and the fog was making it next to impossible to see. I took a deep breath and tried to force myself to focus. Slowly, an idea began to form — this was obviously a nightmare of some sort. Things were still pretty fuzzy, but I remembered being grabbed and then…what?! The fact that I was capable of wondering what was happening meant that at least my neurons were still firing. *I might be unconscious — but I* must *be alive.*

I tried to calm down a bit and focus. *Ok*, I thought, *so if I'm unconscious but bleeding out in a dark alleyway, then what can I do about it?* Calling for help wouldn't do me any good. This was a nightmare, and stopping the bleeding here wasn't going to fix my problem in reality. No, what I needed was to wake up. If I woke up, then I would be back in the real world, and I could try to figure out a plan from there. My mind began to race through a list of things that typically wake you from a dream: the phone, inconsiderate neighbours, irritating alarms. For me, it was usually that something terrifying was happening and I woke with a start. But how was I going to scare myself in a place where there didn't seem to be anything except god-damned fog?

I moved out of the alley; the mist seemed to have engulfed the entire city. I hurried through the streets looking for some way to wake up. The air around me was filled with the repulsive scent of urine and filth that permeates the most neglected parts of any city. Shrouded in the darkness and vapours were people with nowhere else to go — huddled up in doorways as litter blew about them in the slight breeze that had picked up. A sudden inexplicable aversion made me wary of reaching out to them for help.

2

I decided to venture a ways further to see if I could find a break in the haze, but the fog didn't let up. After several frantic minutes of searching, the dull glow of neon lights in the distance drew me towards potential signs of relief. A rowdy group stumbled out of a bar — four against one might be a good way to get the adrenaline pumping. I moved towards the group as they laughed and jostled each other. Hurling a few choice words to get their attention didn't get the result I was anticipating. *They didn't seem to hear me.*

As I moved closer I couldn't help but notice that they still looked cloudy and indistinct. It was weird, but I didn't have time to waste thinking about it. The foursome were now singing loudly, totally blitzed out. Figuring I wasn't loud enough to be heard over their hollering the first time, I changed tactics and reached out to tug on one guy's greasy ponytail instead. Like before with my unconscious body, my hand passed right through the disgusting strands — as if he too was made of air. Desperate to rejoin reality, I began throwing punches. Each time I tried to touch any of the drunks, my hands slipped through them with that same damp sensation.

Reluctantly, I had to admit that this clearly wasn't working. I needed to come up with another plan … but what? Since this dream world seemed to be modeled on the real one, I began running down the street in search of a landmark I would recognize. Maybe if I could figure out where I'd wandered to, I could come up with some other way to wake myself.

While I ran, I was struck by the fact that my steps lacked the wet slapping sound they should have been making on the pavement. It was eerily quiet. Belatedly, I realized that there wasn't even any sound coming out of me. By now I should have been panting like crazy. Instead, my breath came easily, regularly. The silence and lack of a natural physical response weirded me out, so I slowed my pace. It was slightly less unsettling since my brain could accept that less speed would result in less noise.

The streetlamps around me seemed barely able to penetrate the dense mist that enveloped the city, but after a few blocks, I was able to make out an old café I'd been to a couple of times. If I continued along this street a bit longer, I'd eventually come to Banting Memorial Hospital. I hated hospitals. If the goal was scaring myself, then maybe there would be something useful there. It took me another five minutes or so to make my way to the emergency room entrance. Since it already felt like I'd been in this dream world too long, I began to pick up the pace again. I didn't know how much time I had before the blood loss would be too much.

The sterile, antiseptic smell of hand sanitizer and chemical cleaners hit me as soon as I passed through the open doors. Strangely, the thick fog continued inside the hospital — despite the harsh fluorescent lighting. The ER was fairly quiet. I decided to start by seeing if I could get anyone to notice me. I walked up to the admissions desk to grab the nurse's attention. Like the people outside the bar, he looked as foggy and distorted as everything else. As the nurse continued to flip through charts, seemingly oblivious to my presence, I leaned forward over the counter and — in the process — stumbled right through it. Standing there, in the centre of a piece of furniture, I couldn't help but wonder what the rules of this surreal, dream world were.

So far, I seem to be the only solid object, no one can see or hear me, and everything is shrouded in an all-consuming haze. If this hadn't been a life-or-death situation, I might have experimented with what else I was capable of in this eerie shadow world, but I couldn't afford to get distracted. I needed to stay focused on waking up. I looked around and saw a sign for the stairwell. Maybe if I could get to the roof and jump — dreams about falling always woke me with a jolt.

I hurried down the first hallway on my left, following the signs for the stairs. I raced to the end of the hall but hesitated slightly when I reached the door. Slowly, I stretched out my hand to see if it could pass through the metal. The cool, gentle mist let my fingers slide easily into the handle and out the other side. Trying not to think about how weird this was, I quickly pushed the rest of my body through and took the first flight of stairs in several large strides. The building was seven stories high, but I never got tired or out of breath as I rushed upward. When I reached the top, I burst through the door and onto the roof.

Never being a fan of heights, it took a minute for the vertigo to pass before I could move closer to the edge. The air seemed a bit clearer up here, but the light pollution washed out the sky with the dull orange glow of the reflected streetlights. It was eerily quiet. There was the faint hum of some traffic below, but my feet made no sound as I walked across the gravel towards a low brick ledge at the corner of the roof. Cautiously, I looked down and immediately regretted it. My stomach attempted to take up residence in the soles of my feet and my vision grew dark. I stumbled backwards and tried to clear my head.

"This is insane. What the hell am I thinking?" I asked no one in particular. My voice was shaky, and my breath started to catch in my chest.

"Even if this is a dream world, how am I going to get the nerve to jump? What if it doesn't work and, instead of waking myself, I end up brain-dead?"

I didn't have time to waste being afraid. The panic began to spread through my body and my chest got tight.

STOP IT!

Suddenly I was six years old, standing in my parents' kitchen.

"STOP IT!" my mother whisper-screamed at me — her hand leaving a stinging burn as she slapped me across the cheek. "Cut that out right now or you'll wake your father."

That's right, there were worse things than heights. I took a deep breath and stepped towards the edge. Without looking down, I tried to place my foot on the low wall. It seemed to be solid. After another deep breath, I put my weight on my foot and brought myself all the way onto the ledge, staring straight ahead the whole time. The door had been vapour, but the ground was firm. *If I'm wrong, if this fall can't scare me awake, then I don't know what will happen to me — both here and in the real world. But what other options are there? How long has it been already? How much longer do I have?*

With one final breath, I closed my eyes and tilted my weight forward. Instant regret. My eyes snapped open, my arms flailed wildly, reaching for anything that might save me. I was too terrified to scream and this seemed to be doing nothing to wake me up. At least the thick fog made it hard to see the ground that was racing towards me. I closed my eyes again and decided to just wait for it to be over. It wouldn't be long now. I felt pressure building beneath me as I fell.

Am I falling in slow motion? This feels like it's taking forever. I couldn't help a quick glimpse to see how much further I had to go. To my surprise, I was already lying face down on the sidewalk, a discarded piece of gum right in front of my nose.

"Damn it! I survived but I'm still not awake. What the hell do I have to do? Jump again? Jump from higher up?"

This was bullshit. I rolled over and looked back up towards the roof. The darkness and fog only allowed me to see about a storey up. What was I going to do? If this wasn't enough to wake me, then what would be?

Defeated, I decided to make my way back to the alley. If nothing else, I would be near my body for whatever was going to happen next. The sun had begun to rise, but like the lights in the hospital, it did nothing to dispel the mist that saturated everything. A similar veil had begun to descend upon my hopes. As I shuffled along the sidewalk, pondering what my next move would be, I mindlessly kicked at a can laying in my path. My foot passed right through and I was reminded of how powerless I seemed to be in this world. The one bonus so far was that I seemed invincible, and I hadn't grown tired or hungry. At least I didn't need to worry about my more basic needs. That would let me focus on finding a way out.

Loneliness from this sudden isolation began to set in, but I'd been alone before. If there was one thing my parents had done, it was ensure that I never relied on anyone, for anything. I learned very quickly that the only person you can count on is you. I supposed that was part of how I'd ended up in this mess to begin with. When you only look out for yourself, there's never anyone to watch your back.

As I'd made my way back to the alley, the sun had risen enough that some of the bums along my route had begun to stir. Their misty forms moved slowly as they started to gather up their few belongings to face another day. One man mumbled, wondering where he had left his watch, worried that he was late for an appointment. Another grinned, a huge cat-like smile spread across his face as if he were up to no good. I picked up my pace, anxious about how defenseless my unconscious body was, willfully ignoring the fact that there was nothing I could do to defend it.

Since no one seemed able see the conscious version of me, I wasn't too worried about going back down the alleyway by myself. *I wonder if my body's still there, or if it vanished while I was gone.* Suddenly, the things I could picture someone doing to a passed out, defenceless person seemed like they might not be the worst-case scenario. If my body had dissolved into the mists of this world, I'd be trapped here forever.

I ran all the way to the end of the alley, the still rising sun not bright enough to let me see through the fog enough so that I could be sure that my body was still there. I knelt down and tried once again to touch it — *if only I could shake myself awake.* Like the can, I was met with no resistance and my hand passed through the dimly lit air that resembled me.

"I'm sorry for your loss."

Those quietly whispered words had me practically jumping out of my skin, which I guess, in a way, I already had. I turned around quickly and a small girl, probably about twelve years old, was looking down at me with a face full of pity. Not only did she seem to see me, but she was also the first thing I'd seen that didn't appear all misty. I must have looked confused because she repeated herself.

"I'm sorry for your loss."

"You can see me?" I asked, still in shock, not really taking in what she was saying.

"Yeah. I followed you here from the hospital. You looked lost … and now I see why."

"What do you mean? What are you talking about? Why do you look normal?"

Her eyes were soft and her thin lips formed a patient smile. She knelt beside me and gently placed her hand on my shoulder. I could feel its warmth through my sweater. "My name is Ava. Why don't we find somewhere a little nicer to talk?"

Her eyes darted to the blood-soaked areas of my shadow self. She was calm, but I could tell that she didn't want to be there. "We can move to the bench across the street. It's not too far away." she suggested, gesturing behind her.

I stood up and followed her as she led the way out of the alley. Ava had taken my hand like I was a child who needed help crossing the street. I didn't resist — it was the first thing I had really touched in hours. The gentle firmness of her grasp was comforting and felt like a life raft in this sea of anesthetic fog. She was small with dark brown hair braided into pigtails that went to her shoulders. She wore a denim jacket with flowers on it and acid-washed jeans. Her sneakers were fire engine red, and her striped t-shirt looked like a rainbow. The bright colours of her clothing contrasted nicely with the darkness of her skin. She moved towards a wooden bench in front of a boarded-up old deli. It faced the alley, and I could just make out the entrance where the sun had begun to illuminate it.

Ava sat down and patted the spot next to her, indicating that I should do the same. I didn't, partially because I didn't want to, and partially because I didn't know how. Everything else I'd encountered was as solid as a cloud. I didn't feel like falling on my ass and looking like an idiot.

"What's going on here? What is this place?" I snapped. My harshness didn't seem to faze her.

In the same calm and gentle tone she'd used before, she said, "This is the Pale."

"And what the hell is that?"

She paused for a moment and tried to take my hand again. I jerked it away and stared her down. I was done being patient.

The kindness didn't leave her face, if anything, it deepened. She returned my stare with a gaze full of compassion. Then she spoke very quietly, as you might when trying to reassure a frightened animal, "The Pale is where some people go when they die."

Ice ran through my veins. I wanted to laugh in her face and storm off, but everything I'd experienced in the last few hours hinted she was telling the truth. *But she* has to *be wrong. I'm just unconscious, I've lost a lot of blood, but I'll pull through this. If I can keep her talking then maybe she'll give me some idea of how to get out of here.*

"What do you mean some people?"

"Not everyone who passes away comes to the Pale. I'm not entirely sure what the rules are, but I know that those who choose to end their lives don't come here."

"Why?"

"I don't know. I've only been here a little while. There are others who've been here longer, but no one seems to know much about why or how we get here."

Without thinking about it, I sat down. My body wasn't tired, but I was having trouble processing what was going on and suddenly felt like gravity had been magnified. *If Ava is right, then there might be no going back. I could be trapped here. But I'm not giving up that easily, there* must *be a way out.*

"Does anyone ever show up who isn't dead, maybe just unconscious?"

"Not that I've seen. I'm sorry." Her eyes dropped to the ground as she said this. We sat there in silence for a long time. Not once did she try to cheer me up or make me talk. Ava was patient and seemed content to just keep me company while I contemplated this possible reality.

"My name's Alex," I said with an attempt at a less aggressive tone.

"It's nice to meet you, Alex. I'm sorry that it looks like your trip here was … unpleasant."

A harsh laugh escaped my lips. Yeah, that was one way to put it. I'd bled out in an alley. Completely alone. Never to be missed.

A dark figure suddenly blocked my vision and the pain of the stab wound shot through my stomach. I grabbed at his arms, struggling to keep myself upright. His free hand wrapped across my mouth. I still tried to call out for help, but it was growing difficult to stay awake.

A gentle touch on my arm snapped me back to reality as I struggled to shake off the memory.

"Is there anything I can do?" she asked.

Ava's question cleared away the remainder of my flashback, causing the memory to evapourate almost as quickly as it had descended.

"I want to wait for someone to find my body. I'm sure it will be a while. You don't need to hang around." This would buy me some time to think. *There still has to be a way out of this mess, and if I am trapped here, how am I supposed to pay back the monster that did this to me? As much as I appreciate having someone who knows I still exist, I'm sure she's had enough of the way I've been treating her. She's probably trying to figure out a polite way to ditch me.*

"I'll wait with you," she said.

"Have it your way." *I guess I'm not going to get rid of her as easily as I'd thought.*

We continued to sit there for the next few hours. It was hard for me to concentrate. There *had* to be another explanation for what was happening. Ava's silent vigil by my side actually turned out to be kinda nice. She didn't seem to want anything from me, and she never tried to move me along.

The street had gotten busy, but my body had continued to go unnoticed. By about noon the sun lit the passageway all the way to the back. I too had slowly drifted closer, not able to look away from the pathetic mess I'd become. Even though it was now fully visible, I knew why no one had seen my body. Everyone kept their eyes forward, not wanting to see or think about the kinds of people who would take refuge in an alley, not wanting to notice those less fortunate than themselves because they wanted to pretend ignorance. A pair of beat cops doing their rounds eventually spotted me. Neither of them looked fazed. They'd probably seen their fair share of violence in this area. I followed them to the back and the woman bent to check my pulse. She shook her head to her partner, and he called it in. They searched my pockets for ID, but anything of value would be gone by now. It looked like I'd already been picked clean while I was running around the Pale. When I'd returned from my failed attempt to wake up, I'd noticed that my shoes were gone. The rest didn't come as a surprise. It seemed I was destined to be another nameless victim of the city's growing crime problem. I continued to watch them as they sorted through the refuse looking for evidence, but they weren't turning up much.

It looked like I might have to admit that it was too late. *At least my body isn't going to just sit here — hunched over and rotting.* But that wasn't good enough. *No one will come to identify me, no one will mourn me. No one will avenge me.*

Ava had continued to wait back by the bench, although she was standing now. I stood frozen in place as my grim reality descended upon me — but a pity party wouldn't get me anywhere. I needed a plan. To form a plan, I needed information. Luckily Ava hadn't been so easy to get rid of and seemed like the type who was eager to help. While I circled the alley to have another look around for clues as to who might have killed me, she came over and hovered near the opening. Without bothering to turn and face her, I decided to try to get some more information out of Ava.

"You said only some people end up here. You must have a theory as to why we've gotten trapped in this nothing land."

"Well, it could be because we've left something unfinished, some mission we haven't accomplished."

"Then why are you here? It doesn't seem like you'd have been alive long enough to even start anything, let alone leave something incomplete."

She smiled a little. "Maybe that means I have many things to achieve before my time here is done."

I guess she had me there, but this all seemed a little flimsy. I didn't see much point in continuing to discuss theory. What I needed were hard facts.

"So how do things work around here anyway? Can we pop out of paintings or make sensual pottery with the living?"

She laughed again. It was kind of nice making her smile. "No," she said. "As far as I know, we can watch everything the living do, but they can't see or hear us. We don't need to eat, drink, or sleep, but there are limitations too."

"Like what?"

"Well, for starters, we can't touch anything from the living world. For example, if you want to pass your time reading a book, you can't flip the pages. You have to look over someone's shoulder while they read."

"I see. So, no more monster truck racing or working on my needlepoint."

"Sadly, no. Which is too bad because I'm sure you make some pretty interesting embroidery."

I gave her a sly look and she stuck her tongue out at me. Ava seemed to oscillate between sounding a hundred years old and acting like the pre-teen she was.

"Why is it so foggy?" I asked, trying to get the conversation back on track. I'd begun to feel a little claustrophobic, never able to see more than a few meters ahead, never knowing what might be hiding just out of sight. I was also quickly growing frustrated with the misty vapours of this new world that were making it difficult for me to search for clues.

"I've heard a few ideas. No one seems to know for sure. Everything we do know about the Pale is through trial and error or word of mouth. We don't have any way of recording what we learn. One possibility is that since we're no longer trapped in a physical form, we see things more like they are on an atomic level — mostly air and space."

Just then, one of the cops spilled the rank contents of someone's improvised toilet further down the alley — cutting short their cursory search for evidence. Covering their faces, they both rushed for the cleaner air of the street. It didn't look like the police would be much help. Letting out a sigh, I shook my head. *I shouldn't be surprised that, yet again, I'm on my own.*

Ava carried on — almost as if she was trying to distract me from the pitiful circumstances of my untimely end. "But as harmless as it all seems, you still need to be careful."

"What do you mean?" *What around here could possibly be dangerous?*

"If my theory is right, then we're trapped here until we wrap things up and that will be fairly hard to do since we can't interact with anything from the real world. A lot of people drift about aimlessly and their minds deteriorate pretty quickly. You either accomplish what you've left unfinished and move on … or you get trapped here forever and eventually … lose it."

Great! So, according to Professor Ava, unless I can figure out how to get outta here — and soon —I'll end up losing my mind. This isn't exactly reassuring. As far as I'm concerned, my time was cut short way sooner than was fair. Then I arrive in some kind of crappy afterlife, and I find out that the clock is already ticking. Sure, the clock was technically ticking the entire time I was alive — but no one ever bothers to think about it. In fact, we spend a good deal of time and money trying to deny the fact that we won't be around forever. Regardless, there clearly wasn't any time to waste. The longer I stood there, the colder my killer's trail would get. He was obviously my unfinished business, and I was going to do everything in my power to make sure something finished him.

1

The changing seasons made me painfully aware of the months that had slipped by without a single clue. The cops had no leads, and without anyone crying out for the capture of my killer, the case was quickly relegated to the growing stack of unsolved murders in the city. I too was losing the will to hunt him down. It just seemed impossible.

I'd begun to spend more and more of my time randomly wandering and I could feel myself growing numb. What did it really matter if I went crazy? Maybe I'd like it. Anything had to be better than this tediously endless existence of nothingness. *No. I can't think like that. If I give up, then that piece of garbage gets away with what he did.*

Clunky work boots stomp slowly down the stairs. Beady eyes catch a glimpse of me and begin to fill with contempt.

"Come here, Alex."

Instead of moving forward, I back up a step. My backwards movement triggers anger, causing a crimson wave to wash across the face that's quickly hardening into a scowl.

"When I tell you to do something, you better damn well do it!"

I turn and try to get to the back door as quickly as possible. I pass through it and, in the

memory, our yard shifts into a dimly lit street.
Mouth covered by a stinking scratchy glove,
gasping for air through my nose, I try to scream
out. This new tormentor digs the knife deeper and
pulls me further into the alley. It hurts so much
I want to vomit.

Screw that guy. He's not getting off that easily. He's going to pay for what he did. I'm so sick of bullies and dirtbags who think it's okay to hurt people.

I was fired up again, but I was out of ideas. Back in the beginning I'd asked Ava to keep an ear out for anything she might hear about my murder. She tended to spend a lot of time at the hospital and between the cops, paramedics, and newly dead, I was hopeful she would learn something about my killer. Since that night, I'd spread my time between chasing false leads and regular check-ins with Ava. *Perhaps it's time for another visit.*

I found Ava at her parents' place. They were all sitting in the backyard enjoying the sunset — the rest of her family completely oblivious to the fact that she was enjoying it with them. I didn't like coming here much. They all genuinely seemed to care about each other. It always felt like I was intruding on something private, intimate.

As a general rule, I didn't go into people's homes. I wouldn't have wanted anyone poking their nose into my business when I was alive, and the fact that I was dead didn't give me the right to intrude into theirs. Besides, you never knew what you may walk in on behind closed doors — and I didn't need to watch someone dressing their cat, binge-watching TV, or whatever else they might be up to.

Looking over at her, I was reminded of just how young and innocent Ava was. I sometimes wondered if it hadn't been for the best that she'd died so young. She'd gotten out before anything bad could spoil her naïve trust in the world. *No, that's not true. She died a slow and painful death caused by an incurable disease. Still, I think I would've preferred her life to the one I had.*

Being the only two solid beings around, it didn't take long for Ava to notice me hovering by the gate to the yard. She waved me over from her spot under a large maple tree whose leaves had just started to turn with the season. I walked over to stand by her feet, keeping my back to the happy family gathered together on the porch. Ava's gaze was focused on her folks. Her eyes reminded me of what the cross-section the tree she leaned against would probably look like, with rings that gradually shifted from gold to brown as they moved inward towards her pupil.

"Hey, stranger", she said with a smile, "What brings you here?"

Aggravated by the shittiness of the world, and existence in general, my tone was surly. "Just passing through. I thought I'd stop by to see if you'd heard anything, lately."

"No, sorry." Pity filled Ava's face, and this made me even more irritable. I didn't need pity, I needed results.

"I haven't had anything concrete to follow in forever and I can't just wait around for someone else to catch this guy." I swung my fist at the tree but, of course, this did nothing except remind me of how paralyzed this world made me feel. Ava seemed a little startled and I had to keep in mind that even though the tree wasn't solid, she was. I could hurt her, and for the first time, she seemed aware of that.

I immediately bent down to place my hand on her shoulder. I wanted to reassure her, but she flinched away a little. *I am not like those bullies. I can never be like that butcher. I need to make this right.*

"I'm sorry, Ava, I just lost my cool for a minute. I hope you know that I wasn't aiming for you."

"It's ok," she said relaxing a little, "You just surprised me, that's all." Her gaze returned to her family, perhaps avoiding making eye contact with me. "My mom always said, "When all else fails, start again." Why don't you try going back to where it all happened?" Tentatively, she looked back at me to see how her suggestion was received.

Embarrassed by my behaviour, and intent on showing her I could behave, I agreed. "I suppose it can't hurt, it's not like I've got anything to lose." *Except my mind.* I stood up and began to leave the yard.

"Going so soon? Why don't you hang out for a bit? I think my family is going to play charades and they're terrible at it. Maybe it'll be a nice change for you."

"No thanks.*" I'd rather wait in line at Service Ontario than sit here awkwardly sharing in "game night".* "There's no time like the present and the darker it gets the harder it'll be for me to see anything in the alley. Maybe another time." Before she could say anything else, I slipped through the fence and hurried down the street.

*

By the time I made my way downtown, the sun had set, and a cool autumn breeze was picking up. Most of the Vitae, my nickname for the living, had turned in for the evening. The night was dark and cloud-covered: the only lights guiding the way were the small islands created by the streetlamps that lined the sidewalks.

Appearing ahead of me in one of those islands, but still travelling further away, was a pedestrian with warm-ivory skin, chin-length black hair, and an overstuffed messenger bag, wearing jeans and a plaid shirt. She was as misty and shrouded as everything else that still existed in the real world. It looked like she was alone, and this made me a little nervous for her. As I knew from experience, this was a bad part of town and no good would come from being on your own in a neighbourhood like this.

She quickly disappeared, moving out of the light and back into the darkness. I found myself picking up my pace to close the distance between us. It was stupid really — I wouldn't be able to help her if something happened — but it would drive me crazy not knowing whether she made it home safely. My imagination could be very colourful, and it always tended toward the macabre. Suddenly, my fears didn't seem so absurd. A dark figure entered the same patch of light that she'd just left. That decided it: for my own peace of mind, I would follow her to make sure she didn't end up sharing my fate — or worse.

I had made my way closer to both of them now. My pace had quickened to a light jog. I didn't have to worry about being spotted or scaring either of them since they would be completely unaware of my presence. The gap between the man and his apparent target was now only about three meters, with me coming up in between them. He wore a black jacket with the hood pulled down over his face and his hands were in his pockets. He seemed focused on the plaid pedestrian, whom I couldn't help but picture as his inevitable victim.

She wasn't oblivious to the possible danger behind her though. Her steps had quickened from their already brisk pace. Now that I'd caught up with her I could see that she was trying to watch her back out of the corners of her large almond-shaped eyes, using the reflections in the windows of the abandoned storefronts. That was good. If she was prepared for what was likely going to happen, then maybe she would stand a fighting chance at getting out of this.

I glanced around to see if there were any signs of help or safety on the horizon. But as far as I could tell, the street was deserted. There were no other people, no open businesses, nothing she could use as a refuge. I looked back and the man had continued to gain ground despite her increased pace. She sensed that things were coming to a head. I saw her hands tighten on the strap that crossed her body. It made me wonder if she thought her only danger was being mugged.

I'd never felt the helplessness of my situation more strongly than I did right now. My inability to do *anything* to prevent this stranger from meeting the same tragic end that I had was almost painful. I couldn't tear myself away from the scene that I knew was about to play out. One way or another, it would all be over soon.

The man had now completely closed the distance and reached out to grab her — black leather gloves covered his hands even though the weather wasn't remotely cool yet. At that moment, the three of us were passing in front of the opening to an alley. With one quick movement, he dragged her into its mouth.

Only the faintest light from the streetlamps penetrated this dark hole, but I could still make out the general shapes. This mark — who I'd somehow mixed myself up with — seemed to have been more ready for what was coming than her attacker anticipated. With movements as quick as his had been, she spun around, thrust the heel of her hand up into his nose, then kneed him in the groin. I heard muffled surprise and pain escape his mouth.

He staggered backwards and made a failed attempt to keep hold of her as he crumpled to the ground.

She didn't waste any time looking behind her to assess the damage she'd done. As soon as his grasp on her was broken she took off running down the street. The man had fallen back onto the sidewalk, into the light of the streetlamp, blood streaming down his peach-coloured face, obscuring his features. In his hand was a red lanyard that must have been around the girl's neck. He seemed to be in too much pain to get up and chase his *victim* after what she'd done.

In the shock of it all, it took me a moment to realize what had happened and chase after her. The heavy load of her bag seemed to keep her from going as quickly as she wanted to, and it didn't take me long to catch up. After about a block of running, I began to hear voices. She seemed to hear them too and steered her course toward them.

Around the corner was a group of people who'd just stepped out of a bar, and I was once again flashing back to my first night in the Pale. This time was different though — she hadn't died and these people would hear her calls for help. They turned towards the sound of her black combat boots pounding against the pavement. Her breath was ragged as she tried to ask them to call the cops.

The group of people began to close around her. One woman was already dialling 911 on her phone while some of the others looked like they wanted to check out the street she'd come from. A guy asked what the girl's name was while she continued struggling for air.

"Billie," was all she was able to get out between gasps. She flung her bag onto the ground and paced a little with her hands on her hips, still trying to get control of her breathing. Billie seemed to be focused on her surroundings as she continued to glance back down the street every now and then, not ready to let her guard down. She quickly explained to the others what had happened without any hysterics, attention-seeking over-exaggerations, or even a humblebrag about putting a guy larger than her down.

The police arrived pretty quickly, and although it seemed like tonight was a victory over the barbarians of the world, it wasn't until Billie gave her statement that I discovered my devastating mistake.

"Can you describe your attacker?"

"I didn't get a good look at him, but he was about half a foot taller than me, maybe two hundred pounds, Caucasian, and he had a scar that ran along the bottom right side of his jaw. The rest of his face was covered by a hood."

It's late at night and I'm in a rush to grab some food from any place that I can find that's still open. Suddenly someone grabs at my ankle, stopping me in my tracks.

"Can you spare some change?" asks a man covered in rags, squatting against the wall.

"Take your hand off me!" I shake my leg, but his grip only tightens. He looks up at me, his face covered in filth with a long scar that cuts across his jaw.

"Take pity on me, you must have something you can give."

"I've got my own problems, now let go of me before I make you."

Like a flash, he's on his feet and pushing me into a dimly lit alley.

"I CAN'T BELIEVE IT! I had my chance, and I blew it!" I yelled every curse word I could think of at the top of my lungs. *I'd been right there and all I had to do was follow him instead!*

I tried to calm down a little. He hadn't been dressed anything like the last time I'd seen him. This time he'd been in clean dark jeans and an expensive-looking jacket. His hood had been pulled forward to hide his features. After the attack, the blood had so completely covered his face that he'd been impossible to recognize. *That's it! Blood! Hopefully, they'll find some traces of it, and I'll have some way of tracking this guy down. The police might already have a record on him.*

After they'd finished talking to Billie, one officer stayed with her while the other officer went to investigate the scene of the attack. As I followed the cop going down the street, I was sure that monster would be long gone, but a part of me held out hope that he'd still be there nursing his wounds. It was too dark and hazy for me to see much, but the cop radioed back to his partner that it was worth getting a team down to collect some evidence.

All was not lost. I now had two new leads! The cops would surely be investigating this incident and, knowing that this guy had no problem taking a life, I had my doubts that he'd leave a witness walking around. As awful as it was, I found myself hoping that he'd come looking for Billie. Between her and the police, I might actually catch him yet. Of course, I still didn't know what to do once I found him — but I could worry about that later.

Once all of the reports were completed and the formalities wrapped up, the officers offered Billie a ride home. I'd become a reasonably fast runner over the last few months, and they weren't exactly speeding. It was almost as if they were scanning the streets for her attacker on the way. It wasn't too hard to follow along and I was now unwilling to leave Billie until I could figure out where I'd be able to find her in the future. After they dropped her off, I made my way to the police station to see if I could learn anything about the evidence they'd found.

2

The cops hadn't found much. There were a few drops of blood, but it would be a couple of days before any results would be back from the lab. Other than the typical trash, there hadn't been anything else left in the alley.

I figured I couldn't just sit around the police station waiting to hear something. Instead, I decided that Billie would be my best lead. I made sure to get back to her place early the next morning so that I could catch her before she left. She was probably safe during the day, but I needed to learn her routines so that she'd be easier to find in the future.

A little while after the sun rose, Billie emerged from one of several doors at the front of a little brick quadruplex. The bottom two units were businesses — a small engine repair shop and a used bookstore called "Between the Sheets". The top two units looked like they were both apartments. Billie was dressed in the same type of clothes as she'd been wearing the night before but with the addition of a light-grey canvas jacket. Her messenger bag was slung over her shoulder. She chewed on her lip and seemed somewhat unaware of the world around her.

I'd been hanging out across the road from her building and, since she was headed in my direction, I waited for her to join me. We slowly zigzagged through the streets and made our way downtown. The entire time, Billie fidgeted with something in her pocket.

It wasn't long until she'd led us back to the same block as last night. With a determined pace, Billie marched up to the mouth of the alley. She looked around for a minute, then pulled a large, professional-looking camera from her bag. Billie snapped a few pictures, then moved in closer to take a look at the ground. *What is she doing?* I moved closer too, trying to see what she was looking at. Billie took a few more shots and I caught a quick glimpse on the screen — some dark-brown spots that were splattered on the pavement.

After a few more minutes of looking around, she let out a sigh. "There's not much here to go on, is there?" she said to herself.

"It might not be much — but it's more than I had," I answered, even though I knew she couldn't hear me.

Billie put her camera back in her bag and took a quick look at her phone. "Shit, I'm going to be late." She took off again at a brisk pace. After a few more blocks she hurried into a little café. I followed her in, unsure whether this was where she worked or not. As she placed an order, I took a look around. The air was filled with the scent of fresh-baked brownies and hot coffee. Based on the menu and the number of things it was "free" of, I figured it was a vegan joint.

After Billie had her order, half-a-dozen drinks, she left the café and immediately turned to enter the door beside the one she'd just left. Like Billie's apartment, this building had units stacked on top of each other. She rushed up the stairs and entered the only door at the top — it read "Spectrum Publishing".

When I stepped through the door it took me a minute to locate Billie. She was moving through a row of cubicles, handing out the drinks she'd bought downstairs. When she reached the end of the row, she tossed her bag on the floor, handed a drink to the guy who sat behind her and placed the last cup on her desk.

"You're a lifesaver!" the guy said while gripping the cup tightly and inhaling its scent. He had short curly brown hair, the palest skin I'd ever seen, and he wore thick, black-rimmed glasses.

"And you're over-dramatic," Billie laughed as she flopped down into her seat.

Billie's and her co-worker's desks were in the same cubicle but were facing opposite directions, so they'd have their backs to each other while they worked. On Billie's right, there was a large window that looked out onto the street we'd just left. Her side of the window was filled with plants, while her co-worker's side had a bunch of used coffee cups. Their workspaces were just as different as their window space. Billie's desk was neat and organized with a few bobbleheads for decoration. Her partner's was covered in papers, food wrappers, and a single framed picture of him and a blonde woman.

"How was your night, Jesse?" Billie asked.

Still holding his coffee close to his nose, with his eyes closed, Jesse answered, "Uneventful. I had dinner and then mindlessly scrolled through my phone until I went to sleep. How was the awards show?"

Billie frowned a little. "It was fine, but I hate covering that stuff. I'd rather be working on something that actually matters."

Once again, Billie fidgeted with the thing in her jacket pocket. Absentmindedly, she pulled it out and placed it on her desk. It was a travel-sized spray deodorant canister. *That's a weird thing to carry in your pocket.* Jesse seemed to be thinking the same thing.

"Are you planning on working up a sweat today?" he asked.

"Hardy, har, har. Pepper spray may be illegal, but it's not a crime to want to stay "daisy fresh" all day long."

"What are you talking about?"

"When you spray them in someone's eyes, they both accomplish the same thing. One's just against the law and the other isn't."

"Getting a little paranoid, are we?" Jesse's face was skeptical.

"No, just taking precautions. My night was a little more eventful than yours." She began digging through her bag. "By the way, thanks for loaning me your pass." Her eyebrows scrunched up as she continued to look for something.

"What's the matter?"

"I know I had it when I left … what happened to it?" She let out a little grunt of frustration. "Crap. I must have lost it when that guy tried to mug me."

"Wait! What? You got mugged last night? Are you ok?"

"Yeah, I'm fine. I knew it was risky cutting across Utopia Avenue at that time of night, but I was in a hurry. He didn't get anything, except maybe your pass."

"Don't worry about it, it was from the last place I worked anyway. I'm just glad you're all right. Why didn't you say anything?"

"It's not exactly the first time something like this has happened to me. My parents dragged me all over the world. The places that needed their help most usually weren't the kinds of places you'd find on a sitcom."

Her tone was still matter-of-fact, but her face had fallen into a more sombre look. Her eyes stared off into the distance.

They were a captivating mix of grey and gold — like a solar eclipse or the dying light at the event horizon of a black hole.

That explains why she was able to handle herself so well last night. I guess I'm not the only one who's been through some rough times.

Billie shook her head a little and seemed to rejoin the present moment.

"That's the stuff I should be writing about, not some stupid awards show where a bunch of wealthy bureaucrats get to pat each other on the back. I want my stories to mean something, to make a difference in the world."

"Not me. All I aspire to do is pay my bills and afford the latest phone."

Billie was not impressed by Jesse's attempt to lighten the mood. She rolled her eyes, then spun around in her chair and booted up her computer.

"Take a look at this," she said opening a spreadsheet and turning back to Jesse.

"What am I looking at?"

"I was doing some research for a side project on the use of outreach centres. One of the volunteers was telling me about how they're seeing fewer and fewer people show up, even though poverty has been on the rise. So, I did some digging. This is a list of some of the people who've either gone missing or turned up dead in the area over the past year."

Now she had *my* attention. I combed through the list of names, dates, locations, and causes of death.

"So, what?" Jesse asked.

"So… I think they're connected. All of these people went to the same centre. Some used the counselling services, some used the employment services, and some used the hot food counter, but at one point or another, they all visited this same location."

I looked at her list again. At the top of the spreadsheet was the title "New Page Centre Victims". I knew that name. I'd been there to look at the job postings a few times back when the world had still looked solid.

I'm standing in a bland, depressing foyer, staring at a bulletin board. As usual, the only jobs available are mindless, minimum-wage torments for the soul. A man walks up on my right and looks at the board, too.
"Lots of chances to start fresh, eh?"
I say nothing, I'm not here for small talk. He doesn't seem to take the hint.
"Beverage artist sounds like it could be good."
He obviously isn't going to leave me alone. As I turn to walk away, I quickly glance at the man. He's smiling at me, but the smile doesn't reach his eyes. He looks like someone playing a part, performing a role.

"I'm missing from your list!" I shouted. *I need to tell her somehow.*

Oblivious to my outburst, Jesse continued their conversation. "If it's so obvious, then why haven't the police picked up on it?"

"Because all of the victims are from vulnerable groups: street kids, homeless people, sex workers. No one cares enough about these people to see the connection. The killer is careful too. No two people have the same cause of death."

"I don't know, Billie. The ages, genders and races of these people are all different, too."

"Exactly! What better way to hide your pattern than to seemingly have no pattern at all?"

"This seems pretty thin. Are you sure you're not letting your personal feelings cloud your judgement?"

"This has nothing to do with me. People are being murdered and no one is doing anything about it!" Billie's face became indignant. "Just forget it."

She turned her back on Jesse and stared straight ahead but her eyes didn't seem to be focused on the screen in front of her. Jesse said nothing and swivelled back to his desk.

My mind was racing. *I have to find a way to talk to her. Not only does she need to know that she's missing a victim, but she also has no clue who her "random mugger" is.* Panicked, I tried tapping my fingers on her keyboard. Of course, nothing happened. Next, I walked through her desk and stood with my hands inside her computer. *Maybe I can bypass the keyboard and just make a message appear on her screen?* Nothing.

Desperate to get through to her, I yelled as loud as I could, directly into her ear, "YOU'RE IN DANGER! HE'S GOING TO KILL YOU!"

Deaf to my warning, Billie put some headphones on and began blasting heavy metal music.

Nothing is working and this is so much worse than I thought. I wasn't the casualty of some crazy person's bad temper. I was another nameless victim in a long string of people who'd been tossed aside and forgotten by society. But Billie hadn't forgotten us. I needed to warn her and do everything I could to help her catch this guy, for both our sakes.

But why her? Billie didn't seem to fit the pattern. She wasn't homeless or spending most of her time on the streets, which was probably why she hadn't made the connection between what happened last night and the people on her spreadsheet. *Why would he break from his routine to go after her?*

I needed more information, and I needed a way to communicate with Billie. But I didn't have many resources. Ava was the only person I'd spent any time with. She wasn't much, but she was all I had. Ava said we couldn't interact with the Vitae, but there *had* to be a way. There weren't several millennia's worth of ghost lore for nothing. *Maybe if I'd spent more time talking to people in the Pale, I'd have more guidance than a twelve-year-old kid.* Once again, doing everything on my own wasn't helping my situation.

I figured it'd be safe to leave Billie at work for the next few hours, so I took off to the hospital, hoping I wouldn't have to waste time running all over the city looking for Ava.

For once, luck was on my side. She was predictably hanging around the intensive care unit. I had a sudden dark image of Ava in a hooded black robe, standing silently with a scythe, a cold emotionless expression on her face as she waited to take the lives of those she watched over. The wail of sirens outside the hospital brought me back to reality. That vision couldn't have been further from the truth. Standing there in the same bright outfit she'd worn since the day I met her, Ava's face lit up when she saw me coming down the hall.

"Hey, Alex. I didn't expect to see you again so soon. Have you finally come to help me with the new transfers?"

"No, I have a problem and I was hoping you could help."

"What's up?"

"I finally have some information on the guy who killed me. The problem is, it looks like I'm not the only one he's killed. I need to warn someone before he can hurt anybody else."

Surprise and worry wrinkled Ava's brow. "I'm so sorry, Alex, but I don't know what you can do about it."

"There must be something. Think!"

Ava was quiet for a few minutes. The person clinging to life on the gurney beside her was restless and mumbling in his sleep. Suddenly, her eyes widened.

"Well," she said, "there is this one thing that might work."

"Let's hear it."

"It's a long shot."

Come on, I haven't got all day. "What have I got to lose?"

"My brother gets these really bad nightmares, sometimes. A little while ago I was watching him sleep, and even though I knew he wouldn't feel it, I bent down to kiss his forehead, you know, just to let him know he was safe, that he wasn't alone."

"And …"

"And as I bent down, I thought I heard him say something, so I turned my ear closer to listen. As I turned, my head passed through his. I saw these images and flashes of light. At first, I was startled and jumped back, but after a minute I tried lowering my head again."

Come on, come on, come on. Get to it already.

"This time I laid my head fully inside his and I couldn't believe what I saw. I was in his nightmare. And it wasn't like here in the Pale where everything is so dull and hard to see. It was like being back in the living world. It was bright and real."

"But I don't see how eavesdropping on people's dreams is going to help me, Ava."

"I'm getting to that. I was so upset by what I saw that I wished I could take him away, take him to the treehouse in our backyard, and then suddenly that's where we were in the dream."

"Interesting."

"It won't be easy … but maybe you can figure out a way to show someone who this guy is."

"Why would I have to show them? Couldn't I just tell them?"

"No. I've tried talking to my brother. He doesn't seem to be able to see or hear me. All I can do is change the setting of his dreams, make them a little more pleasant."

It isn't what I'd hoped for, but it's better than nothing.

"Thanks, Ava. I'll have to give that a try." I turned to leave, but Ava stopped me.

"Aren't you going to stay for a little while?"

She looked so innocent and hopeful. I began to feel bad about constantly ditching her the second I had what I needed.

"No, I've gotta run. I'll see you around, though." I ran out before this newfound guilt could distract me from everything I needed to figure out. The trip from Billie's work to the hospital had taken longer than I'd thought, and I still needed to make it back before she left. I was already starting to feel anxious about being away from her. I'd begun to imagine Billie leaving early or going out on an assignment and disappearing forever. Without knowing her routines, I stood a greater chance of losing track of her, and I didn't want that murderer catching up with Billie before I could.

Running along the streets, I tried to force the noisy symphony of the city to fade so that I could concentrate. A lot had happened in the last day or so and I needed to start thinking about the long game.

Problem #1: My killer is on the loose and I don't know where to find him.

Problem #2: Billie needs to be warned, but I can't talk to her.

Problem #3: I need to figure out what I can do about this monster when I eventually find him.

Problem #4: I don't know how long I have before the Pale makes me lose my grip on reality.

Unfortunately, I didn't have any clear solutions. I needed to concentrate on what I could do. It seemed my only option, for now, was to stick with Billie and try out this dream walking thing. *How the hell am I going to make a setting that says, "You're being targeted by a serial killer!"?* Key scenes from a few movies popped into my head. *I wonder if she's a film buff.*

It wasn't much, but at least it was a plan. Tonight, I would break my rule and follow Billie into her apartment. Once she fell asleep, I would try my best to warn her.

3

Billie's walk home was uneventful. She'd continued to fidget with the deodorant canister, and she'd chosen a route that bypassed the alley. When we arrived at her place I expected her to head in but, instead, she went through the door beside the one she'd used last night. It led to the used bookstore. The bell on the door clattered to announce her entrance. I followed closely behind her.

"Hey, Al, it's me," she shouted towards the back of the store.

Just then, a balding man with skin the colour of desert sand, and tiny glasses perched on the edge of his prominent nose, poked his head out of an office in the back. "Great! You're just in time," he responded with a warm smile.

"Oh really? For what?"

"We ordered dinner and we're not taking no for an answer. You spend too much time alone, up there."

Billie looked embarrassed and quickly changed the subject. "I've actually got plans. Sorry, I'll have to take a rain cheque. I just wanted to return the novel I borrowed." She pulled an old cloth-bound volume out of her bag and placed it on the counter next to an ancient-looking cash register. The smell of musty books was taking me back to my childhood again. Whenever the weather wasn't nice enough to be outside, I'd spent the bulk of my time in the public library.

"What have you got there little one?"

"It's called *Brave New World*," I replied, eyeing the old woman suspiciously.

"I think you're a bit young for that. Why don't you try something from the children's section? They have some very fine picture books."

"Why don't *you* mind your own beeswax?"

She let out a huff, "Well, I never!"

She turned on her heel and left me to my tale. Some kids in the stacks next to me snickered but were quickly shushed by their mother, who gave me a dirty look.

Who cares? They're no one to me, and she sure ain't my mother … not that she seems like a bad one.

When I was older and had exhausted the local library's resources, I moved on to the library at the University. I quickly discovered that, if you played your cards right, it wasn't just the libraries that were open to the public. Just about anyone could sit in on a lecture if the hall was large enough. The professors had no idea who belonged there and, frankly, didn't seem to care. I may not have gotten an expensive piece of paper, but I certainly got an education.

The title of the book Billie had placed on the counter was hard to make out since the writing was faded, and the haze of the Pale didn't exactly sharpen my vision.

"How about next week then? We may need to take you up on your offer to help. The website's coming along slowly. It's taking forever to catalogue everything we've got in here."

"Sure thing. It's the least I can do considering the unrestricted access you give me."

That's interesting. I wonder what kind of stuff she likes to read. Maybe I know some of it, not that it matters. She's just a lead.

Billie turned, aiming for the door. "Just let me know when you want help, and I'll pop down." With that, she was back on the sidewalk, digging for something in her bag. She pulled out her keys and opened the entrance next door very carefully. Billie tiptoed up the stairs like she was trying not to make any noise.

That's a weird way to enter your home. Since dropping in on her dreams would be pretty hard to do from outside, I broke my rule and followed her up the stairs. Billie's ascent was slow. She seemed to pick her footing carefully. When she made it to the top, I noticed there were more stairs on the other side of the landing that descended to a back entrance. Billie turned to her right and quietly opened the door of her apartment. She crept through the opening, then gently eased the door shut and clicked the lock. *She's certainly going out of her way just to avoid a dinner invitation. I guess she didn't think the free food would be worth listening to more advice about how she should be living her life.*

Billie removed her boots, dropped her bag, then went into the room on the right. She flopped onto a couch in the middle of the room without turning any lights on. Billie lay there with her eyes closed for a minute or two. The sun hadn't quite started to set, so I had enough light to see around the room. Across from the couch were a TV, gaming console, and two overflowing bookshelves. I examined the titles, but I couldn't figure out what her organizational system was. The subjects were random and included anthropology, biographies, classic literature, graphic novels, and a bunch of books that weren't even in English.

Tucked into the left-hand corner was a closet with bi-fold doors that stood open. Inside the closet was a pile of stuff that varied from tools to climbing harnesses, to a large black case about the size of a small child. Behind the couch that Billie was laying on was an electric drum kit, and a wall of even more bookshelves.

While I stood there surveying things, a large fluffy calico cat came into the room and hopped up onto the couch at Billie's feet. The cat slowly made its way along the back of the couch, then down the arm on the opposite side, until it was beside Billie's head. It began treading its paws in her hair.

"Hey, Taco," Billie said without opening her eyes. "How was your day?"

Taco continued to matt-up Billie's hair until she finally sat up and moved the cat to her lap. They sat there in silence for a little while, seeming to just enjoy each other's company. After a minute I saw Billie repeatedly wipe her hand under her eyes. *Is she crying? I wonder what's got her down.* As if she'd heard my wondering thoughts, she spoke to Taco again. "Yeah, you know how it is, don't you? Alone up here all by yourself day after day. I really should get you some company, shouldn't I?"

If she's lonely, it must be her choice. Everyone I saw her with today seemed to like her. If anyone can understand keeping people away, I can... but look where that got me.

Billie's phone chimed, startling Taco off her lap and snapping me out of my train of thought. I hadn't realized how still and quiet the apartment had felt until that harsh electronic bell sounded. Billie pulled out her phone and unlocked the screen. The message read, "Don't forget about Sunday. I know things have been hard, but you can't let what happened to your parents rule your life. He needs you."

Billie turned her screen off and tossed the phone to the other end of the couch. *I wonder what happened to her parents. This girl becomes more of a mystery the more time I spend with her.* With a sigh, Billie got off the couch and moved back into the hallway. She finally flicked on some lights, illuminating an outdated kitchen across from the front door. The linoleum was a pattern of white and pale mint-green diamonds. The cupboards were a similar mint green, with black wrought iron handles, and the counter had a bland marble veneer. Everything was old but clean. Billie began gathering some tortillas, vegetables, and glass containers from the fridge. Everything in there was either fresh fruits and veggies or had "organic" or "plant-based" plastered across the label.

While Billie cooked, I took the opportunity to look around a little more. The apartment was very quiet except for the low hum of her fridge and the sounds of cooking. Plants filled the kitchen window. Based on the aroma hanging in the room, I guessed they were herbs, perhaps basil and dill. There weren't any decorations on the walls, but the fridge held a few pictures of people I didn't recognize. The photos were older; a little beat up around the edges. Only one had someone in it that I figured was a younger version of Billie. She was holding a baby and there was a man on her left and a woman on her right. The baby's skin was light brown, whereas Billie's and the man's were golden beige and the woman's was pale pink. All of their eyes focused on the baby instead of the camera. The man and woman were smiling but Billie's expression was harder to read. I couldn't tell what she thought of the little bundle she was holding.

The cat, inexplicably named Taco, came in and began winding itself around Billie's ankles.

"You hungry too?"

Taco answered in the affirmative and Billie peeled open a can of food. She took both their plates back out to the living room. The smell of Taco's cat food mixed unpleasantly with the fragrant odour of Billie's falafel wrap. Billie seemed to spot her phone where she'd left it. Her mouth puckered and her eyebrows scrunched in towards each other.

"What do you think?", Billie asked Taco, who'd already practically inhaled the cat food. "Mom and Dad are dead. Shouldn't I be entitled to become a grumpy old hermit and hide out in my apartment?"

The only response that Taco could offer was to scamper over to Billie and immediately plop down on her lap. Absentmindedly, she began to stroke the cat.

"Yeah, I guess you're right. It's selfish and I'm not being fair to Sam."

That seemed to be the end of the one-sided conversation. Yet again, I'd learned something new that only resulted in more questions: *How did her parents die? Who is Sam and what does he want? Who was the baby in the picture? Why do I care?*

Billie turned on some old black and white film and began picking at her dinner. She seemed more lost in thought than focused on the movie or her food. As time passed, her features relaxed and her eyes started looking a little droopy. It wasn't long before she was passed out on the couch, fast asleep, with Taco curled up on her lap.

Ok, this is what I've been waiting for. Given the limited means of communication I had available, the best I could come up with was to hope that Billie was familiar with movies about serial killers. Maybe if I filled her dreams with human monsters, she'd realize the danger she was in.

I moved towards her. Standing behind Billie, I hesitated. *This feels wrong. It's bad enough that I'm walking around in her apartment, let alone literally nosing around in her head. But what other choice do I have?*

Just then, Billie's face scrunched itself up again. She let out a whimper and her head twitched to the side.

As if she hasn't had enough stress, she can't even catch a break when she's asleep?

I tried to remember what Ava had told me she'd done. *All she said was that she'd laid her head in her brother's. But it can't be that easy, can it?*

Billie's head flopped back against the couch. Her mouth was open just the slightest bit. A low sob escaped from her lips and suddenly all I wanted to do was make things a little better for her. I bent down, hovering a few centimetres above her petite nose, then plunged my face into the misty space where her head was.

Disoriented, it took me a minute to get my bearings and grasp what I was seeing. For the first time in I don't know how long, I looked around at a world that seemed relatively normal. It was night and tall lights illuminated an empty, damp street. There didn't seem to be much of a world outside of the spaces lit by the lamps, but it all looked deep, rich, and solid. I heard a startled scream. It had come from behind me, and I ran towards the sound.

Not far away was a flickering light that flooded the entrance to an alley in the brief pulses when it flashed on. Another scream, this one more terrified than the last, burst from the mouth of the alley.

When I got there, I could clearly see what was happening. This time Billie hadn't won her match with the *mugger*. She was shoved against the wall. His one hand was now over her mouth and the other held a gun pressed into her stomach. His face was hidden in the depths of his hood, and he didn't seem to be demanding anything. He just stood there jamming the gun deeper and deeper into her stomach. *The attack must be bothering her more than she's been letting on.*

I ran at him at full speed, but I was as powerless here as I was in the Pale. Everything may have looked solid, but I wasn't technically a part of this dream. *Ava told me that she couldn't do anything except change the scenery.* Muffled sounds of agony escaped the hold the mugger had over Billie's mouth and I knew I needed to do something to stop her suffering. *I have to get her out of here, but where am I going to take her? It doesn't matter. Anywhere is better than here. How the hell am I supposed to do this?*

I tried to focus, to bring somewhere pleasant into my mind, but it was hard to escape the memories that were fighting for my attention. Before I could choose something, the dream started to shift. The light got brighter and walls began to form around us. Everything was decorated in muted tans and beiges. The mugger evaporated and was replaced by a table covered in white linen. On the table were two vases, each with a photograph beside it. No, not vases, urns. The people in the photos resembled the people in the picture on Billie's fridge, but they were older. *This must be her parents.*

The horror on Billie's face slowly shifted to intense sadness. Silently, tears streamed down her cheeks as she struggled to hold back sobs. Somehow, the pain on her face seemed so much worse than the fear that had held it a moment ago. *I need to think. Where can I take her to make this stop?*

Closing my eyes so that I could concentrate, I began to picture a rainforest I'd seen in a documentary. I opened my eyes, but we were still in the funeral home. Billie had fallen to her knees

44

and was hunched over, holding her sides like they might explode if she didn't grip with all her strength.

What did I do wrong? Ava made it sound so easy. Closing my eyes again, I worked harder. This time I tried to picture specific details. I imagined the fresh scent of the leaves in the hot dense air, the gentle patter of the rain as it slowly trickled down from the canopy above, and the astonishing number of shades of green that nature was capable of producing. For a minute, I swore that I could hear the distant croaking of frogs further off in the jungle.

My eyes shot open when I heard a loud gasp. Still crouched on the ground, Billie was now surrounded by a thick bed of ferns. Her hand reached out to touch one of the leaves and the pooled water in it came spilling out. A smile began to pull at the corner of her mouth. *I did it! I can't believe that worked.*

After a few minutes of enjoying the hushed tranquillity of the forest, I remembered what had brought me here in the first place. I couldn't just leave her here to enjoy a peaceful sleep. I had a job to do and putting it off wouldn't make things any easier. *She needs to be warned.*

Once again, I tried to concentrate on an image. This time I pictured stone walls, a cot, an aluminum bench, and a wall made of plexiglass with holes for air and sound to pass through. I tried to imagine the smell that would accompany being in a row of subterranean cages.

When I opened my eyes it was all there, just as I'd pictured it, but there was no one in the prison cell. I tried with all my might to conjure a man, his arms restrained, a large scar jagged across his jaw, but nothing appeared. *Ava had said she could only change the setting. Does that mean I'm restricted to just creating inanimate objects?*

Billie was looking around, her brows pinched together in confusion. She stepped closer to the plexiglass, and I tried to remember what else belonged in the cell, but it'd been years since I'd seen the movie.

Losing interest, she proceeded down the hallway and reached the gate at the end. *Maybe a prison cell was too generic. What else might she recognize?* On the other side of the gate, I quickly created a musty old basement. I filled the space with sewing mannequins and cages of butterflies. Billie didn't take much notice of these things and continued towards an open doorway. Through the door, I made a deep pit lined with stone. Billie glanced down into the pit, but it was too dark to see anything.

This isn't working. She must not know this one. She was watching a black-and-white movie when she fell asleep. Maybe I need to try something older.

Trying to recall specific details, I began to create a new environment. A monochrome scene, with a gravel road that ran alongside an old motel. One of the rooms' doors stood open with a light on inside. Billie moved towards the light and entered the room.

Following behind her, I struggled to remember how this movie went. I needed to draw her toward the bathroom. I tried mentally turning on the shower and to my surprise, it actually worked. The steam from the shower began to roll out into the bedroom. Billie drifted further in. Once she'd reached the bathroom, I played the iconic slasher music and splattered everything inside the tub with bright red blood. This startled Billie. With a shaking hand, she reached forward to pull back the shower curtain. I held my breath. I didn't know what she'd find behind it since I didn't seem to be able to create people.

But before I knew it, the scene had disappeared, and I was staring down at a couch made of mist. Billie'd woken up and was hunched forward with her head in her hands.

"I've gotta stop falling asleep with the TV on. The dreams are too weird."

That's it? After all that, she just writes it off as weird dreams? I don't know why I'd expected anything different. Why would Billie assume it'd been anything more than a dream? But I wasn't giving up that quickly. *When has anything ever been easy for me? It was just a first attempt. I'll have to come up with a new strategy and try again.*

4

I gave Billie some privacy while I worked on formulating a new plan. She moved about the apartment getting ready for bed and I hung out in her living room, pondering my options. *When you think about it logically, from her perspective, Billie would have no reason to know that there was anything special about those dreams. I need to make them more real, more personal.* In order to do that, I would have to get to know her better. The dreams I'd created were lacking details that would catch her attention, details specific to her.

But this wasn't my only issue. I was slowly beginning to realize that outside help might be necessary if I was going to find a way to warn Billie. This dream stuff was going to take time: time that Billie didn't have. Ava's limited knowledge and my minimal experience weren't enough for the monumental task I had ahead of me. As much as I hated to admit it, I was going to have to "make friends" with more people in the Pale and see what I could learn from them. My overall experiences with people had not been great. Generally, they were either judging you, using you, or pretending you didn't exist. So, I was less than thrilled at the prospect of going out and purposely making contact with anyone other than Ava.

Without any specific details for manipulating Billie's dreams, I didn't see the point in invading her privacy anymore, tonight. It was time for me to go in search of others that I could learn from. But I didn't want to be gone for long. With tomorrow being the weekend, I had no idea where to look for Billie if she left before I got back. As I passed through the door, I looked back at Billie sleepily shuffling about and hoped that she would be able to get some rest.

Although my experiment — that first night at the hospital — had taught me I could survive great falls, I still preferred to use the stairs. The idea of simply walking out Billie's living room window and dropping to the sidewalk did not appeal to me whatsoever. My fear of heights hadn't decreased with my newfound immortality.

Once I was back out on the street, the chilly night air cleared my head and helped me focus. *If I were a dead person, where would I hang out?* Unfortunately, I *was* a dead person and I never really saw other post-corporeal people in any of my usual haunts. Just like the living, we probably each had our own places we liked to be. With the elimination of material needs, I could probably rule out spots like grocery stores and coffee shops. *Maybe somewhere touristy?*

As far as I was concerned, there was nothing worth seeing in this city, but I didn't have time to travel too far away. I needed to make sure that I'd be back before Billie could leave the next morning and, even running, it still took me forever to get anywhere. The best I could come up with was the waterfront. At this time of year, it wasn't likely to draw too many visitors, but I couldn't think of anywhere else that was close enough. As it was, it would probably take me close to an hour and a half to get there.

With no time to lose, I took off for the beach. While I ran, I tried to come up with a strategy for getting the information I needed. *My story should be simple, believable, and sympathetic. I should be brand new to the Pale so that I don't have to waste time giving away information in return.* I continued to refine my backstory as I made my way through the dark, misty streets. Apart from a few motorists, I didn't pass anyone, living or otherwise.

I eventually got to the marina and followed the footpath along to the picnic area that separated the sandy shore from the parking lot. The beach was several kilometres long, but the haze of the Pale restricted my vision. I slowed down so that I'd have time to see if anyone was coming. I began a tedious zig-zag pattern, looping back and forth between the water and the walking trail.

The moon shone brightly and lit the waterfront in a fluorescent glow. Seagulls strutted across the sand, picking through the trash people had left behind. By the time I reached the end of the beach, I hadn't come across anyone other than a few Vitae who were stargazing. *Maybe Ava will know where people like us hang out. I might have to spend some time with her before I ask. She's probably getting tired of never getting anything out of this relationship.*

Just then, I heard some laughter in the distance. Looking up, I was able to make out two solid forms silhouetted against the early light of dawn. *Ok, time for my performance.*

"Help! Anyone, please!" I shouted in the most scared voice I could muster. I tried to look lost and panicked, opening my eyes wide, looking in every direction.

The two forms ran up to me. The first was a terra-cotta-skinned woman who'd probably been in her forties when she bit the dust. Her thick, dark hair ran all the way to her waist. The second figure was a man who'd probably been around seventy when he arrived in the Pale. His beard was flecked with grey, and his skin was like the night sky. When they got closer I amped up my performance and began gasping for breath as I begged for their help.

"Please, please. You have to help me. My friends are still out there. We need to get help."

"Whoa now," said the man, "slow down a minute. Tell us what happened."

"We were out in the boat, and it got dark faster than we thought it would. There were no lights, and we were trying to make our way back to shore. We hit a rock or something. Please, you have to help me. My friends must still be out in the water."

The man turned and gave a concerned look to the woman. "What is your name?" she asked with a slight accent I couldn't place.

"Alex. Please, we don't have time. They need help."

"I'm Zyanya and this is Jo," she said gesturing to herself and the older man. "I need you to calm down a little. What I have to tell you is not going to be easy."

"What are you talking about? We need to call someone for a rescue crew."

Jo placed his hand on my shoulder. "I'm sorry, my friend, but that isn't the type of help you need anymore." I made my face look confused and waited for one of them to continue. They slowly walked me through the fact that I was dead and that there was nothing I could do for my friends now. If I was lucky, they'd survived, and if I wasn't, then I might be able to find them around here soon.

I quickly started to regret creating a lie that made me so new to the Pale. I hadn't thought about the fact that it would take time to realistically fake acceptance of my fate. The sun was already rising, and I hadn't gotten anything useful out of them yet.

After about as much time as I could stand, I started to dig for information that would be a little more helpful. "I still need to let someone know about my friends. How do we tell people that they need help?"

Zyanya frowned a little and shook her head. "I'm sorry, Alex. Your ties with the real world are gone. There is nothing we can do for them now."

I didn't have to fake my disappointment. This was not the answer I'd hoped for, but I didn't give up that easily. *Maybe I'm being too specific. An open-ended question might get me some information I can work with.*

"So, what am I supposed to do now? What *can* I do?"

Jo smiled and looked out towards the sun rising in the distance. "Now … you do whatever you want. You're free."

"Well, that isn't exactly true," Zyanya corrected.

She then went through a list of all the things I couldn't do, and these matched up with everything I already knew.

"This doesn't sound like freedom at all," I complained. "This sounds like punishment."

Jo looked at me fondly as if he was about to explain something very simple and obvious. "This existence will be what you make of it. If you let it, it can feel like a prison that forces you to look back at everything you've lost. *Or* it can be a playground of endless possibilities."

Like Ava, Jo seemed to be an optimist.

"What kind of possibilities? If I can't do anything, then what's the point?"

"We never said you can't do anything," Jo said with a knowing smile spreading across his face.

I hope I'm finally getting somewhere with these two. I don't know what time Billie gets up on weekends and I never found out if she had any plans. She could be leaving her apartment any time now.

Jo began to pace as he continued. "There's a whole wide world out there and it's yours to explore. Hop in a car and travel the country. Jump on a plane and see another continent. Take a walk into the depths of the ocean. You can see it all!"

I was about to ask him how exactly I could do all this travelling when everything is as solid as a cloud, but then I remembered that I wouldn't know that yet. According to my story, I had woken up onshore and hadn't been anywhere else. I waited for Jo to elaborate, but Zyanya cut in.

"And it's not like you need to give up everything you enjoyed when you were alive. You can go to the movies, attend concerts, you can even go out dancing if you want."

Clearly, these two had no idea how much all this sightseeing would cost them. Here they were, wasting their time clubbing. With each moment that passed, they got closer to all-consuming madness.

Speaking of time, mine was growing short. Once again, separation from Billie was causing me some anxiety and all I could think about was getting back to her. Then it hit me — a way to break away so I could get back to Billie's apartment *and* a way that I could ask how the travelling worked.

"I want to go look for my friends. You said that I could explore underwater. How am I supposed to do that? It's not like I can rent a boat and some scuba gear?"

My ignorance seemed to amuse both of them, but Jo answered my question.

"You're dead, and *that means* you don't *need* to breathe. In fact, you're not actually breathing right now. Your chest rises and falls, but that's just a subconscious habit."

I had noticed that I never got winded when I ran, but it had never occurred to me that it was because I wasn't breathing at all. And, as interesting as this was, it didn't give me any information that would help me catch a killer.

"Ok, but what about a boat to get out to where I think we were? It's not like I could swim all that way."

Zyanya answered this time. "Technically you could "swim" or walk there since you don't have muscles that get tired, but it would take a long time. You could join one of the boats leaving the marina and see if it heads in the right direction."

Again, this didn't give me any clue as to how I would keep from just falling through the boat into the water. Luckily, Zyanya continued with her explanation.

"But you must make sure to concentrate. Things work a little differently now that you are dead."

"Concentrate on what?"

"The vehicle you are riding in. I guess you would not have noticed yet, but those who have passed are the only solid things on this plane of existence. Everything else you'll see will look like a nebulous version of itself: like it's made of mist. If you're going to ride in a boat, you have to remember what it's like to walk on the deck, to stand at the bow. You must be conscious of yourself moving where it moves."

I must have looked confused. Jo tried to simplify what Zyanya was saying.

"I like to picture that my feet or my pants are glued to the vehicle. When I want to get out, I just dissolve the glue."

I mulled this over. *I guess I should have figured this out before. It's the same as me sitting on a bench or walking up the stairs. I'm not actually doing those things; I'm just picturing myself doing them. And I fell from the roof of the hospital because that's what I expected to happen.*

Although the travelling thing would come in handy, it wasn't going to bring a serial killer to justice from beyond the grave. However, the possibilities this new perspective offered definitely warranted some consideration. In the meantime, I had to ditch these two. I hoped they wouldn't find my sudden urge to be rid of them suspicious.

"Thanks, I'll remember to do that."

As I began to move towards the water, Zyanya stopped me.

"Are you leaving so quickly?"

"I really want to find my friends. I need to know what happened to them."

"We can come with you," Jo offered.

"Thanks, but I think I need some time alone. You know … to process everything."

"Suit yourself. We're grabbing a tour bus to Niagara Falls this afternoon if you want to join us."

"Ok, I'll think about it. Thanks again for your help."

And with that, I turned to step into the lake. I figured I could walk along the bottom a little ways and come out on the northern shore. The murky haziness of the Pale would hide my departure and I'd be free to drop the charade.

I struggled more than I thought I would with remembering that I didn't need to breathe while I was under the water. My instinct was to hold my breath.

The man's car careens off a bridge and plummets into a river. The water quickly rises, and he presses his face to the ceiling, trying to capture one last gulp of air before his head is completely submerged. He struggles to unclasp his seat belt and open the damaged door.

My focus on the screen is broken as my grandmother shakes my shoulder.

"Breathe, Alex," she says with a laugh. "It's not real, it's just a movie."

I take a shallow breath, but it's hard to remember that this dingy movie theatre isn't the dark depths of a river. The man kicks at the glass and eventually smashes through. His head breaks the surface of the water, and at the same time, we each fill our lungs with as much air as they can take.

I just wasn't able to wrap my brain around what it would feel like not needing to breathe. My chest grew tight and the urge to raise my head from the lake was all I could think about. *Calm down. This can't actually hurt you.* I tried to focus. If I couldn't picture what it was like to not use my lungs, then I could try something else. I thought about fish and how their gills allowed them to pull oxygen from the water. *I'm like a fish. I can get the air I need from within the lake.*

Very carefully, I opened my mouth slightly and inhaled. Nothing happened. My mouth wasn't flooded with water. I didn't begin to drown. I was fine.

Relieved, I followed the slope of the lakebed downward and moved deeper into the lake as I tried to calculate roughly where I would need to go in order to come out where I wanted.

When I'd eventually ascended the rocky revetment and breached the surface, I immediately started running towards Billie's apartment. I hadn't come out exactly where I'd hoped, and I didn't have time to experiment with any other means of travel.

My route took me by City Hall and, as I passed, I glanced at the clock. *Nine forty-five! Shit. It's even later than I thought.* I didn't know if Billie was the lounge-in-bed or early bird type of person. I wished I could move faster. *And why shouldn't I? If I was wearing rollerblades I'd be moving at a nice brisk pace.*

As I ran, I tried to change my stride as if I were on rollerblades instead of just running. It felt weird at first, but as soon as I stopped looking at my feet and focused more on what the movement would feel like, I began to glide quickly along the sidewalk. For the first time since I'd arrived in the Pale, I found myself actually enjoying the moment. This felt like the first real success I'd had in a very long time.

My euphoria didn't last long though, as I quickly remembered my reason for hurrying.

5

When I reached Billie's building, I ran up the stairs two at a time and burst through her apartment door. Everything was quiet. The kitchen and living room were empty. *Maybe she's still in bed.* Not wanting to intrude more than I already had, I'd avoided exploring the back half of Billie's apartment the night before. I was hesitant to put myself in a situation where I might walk in on anything private but, right now, I was more concerned about the fact that it looked like Billie might not be here at all.

Turning left, I hurried towards the room directly at the end of the hall. The door stood open, revealing a small bathroom with tiny black and white squares in a retro pattern that covered the floor and wrapped halfway up the walls. The sink and vanity were clear of anything except a single toothbrush, a tube of toothpaste, and some hand soap. A deep purple shower curtain was drawn partially shut, obscuring the left side of the bathtub. The air was warm and damp, with an artificial citrus scent hanging in the air. *It seems like she showered recently. Maybe I haven't missed her.*

The only place left to search was Billie's bedroom. I passed through the wall that divided the washroom and bedroom. *Empty. Dammit. Maybe there's a hint as to where she's gone somewhere around here.* Like the rest of the apartment, everything was orderly and tidy. Billie didn't seem to have many pictures or knick-knacks.

Most people's homes are cluttered and full of stuff. Billie's home, on the other hand, looked like she could pack up in a matter of minutes, except for the books.

The only furniture in here was a dresser, a night table and a bed. A white comforter covered in a variety of colourful birds was stretched neatly across the bed. The night table had more books, a small reading lamp, and a picture of Billie's parents. On the dresser was an old, ratty stuffed panda bear, a frame filled with plane tickets from around the world, and what looked like a set of wedding bands.

Not finding anything that indicated where Billie may have gone, I was about to search the rest of the apartment for a clue when I was stopped by the sound of a thunk, followed by a strange clanging noise, then some swearing, coming through the bedroom window. *That sounded like Billie!* Relief washed through me. The window was at the back of the building and looked out onto a neighbour's yard. I stuck my head out and tried to catch a glimpse of Billie. There was a narrow alleyway behind the building but all I could make out was the fence that bordered it. Just then, I heard another thunk-clang but this time it was followed by a grunt of frustration.

Hurrying down to see what was going on, I found Billie in the back alley. She was at the far end, to my right. Billie collected something from the ground, then sullenly marched her way back to the doorway where I stood. I thought that maybe she would come in but, instead, she turned to glare at the spot she'd just left.

Billie seemed to take a minute to compose herself. Closing her eyes, she took a deep breath, then opened her eyes again. Unexpectedly, her arm flew forward and I heard the same thunk as before, but this time without the clang. Before I could figure out what she was doing, her arm shot out again, resulting in another thunk. The third time her arm began to fly, I caught a glimpse of something metallic and reflective in her hand. This throw resulted in another clang and Billie growled as she stomped down to the back of the alley. Following her, I finally figured out what she was up to. She'd been throwing knives at a target, and the noise that had triggered her frustration was the only knife that hadn't found its mark and had, instead, tumbled to the concrete.

She collected the blades and made her way back to the doorway to try again. *What the hell? Who actually keeps a set of throwing knives around? I thought that was just something spies in movies had. Billie's a bit of a badass!* I was impressed. What was even more impressive was that the majority of them stuck pretty close to the centre of the target. Unfortunately, Billie seemed to focus more on the odd miss, which inevitably infuriated her.

After a few more rounds, Billie found a rhythm and the knives stopped crashing against the pavement. She looked like she was relaxing a little, but I wouldn't say that she was enjoying herself. Just then, a car pulled into the alley and Billie turned to see who it was. The car parked right at the opening, keeping its distance from Billie and blocking any other cars from being able to pull in.

Al, the shopkeeper from yesterday, stepped out of the car and held his hands up in mock surrender.

"I'm unarmed and come in peace. I just wanted to unload some boxes and then I'll be on my way."

Billie gave him a half-hearted smile. "Do you want a hand with those?"

"That would be great."

As they moved to the back of the car, I noticed Al's concerned eyes as they secretly assessed Billie when she wasn't looking.

"Is everything okay, kiddo? I haven't seen you out here abusing my fence in a while."

"I just needed to blow off some steam. I called the police station for an update this morning and they've got nothing … at least nothing they would tell me."

Crap. I wish I'd been here so that I'd know exactly what they'd said.

"I didn't really expect much since they had so little to go on, but it's still frustrating."

Their arms now filled with boxes, Billie and Al moved towards a door that must've been a back entrance to the store. Al still looked concerned.

"Unfortunately, things like this happen all the time around here. You may not get a resolution."

"I know. Don't worry about me, I'm just extra irritable this morning. I didn't get much sleep last night. What are you and Kaz up to, today?"

Al had set down his boxes and was fumbling with his keys. As he was doing that, the door swung open. A person with shoulder-length black hair that was shiny like silk, and tanned skin the shade of an acorn, held the door for Al and Billie.

"Speak of the devil! Billie was just asking about you."

"I hadn't heard any cussing for a little while so I figured it might be safe to come out and see if Billie'd finished with the alley."

Billie blushed a little. "Sorry, Kaz. I didn't realize I was being that loud. Just knock next time and I'll know to tone it down."

"Don't worry about it. I don't think any of the customers could hear you."

The three of them went inside with the boxes.

"Actually, I'm glad I ran into you. Would you mind if I borrowed your car tonight? Mine's still not out of the shop and I wanted to avoid walking home from work after the expo. It's all the way down at the amphitheatre."

"Of course. The car is yours any time you want, just ask."

"You two are the best. I'll make sure it comes back with a full tank and some of those donuts you like from the place downtown."

"In that case, you should borrow the car more often." Al gave Billie a wink and a set of keys.

After spending some time helping Kaz and Al unpack all of the boxes, Billie went back up to her apartment. We spent the day hanging out in the living room. Billie read for a while, and I joined her by reading over her shoulder. She'd just cracked open a book by Zora Neale Hurston, so I was lucky enough to get to start at the beginning.

By the time the afternoon was drawing to a close, and the light outside began to dim, Billie went to her bedroom. I guessed that she was getting ready for work, so I stayed in the living room with Taco.

I need to get a better system. Each time I leave Billie, I risk missing out on information like the call with the cops. But at the same time, I need to keep exploring the Pale so that I can figure out how to stop this monster. My newly increased travelling speed would help with this, but it wasn't enough. I would need to be more careful about the time I spent away.

While I pondered my predicament, Billie came back out to the living room.

"All right, Taco, I'm heading out for the night, and you're forbidden from throwing any wild parties while I'm gone."

Taco did not seem amused by Billie's joke. She scratched the cat under the chin, then turned to leave the apartment. I followed behind as we descended the back staircase. Al's car was still in the alley where he'd left it earlier in the day. There were no safety lights and the glow from the streetlamps barely created enough light for Billie to see, causing her to stumble over something left lying on the ground.

Passing through the door, I sat down in the front on the passenger's side. *Ok, my ass is glued to the seat. My ass is glued to the seat.*

While I focused on that lovely visual, Billie started the engine and backed out of the driveway. *So far so good.* The car moved through the busy streets. Lots of people were out taking advantage of the last of the warmer weather. As we drove along I people-watched out the window.

We'd been driving for about five minutes when, while stopped at a light, a man on the sidewalk begging for change caught my attention. He was hard to make out in the dull glow of dusk, but the stoplight was a long one, so I continued to stare. After a few minutes of watching him, trying to make out his features, I realized that we should have been moving by now. Looking up at the light, I saw that it was green. I turned to see why Billie wasn't pulling forward and realized what I'd done.

Shit! I was so focused on the beggar, that I forgot to pay attention to the car. This sudden, unexpected separation from Billie caused me a moment of panic. *How am I supposed to find her? What if something happens to her? She isn't exactly headed to the best part of town.* Then it hit me: I knew where she was going. She'd told Al and Kaz she was working at the amphitheatre. I immediately started to calm down. *I can catch up to Billie ... and I can take a minute to check out that guy on the corner.* But when I looked back, he was gone.

Not wanting to waste any more time, I tried to think of the fastest way to the amphitheatre. *What about a transporter? But how would that work without a Scotty to beam me up?* Breathing underwater and gliding on rollerblades worked because I was able to picture the mechanics of them, but transporters were science fiction. Like with the fish, I decided to try using my knowledge of something real to make something crazy happen.

I closed my eyes and pictured myself as a group of particles. No, not particles, signals. Just like using Morse code to send a message along communication lines, I would turn myself into a signal that could travel great distances at rapid speeds. I carefully pictured the concourse by the amphitheatre. The city had painted the benches so that they were each a different colour. I pictured myself as a pulse travelling along an invisible cable that led from where I stood, directly to the red bench on the concourse.

Tentatively, I opened one eye. *Holy shit! I can't believe that actually worked!* My excitement at the success of my experiment quickly subsided as I took a closer look at my surroundings. *This can't be right.*

All around me were strange creatures. Closest to me was something that looked human, but a zipper ran across its face. The zipper was undone, revealing the blood and tissue that are normally encased in skin. Next to that was a creature with wings that looked as though they were made of knives, its body coated in leather armour.

What's happening? What did I do wrong? Where the hell am I? As my brain tried to process the disturbing images in front of me, it presented an explanation I didn't want to accept. *This is it. I took too long, and I've gone crazy. I should have seen it coming, thinking I could breathe underwater or travel at impossible speeds.* Distraught, I moved through the crowd, each being I encountered more bizarre than the last. *I'll never catch him. Billie will be murdered.*

Overwhelmed, I sat down on the sidewalk and tried to clear my head. My chest grew tight as the fear started to take over. I'd only been this frightened one other time before.

The truck had come to an abrupt halt. I knew this
was my fault and there'd be hell to pay. Rough
hands wrapped themselves around my throat. Anger
made their grip tighter than a vice. My fingers
clawed at the ones interlaced around my neck,
unable to loosen their hold.

No! I forced that memory away. My whole body was shaking now. *What am I going to do?* I was on the verge of tears. I was utterly alone and had almost completely lost my grip on reality. *How long until I can't even remember who I am? Who I was?*

Then, unbelievably, I heard a sound sweeter than the most beautiful symphony.

"Can you tell me where the judging is taking place?"

It was Billie! I looked around but I couldn't see her from my spot on the ground. Although the crowd was densely packed, she sounded like she was right beside me. I waded through the monsters but, without her voice to guide me, I wasn't sure where to go. I began to worry that the sound of her had been a delusion, but then I heard it again.

"Thanks. Do you think they'll be starting on time?"

I rushed through the horde of nightmares and found her at last. Billie looked the same as when I'd left her. She still wore her usual jeans and plaid shirt. She was pushing through the crowd towards the main stage, and that's when I realized that the creatures were misty, just like her. I'd gotten so used to the foggy look of everything that I didn't make the connection to what I was seeing. Billie bumped into a man clad in chainmail and quickly apologized. *She can see them.*

As this new piece of information sunk in, I tried to look around the mob we were passing through a little more closely. In the distance, I spotted someone with elf ears and a green tunic. Emblazoned on their shield was a design I recognized, the symbol of Hyrule.

The overwhelming relief I felt made me break out into hysterical laughter. *We're at a bloody convention!* My laughter was so loud and so manic that I began to sound as unhinged as I'd feared I'd become earlier. *Ok, get a hold of yourself, Alex. Don't lose track of Billie again.* Calming down a little, I made sure that I could still see her as we made our way through the crowd. I continued to chuckle, every once in a while, at just how much I'd let my imagination get the better of me.

It looked like Billie had only come to cover the costume competition. I always admired nerds, geeks, whatever you wanted to call them, because they weren't afraid to be who they wanted to be. They were passionate about something, and they didn't let other people's petty thoughts get in the way of that passion. I never cared about anything in my entire life as much as these people cared about the various fantasy worlds they were dressed up to represent.

We didn't hang around for long after the competition was over. It was pretty late by that point and Billie looked like she was dead on her feet. During the ride back to her apartment I made sure to stay focused on Billie. I figured, that if I paid attention to her,

then I couldn't get distracted by something that wasn't moving
along with the car. Sure, I could have just beamed myself there,
but then I might have missed out on something important.

I found myself *really* looking at her. I watched the way the
breeze from the open window twirled her inky-black hair. For the
first time, I spotted a tattoo peeking out from under her chunky
watchband. It was hard to see, but it looked like it might be a
compass rose. I also noticed that she tended to chew on the insides
of her cheeks. This action was frequently followed by a sigh, so I
figured it must be a stress habit, like biting your fingernails. I was
so focused on Billie that I didn't even realize we were parked until
she unbuckled her seatbelt and reached back to grab her messenger
bag. Using the back entrance, Billie slowly trudged up the stairs,
barely able to keep her eyes open.

6

When we came through the door, Taco hurried over to greet us. Once again, I hung out in the living room so that Billie could have some privacy. After it had been a while since I'd heard any movement, I ventured into her room. The lights were out and the curtain was drawn shut. The haze of the Pale combined with the almost absolute darkness of the room made it difficult for me to orient myself. I was glad that I'd already been in here earlier, in the daylight.

After a moment, my eyes adjusted to the little light there was. I found Billie and lowered my head to listen to her breathing. The rhythm was slow and steady, so I figured it was time for another attempt at dream walking. *Hopefully this time I won't be walking in on a nightmare.*

I crouched and placed my head where hers was, but nothing happened. *Did I miss?* It was dark, but I was sure I'd lined myself up correctly. I tried again, still nothing. *What's going on?* I began to worry that I'd lost the ability to see her dreams. I sat there for a few minutes, my head still occupying the same space as Billie's, while trying to remember every detail of what I'd done last night. I wracked my brain, but I couldn't come up with anything I was doing differently. Then, slowly, colours began to swirl in front of my eyes. *Of course, you dummy, sleeping doesn't equal dreaming.* I'd forgotten that dreams only happened during the REM cycle.

The brick walls of an alley were forming, but this time it was the middle of a grey, overcast day. An old station wagon with wood panel siding was parked facing towards the alley's opening, a set of dumpsters at it's rear. A little girl, who looked like a younger version of Billie, hopped down from the rear driver-side door. She was wearing a denim-overall dress with a red t-shirt underneath. The shade of her blue sneakers matched the denim almost exactly. Little Billie moved to the back of the vehicle, then turned to shout towards the front of the car.

"I don't see anything back here. What am I supposed to be looking for?"

Just then, an alligator began to creep forward from behind a dumpster. Little Billie's back was turned so that she couldn't see what was coming for her. At the same moment, I heard the door locks on the car click shut.

Hearing it too, Billie turned to discover the monster gator, three times her size, advancing towards her. With a frightened look, she ran back towards the car, but it had already started to pull away.

"Please! Mom, Dad, don't leave me here!"

Screaming and crying, the small girl ran after the car as quickly as she could. With the kind of physics that are only possible in dreams, the alley continued infinitely in both directions, the car always just out of reach and the alligator always snapping at her heels, missing by a hair.

Closing my eyes, I concentrated on emptying the alley. I pictured the car and the alligator disappearing in a puff of smoke. When I opened my eyes, young Billie was standing there sniffling and looking terrified. Remembering the bear on her dresser, I conjured up a stuffed panda roughly the same size as Billie. I made it softer and less worn than the version I'd seen this morning.

Spotting it, Billie immediately hugged the bear around its neck and dissolved into tears.

Slowly, the sobbing began to quiet, and Billie gradually morphed into her current self. Her clothes changed too. She was now wearing black leggings and a long, thick, purple knit sweater. As she sat on the pavement, clinging to the bear, I tried to formulate a plan. *I can't say I remember any of the pleasant dreams I must have had, but I certainly remember my nightmares. Maybe I need to try communicating with Billie while she's still upset.*

Picturing a can of spray paint, I began to write a message on the brick wall across from her.

He's coming for you!

Billie wiped her nose on her sleeve as she read the message. She stood up and glanced down the alley, then looked back at the message.

Good, I've got her attention. I was about to add to my graffiti, but I was having trouble figuring out exactly what to say. *What do I even call him? I don't think Billie had given the killer a name.*

Mugger = New Page Killer

Again, Billie checked to see if anyone was around her. I couldn't tell what she was thinking, and I had no way of knowing if this was getting through to her.

The setting began to shift and morph around us. *She must have taken back control of the dream.*

But I was wrong, it wasn't Billie changing the scene, it was a change in her sleep cycle. Everything faded to black, and I was back in her room staring down at her pillow. Billie had rolled over, turning her back to where I was sitting. *Crap. I'll have to wait until she starts dreaming again.*

The night was long, and Billie's sleep was restless. I too was restless and paced back and forth while I waited for another opportunity to warn her. I wasn't able to catch Billie dreaming again for the rest of the evening. By morning, she awoke as groggy and exhausted looking as when we'd come home the night before.

I hungrily waited for some sign that my warning had gotten through. Unfortunately, with no one but a cat to talk to, Billie didn't really have any reason to chat about how she'd slept or what she'd dreamt of. I had no way of knowing if she even remembered the dream at all.

As Billie made breakfast, I considered my dilemma. *Maybe I don't need to wait for another dream. Maybe I can figure out some way to talk to her while she's awake.* I thought about the ways I'd been able to travel at impossible speeds by thinking outside the box. I'd already tried semi-conventional methods of communication. Perhaps there was a creative solution that was eluding me?

After breakfast, Billie got dressed and began gathering things from her living room closet as I watched from the couch. One of the items she grabbed was the large black case that I'd noticed earlier. She also pulled out a big blanket, some sunscreen, and rubber boots. *What on Earth is she getting ready for? This collection of stuff is more random than the rollerblading T-Rex I saw on Birch Street the other day.* Billie packed some food and everything else, except the black case, into a backpack, then sent a quick text.

We headed out and Billie quickly popped her head into the bookstore to let Al know she'd gotten in late last night, so she'd be grabbing his donuts, today. We then headed down the street on foot. About a block away, Billie went inside an office. If the sign out front hadn't made it obvious, the scent of gasoline and oil mixed with dust and exhaust would have given me a hint as to why we were here.

"Hi Andy, please tell me I can finally have my car back?"

The fair-skinned woman behind the counter gave Billie an apologetic smile. "Sorry for the wait honey, but when you drive a car more than three times your own age, you've gotta be patient when it comes time to scrounge up parts."

Billie cracked a smile and pulled out her wallet. "What's the damage?"

Andy passed her the invoice, then turned to grab a set of keys off the wall. After everything was settled up, we went to a lot at the side of the building. I tried to guess which of the various cars was Billie's. She made her way over to a classic VW beetle. The exterior had an opal paint job that shifted colours in the sunlight. All of the metal had a shiny chrome finish. The interior was entirely tan and spotless. Billie had clearly taken care of this car.

We both hopped in, and Billie pulled out of the lot. As we drove she drummed her fingers on the steering wheel and hummed along to a tune in her head.

♫ "Fa-fa-fa-fa-fa-fa-fa-fa-fa-far better. Run, run, run, run, run, run, run away oh oh oh." ♪

Is she singing what I think she's singing?

♪ "Psycho Killer. Qu'est-ce que c'est?" ♫

Billie quickly went back to just humming the Talking Heads tune. She'd been going about her day calmly and I'd given up on the prospect that my warning to her last night had gotten through. But this absent-minded singing gave me some hope that maybe, at least partially, she remembered. This was good news, but I couldn't get distracted while we were in the car: this time I had no idea where she was headed.

After about twenty minutes, we pulled into the driveway of a small two-storey brick house. As we got out of the car a short woman wearing a teal hijab and a long flowing dress came out to meet Billie. Her huge friendly smile reached up and crinkled the light beige skin at the corners of her eyes.

"Welcome, Billie. I'm so glad you came."

Billie looked down at the ground and muttered just under her breath. "I said I'd be here, Asra."

A tall red-haired woman covered in freckles was next to come out to the driveway, followed reluctantly by a small boy, probably about eight or nine years old. With his head hung down, some of his wavy dark-brown hair obscured his face. His warm golden-skinned hands played nervously with the straps of the backpack he was wearing.

The freckled woman stopped beside Asra. Her face was stern, and she looked accusingly at Billie.

"Nice to finally see you again, Billie." Her tone made the words sound more like judgment and less like an actual welcome.

"Hi, Frankie," was all that Billie replied as she stared Frankie down.

The boy hovered behind Asra and Frankie. He kept his eyes on the ground the entire time. Billie's gaze shifted to him and she seemed to make an effort to soften her expression.

"Hey, Sam."

Sam timidly peeked up at Billie. "Hey," was all he said.

"I think you're going to like what I've got planned for today. Are you ready to go?" Billie looked like she was in a hurry to get away from the death glare coming from Frankie.

"Sure."

Sam kept his head down as he got into the back seat of Billie's car. When his door closed Frankie took a step forward like she was about to say something more, but Asra moved ahead of her before she could open her mouth.

"Thank you for coming to spend some time with him today. I know that things haven't been easy for you."

"And they sure haven't been easy for him either." Frankie added. "You're not the only one who lost their parents, and just because he was adopted and you weren't, doesn't mean that this hurts him any less. If anything, he's suffering more. He's now lost two sets of parents. He doesn't need to be abandoned by his sister on top of all that." Frankie looked like she was barely able to keep her anger from escalating into a full-blown rant.

Billie glared back at Frankie. "I'm not abandoning him. I hardly *know* him." Billie growled, trying to keep her voice low, presumably so that Sam wouldn't hear their argument.

"And whose fault is that?"

Asra moved between Billie and Frankie. "It sounded like you had a nice day planned, Billie. Let's not keep Sam waiting."

With that, Frankie scowled at Billie one final time, then turned and strode back into the house. Asra smiled and waved at Sam in the back seat and Billie slammed the door as she got in the car. This made Sam jump, which Billie seemed to catch in the rear-view mirror. She made an effort to paste on a smile. "Today really should be fun. We have a bit of a drive, but it'll be worth the wait."

We drove in silence for about forty-five minutes. Billie had quickly abandoned her futile attempts to engage Sam in conversation. The city slowly disappeared as we took the highway, followed by some side streets that eventually turned into a gravel road. Eventually, we pulled into a long narrow driveway that ended at a sort of barn-shaped building. Billie parked next to a few other cars.

"Wait here, I'll be right back."

While she ran into the building, I decided to wait with Sam. The poor kid had looked on the verge of tears when we'd first gotten in the car, but he was calmer now. He was looking curiously out the window. I couldn't make out much of our surroundings. Other than the misty barn in the distance, the only other thing I could see were trees. It looked like we were on the edge of a forest.

Billie got back in the car and drove it around to the rear of the barn. She parked, then got out and began to gather her stuff from the back seat, and switch her shoes for the rain boots. Sam hopped out and stretched a little in a not-so-subtle attempt to get a better look at the place. The new surroundings appeared to be causing curiosity to win out over his brooding. "So, what are we doing here, anyway?"

Billie smiled but said nothing. Instead, she walked around to where Sam was standing and lay the big black case on the ground. When she flipped the latches and opened the cover, I could see a bunch of parts to something, each one individually embedded in the protective foam that filled the negative spaces of the case. "Do you know what these are?"

Sam looked hard for a minute then shook his head. Billie began removing the pieces and assembling them. After a moment or two, she had built two bows, one larger than the other.

"Have you ever done archery before?" Billie asked.

Again, Sam shook his head. He looked a little nervous. Billie handed him the smaller bow, taking the larger one for herself. She grabbed a handful of arrows that were in another compartment, then threw the case back in the car. She led the way to a small open field with targets on hay bales at various distances. The field was covered in soggy patches, and I finally understood the need for the boots.

"Dad taught me on the bow that you have when I was about your age. We'll go over the rules, and then I'll show you some basics, like how to stand, where to hold your arm, that kind of stuff."

Sam's face lit up a little and I didn't blame him: I would have loved to learn something like this when I'd had the chance.

I spent the morning enjoying the warmth of the sun, the smell of fresh-cut grass, and the gentle twang of the bows as they let loose the arrows. Unfortunately, I couldn't help but feel a little preoccupied. All the time I spent hanging around Billie when nothing was happening was time I was wasting: time I didn't have. I'd let myself forget everything else that was going on, which made it so much worse when I came back to reality. I was growing frustrated with Billie too. Why wasn't she pushing the cops to do more? Why were we wasting our time here, when there was a killer on the loose? Didn't she care about those victims on her spreadsheet?

I began pacing around the archery range. I was slowly growing more aggravated, and I had nothing productive to focus my energy on except people-watching the archers that had slowly trickled in. Sam seemed to be enjoying himself, at least. He'd relaxed after some of his arrows finally started to hit the target, instead of floating off into the grass. His arms had begun to look like they weren't exactly up to the task of pulling the bowstring anymore, but he didn't seem willing to tell Billie, yet. By early afternoon, the range was pretty much full. At least I didn't have to worry about being in anyone's way as I restlessly paced back and forth, almost wishing one of the arrows could actually hit me.

Some guy dressed all in camo with a literal red neck kept trying to catch Billie's eye. He'd finally given up on hoping she would notice him and came over to talk to her. Billie was polite, but I could tell she wasn't interested. He, however, did not seem to take the hint. He'd been yammering at Billie for a few minutes when she suddenly noticed Sam was missing. Panic swept across her face as her eyes desperately scanned for him.

I ran around trying to find him too. *I don't know what good you think that will do. It's not like you can do anything if you do find him.* I ignored the snide voice in my head and continued to look for him. Since I could freely run around on the course it didn't take me long to spot Sam hidden behind one of the targets. He was crouched down looking at the grass, probably searching for an arrow that had missed.

I relaxed a little since nothing serious had happened to him, but my inexperience kept me from knowing the danger he was in. I heard Billie yelling his name and calling for the other archers to wait. I came out from behind the target so I could see why she sounded so scared. Just then, I saw a man taking aim at the target Sam was hidden behind. Others at the range seemed to realize the issue and were yelling at the man that the course hadn't been cleared yet, but he was wearing headphones and didn't seem to hear them.

Everything suddenly happened in slow motion. As the camo guy ran towards the ready archer, Billie sprinted towards Sam. By this time, he'd looked up to see what she wanted, but he was still partially hidden by the target. Billie dove full force into him, knocking Sam to the ground just as an arrow whizzed by him and off into the trees.

A group had formed around the archer and several men were shoving him off the course towards the parking lot. I could hear shouting and it sounded like a fight might break out.

"You drunk, asshole! You could have killed that kid."

Billie knelt on the ground anxiously checking Sam over. "Are you ok? Did you get hit?"

Sam was dazed. Billie had probably knocked the wind out of him in her rush to get him out of the way. "I'm fine," he eventually stammered.

As soon as I knew they were both safe, my frustration at Billie came pouring out. Rationally, I knew that she had been only thinking about protecting Sam, but I was furious.

"You are the only person who is even looking into the guy who killed me," I yelled at her, even though I knew she couldn't hear me, "You can't go and get yourself killed too! You're too important."

Billie and Sam were standing now.

"I think that's enough excitement for one day. Why don't we head back?" Billie's voice shook as she tried to make light of a situation that had clearly shaken her.

Sam nodded his head in agreement, and they went to collect their equipment. The drive back was quiet, Billie chewing on her lip the entire way. The bright sunny day had quickly shifted to dark and overcast, with thunder rumbling in the distance. By the time Billie pulled into the driveway at Asra and Frankie's house the rain was pouring down, creating a thick curtain of water. Billie turned off the engine and glanced in the rear-view mirror at Sam. The two of them sat in silence, neither one knowing what to say to the other. Finally, Sam spoke. "I'm sorry for screwing everything up for you all the time."   Billie looked puzzled and a little hurt. She turned to face Sam in the back seat. "You don't screw things up for me, and what happened today was not your fault. No one is supposed to take aim until the course is clear." She paused for a moment, then continued. "What else do you think you've done wrong?"

"I don't know, but I *do* know that you can't stand me."

Billie dropped her eyes for a moment as a guilty look swept across her face. "I'm sorry I've made you feel that way, Sam. I don't dislike you."

He didn't say anything, he just looked out the window at the ribbons of water that streamed down the car.

Billie let out a deep sigh. "Things with Mom and Dad, before you came along, were very different than what they were like after you came to live with us. Their work always came first, and they dragged me all over the world because of it. I got used to always being the new kid and never hanging on to any friends. I accepted that that was just the way things were. But then they met you, and everything changed."

Sam quickly glanced at Billie, then went back to silently staring out the window.

"Mom helped your biological mother deliver you but she didn't survive it. Mom and Dad did everything they could to try to track down her relatives, but when they found out that you were all alone in the world, they couldn't stand the thought of leaving you. They'd fallen in love with you right from the start." She smiled at Sam before continuing. "The adoption process took years, but they fought it out in order to give you a family and a home."

Sam looked at Billie again. This time there were tears in his eyes.

"By the time they were allowed to pick you up, they had decided to take a break from all of the travelling and settle down. They'd already signed me up for a year in Germany in an exchange program, so the three of you got to have a nice little life, while I was shipped off to yet another country. I envied you. It looked like you were going to get the life I'd always wished for, instead of being some homeless nomad forced to wander the earth."

"So, you *do* hate me."

Billie reached back to put her hand on Sam's knee. "No Sam. Sometimes I wonder why I was never important enough for them to give me what they gave you, but I don't ever blame you for their choices. Mom and Dad were complicated people, just like everyone else. By the time I came back, I had decided that if I wanted a home, I would have to make one for myself. So, I got my own place. I've just spent so little time with you that I haven't really gotten the chance to know you. But I want to try to fix that."

Sam tentatively smiled at Billie. "Ok" was all he said.

After Sam went inside, Billie picked up Al's donuts and drove home. She chewed on the insides of her cheeks the entire ride. I could only guess that her conversation with Sam was replaying in her mind. She didn't sing or talk to herself, so I had no way of knowing what was actually going on inside her head. I had to admit, their conversation was taking up more of my mental focus than I would have thought it would.

I'd gained new insight into Billie and her life from before I came barging into it. Being someone who had always felt like a loner and an outsider, I could sympathize with how she must have felt. Feeling like no one really knows you, like you have no one to turn to, makes all the bad things in life that much harder.

I'm staring at a closed casket, but I don't really see it because my eyes are so full of tears. A heavy hand grabs my shoulder and begins to drag me to the side. He says nothing to me. He just pulls me away from the only person who had ever really shown me kindness, compassion, and love. I'd never felt more alone in my entire life.

At least I had my grandmother for a little while. It didn't sound like Billie had ever had anyone. I could picture her always in a strange place. Constantly being left on her own to make her meals and eat alone while her parents worked late. Never having their full attention as the burden of their day continued to weigh on their minds when they *were* around. Never having the time to form any kind of relationship before being moved on to the next place where the cycle would begin all over again.

It didn't exactly look like settling in one spot had changed any of this for Billie, either. She seemed to be on friendly terms with the majority of people she interacted with, but no one ever came to her apartment. No one ever called or talked with her about anything deeper than the superficial small talk that was required by polite society. *I wonder if, like me, she's found it's better to just keep everyone else out?*

Someone's car horn startled me out of my distraction. Panicked, I looked to see if I was still sitting next to Billie. It seemed that the rude honk was meant for her, as she looked just as surprised. She checked the rear-view mirror, then glanced up at the green light ahead of her. She quickly pulled forward and I did my best to stay in the present for the rest of the ride back to her apartment.

7

That night, Billie and I repeated our nocturnal routine. This time my message had to be scrolled in the sky. I used an airplane on fire pulling a banner with the same words as the night before. It flew past the window of the jumbo jet that Billie was riding in. At first, my plane wasn't on fire, but I needed to draw her attention away from the completely empty seats that surrounded her. I'd hoped that the frightening image of a flaming plane dragging an urgent warning would be more likely to stick with Billie when she woke up than the graffiti had. Something must have stuck because this morning Billie was singing "Girl on Fire" on her drive in to work. Unfortunately, the playlist my dreams were generating wasn't doing anything to help the situation in the real world.

When Billie got to work, I realized how early she was. We'd arrived before anyone else. Billie peered over the tops of the cubicles as if looking to see if she was alone. Satisfied that she was on her own, Billie logged in to her computer and turned the monitor so that anyone who came in wouldn't be able to see her screen. Her suspicious behaviour had me curious about what she was up to.

After activating some privacy settings and logging in to a few more programs, Billie began to scour some pretty dark parts of the internet. Some of her search terms brought up contact lists for human traffickers, black market organs, and even mail-order meals for cannibals. I was getting pretty concerned about what she might be into. She had just typed in the terms "snuff films shot in my area" when a pointy-faced little blond appeared at the entrance to Billie's and Jesse's cubicle, startling both Billie and me. With a few rapid keystrokes, Billie closed all of her programs and brought up a screen with details about the comic book event from the other night.

"What are you doing here so early?" the blond sneered. "Trying to earn brownie points with the boss? Or is your life so pathetic that work is all you have?"

Billie kept her face a lot more composed than I would've been able to if someone were speaking to me like that. She replied with feigned innocence, "Good morning, Sheila. It's always a pleasure to see you."

Sheila seemed furious that this was the only reaction she had elicited and stomped off. Billie crumpled her face and made a hand gesture that I'm sure HR would not have approved of. As she was doing this, Jesse walked in and caught the tail end of her farewell to Sheila.

"Starting your morning off with some new kind of Tai Chi I'm not aware of?" Jesse asked.

"Yeah," Billie scowled, "It's called Daemonous Repelum."

"That sounds more like a spell you'd learn at Hogwarts."

Jesse's joking wasn't able to break through Billie's bad mood. She let out a big sigh, then straightened her monitor. *I guess she's given up her terrifying tour of the internet.* Just then, Jesse interrupted my train of thought.

"So, what are you doing here so early? And without any caffeine too?"

Billie still looked angry at the rude greeting she'd received. She grumbled her reply to Jesse. "I *was* trying to get answers as to where some of my missing persons may have gone."

That's a relief, and it makes a lot more sense with the version of Billie that I've created in my head. I'd started to worry that I'd gotten Billie all wrong and that she was actually some kind of well-disguised sociopath. Like my panic attack at the convention, I should have realized how insane that idea was.

Paranoia isn't crazy, it's a means of survival.

"Shut up," I whispered at the voice in my head. I'd noticed it butting in where it wasn't welcome more and more frequently.

Talking to yourself now, Alex?

I did my best to ignore the voice. It looked like Jesse had noticed the unconventional position of Billie's monitor. "You didn't happen to be using company equipment in a way that might wind up getting you in trouble, did you?" Jesse poked Billie in the shoulder as he said this.

"Come on," she whispered, "I know how to be careful."

"May I make a recommendation?"

Billie looked suspicious. "What?"

"The next time you need to do some questionable research, I suggest you use Sheila's computer and be a little less careful."

They both laughed but Billie shook her head. I doubted that she would ever do anything so malicious, even if the person might deserve it. Jesse sat down but didn't seem in a hurry to get to work. "So, did anything exciting happen to you this weekend?"

Billie shrugged her shoulders. "I worked the convention and then Sunday I took Sam out to the range. How about you?" Apparently almost being skewered by an arrow didn't count as exciting.

Jesse's face shifted and it looked like he had something a little more interesting to tell. "I came home from work Friday to find that my house had been broken into. The entire place was trashed but they didn't take anything. I got to spend most of my evening feeling like I was smack in the middle of some crime drama."

"Geez, are you ok?"

"Yeah. I was pretty pissed at the time, but like I said, nothing was missing. It was mostly just a big pain to have to clean up."

"Weird, I wonder why someone would break in just to mess things up?"

"Maybe it was some kids being jerks. I don't know. I went out and got some new window locks on the weekend. Whoever it was probably realized that I didn't have anything worth stealing."

Billie and Jesse may have been stumped, but I had an idea as to why someone would have broken in on Friday; the day immediately following Billie's attack; the day after she'd had Jesse's ID ripped from around her neck. *This isn't good. He's hunting her.* Nervous adrenaline began to race through my body. *I can't just sit here waiting for Billie to figure things out. He must know by now that she doesn't live at Jesse's place. What if he's figured out where Jesse works? It won't take him long to track her here.*

I needed to take action, but I was still powerless against anything happening in the real world. *If only I knew his name, then maybe I could warn Billie or alert every cop in the city through their dreams.* The only real lead I had was the one Billie had given me. She thought that all of the victims were somehow tied to the New Page Centre. With my dramatically increased travelling speeds, I decided that I could risk leaving Billie to see if there were any clues at the centre. She would likely be here for a few hours at least and then maybe I would have something more useful to share with her tonight.

After a thorough search around the outside of the office, I zapped myself to the concrete steps of New Page. The red-brick exterior was grimy and tinged from over a century's worth of pollution. It looked as dirty and run down as the people who were already forming a line at the side entrance, where they distributed hot meals. Heading up the stairs at the front, I decided to check the foyer with the job postings, first. Unfortunately, for the most part, the building was still empty. It was early in the morning, and employees and volunteers were only just starting to filter in.

I spent the majority of my day popping back and forth between Billie's work and the centre. I closely examined every man who walked through the doors, but no one had the tell-tale scar that both Billie and I had spotted. When it was about time for Billie to be heading home, I did a final sweep of the building. That's when I heard it. The last voice that had spoken to me before my heart stopped beating.

"See you later, Taylor."

"Goodnight, Rodger. See you Wednesday?" A friendly, tanned blonde woman replied.

"Sure thing. I'll be here at eight o'clock sharp."

There were about a dozen people in the room, so it took me a minute to figure out which Vitae the cheerful woman behind the desk had been talking to. Just as I caught a glimpse of a man disappearing around a corner into the mists that limited my range of vision, I felt something tapping me on the shoulder. Surprised at feeling anything at all, I instinctively turned towards it.

I was more than a little stunned to see a pale, almost sickly-looking man standing right beside me. It only took a moment for me to realize that, regardless of the rarity of meeting other dead people, I had much more important things to be focused on at the moment. I immediately turned to follow the direction I'd seen Rodger going, but he was already gone. I tried to follow him, but the light suddenly got dim. My vision went dark, and I stumbled to the side. Cold clammy fingers had suddenly locked around my wrist. The icy touch released, and my head cleared a little.

"Sorry if I startled you. I don't see many of our kind," the dead man said as he tried to move back into my field of vision. "Are you new, here?"

Tripping over my feet, I moved towards the corridor I'd seen Rodger disappear through. It was no use. He was gone. Exhausted, I slid to the floor, completely disoriented. *What the hell is happening to me?*

The dead man had followed closely behind me as I'd tried to run towards the passageway, but he backed up when he saw that I had collapsed into a puddle on the floor. My senses slowly started to return. This unexpected bout of weakness bothered me. I couldn't afford to be vulnerable, especially not now. Annoyed that the killer had slipped through my grasp once again, I turned and scowled at the man I wanted to call "Casper". I stared pointedly into his eyes as I struggled to make the room stop spinning.

"Sorry, how silly of me. I haven't introduced myself. I'm Broden."

Has this guy not even noticed that I practically just passed out? His reaction didn't make sense, but I was still having trouble mentally focusing. Since I'd already lost my chance at following Rodger, I figured I might as well see if Broden could be of any use, but I didn't have much time. Billie would be leaving any minute now, and I didn't know if I could count on her to go straight home.

I also didn't like the fact that Rodger could be headed straight for her.

Calm down. If he knew where she was, why would he spend all day here, instead of watching for an opportunity to silence her?

The voice made sense. However, he might already know where she works or lives, and had just been biding his time until she wasn't in a public place. I wanted to hurry, but I also needed to try to learn as much as I could from the limited resources at my disposal.

"I'm Alex." I didn't bother with any pleasantries. "How long have you been here?" My curt tone didn't seem to phase him. He giggled a little at my question and I began to wonder if, however long it had been, was already *too long.*

"I'm not entirely sure," he said, looking off into the distance. "I think I only remember one winter here, but it's getting hard to be certain. All the days just sort of blend together, you know?"

"Sure," was the only answer I could muster. I didn't really have any patience, so I decided to just cut to the chase. "Hey, do you know if there's any way we can talk to the living?"

This question seemed to surprise him. I waited for his answer, but his eyes had become very distant, like he'd gotten lost in thought. I stood and moved forward to try to get his attention and immediately felt dizzy again. If I'd still been alive, I would have figured the blood had just rushed to my head too quickly but, even though I was solid, I wasn't sure that there was still blood flowing through me. I waved my hand in front of his face, but it was like he wasn't even there, anymore.

"I don't have time for this," I muttered under my breath. I felt awful, and the increasing possibility that Billie could be in danger had my anxiety levels rising. With one last glance in the direction that Rodger had left, I gave up my search and beamed myself back to Billie's cubicle. Being back at the office already had me feeling better. My head cleared and I remembered that all was not lost.

I think that Rodger might find his sleep a little less restful, starting Wednesday. I'll need to figure out how you interrogate someone when you can't exactly ask them any questions.

The beginning of my planning was cut short when I realized that Billie's cubicle was already empty. Quickly, I shot myself down to where she'd parked her car, and I was relieved to find her buckling her seatbelt. I took my spot in the passenger seat as she began to pull out of the lot. She drove and I scanned the limited area I could actually see for anyone who might match Rodger's general description. A growl of frustration escaped my clenched jaw as I tried in vain to see past the damn fog restricting my vision. For all I knew, he could already be in the vicinity, stalking Billie from just out of sight. My near-miss with Rodger and the episode with Broden had put me that much more on edge.

8

Tuesday had followed much of the same pattern as Monday. I accompanied Billie to work, and spent my day shooting back and forth between the centre and the publishing office. Billie's sleep was still restless so my chances to warn her were pretty limited. I'd tried placing her at New Page, but with no people to populate the space and no solid lead on the killer's identity, this warning seemed to be the least effective out of all of my attempts. I'd thrown the name "Rodger" in, but without a last name, I didn't have much hope of it leading to anything. The next night I'd placed her back in the alley where I'd made the graffiti in the hope that a recurring dream would have a better chance of sticking with her when she woke up. Unfortunately, Billie was not the type of person who constantly needed to talk about herself, so I had no way of knowing what was going on in her head. It certainly didn't seem like I was getting through.

As Billie drove in to work on Wednesday morning, I found myself antsy for her to hurry up and get there. She usually arrived a little before eight, but she was running behind today and I didn't want to leave until I'd seen her safely deposited somewhere I could count on finding her.

The moment she stepped through the door of her office I was standing at the reception desk of the New Page Centre. I checked the clock in the lobby and wondered how punctual this cold-blooded murderer would be. The clacking of Taylor's fingers typing out responses to emails seemed to echo through this relatively empty space, and it grated on my nerves. There was also a dank scent of must and body odour that hung in the air from the few patrons who had already entered the building. As the seconds ticked by, the atmosphere became more and more oppressive, and all I wanted to do was grab a breath of fresh air from outside.

Just when I thought that I wouldn't be able to stand it any longer, the door blew open and slammed against the wall. A pile of early fall leaves skittered across the floor, and I was grateful for the clean scent the sudden gust of wind had brought with it. Taylor tsked at the mess and quickly hurried over to close the door, almost slamming it in a man's face as she attempted to push back against the strong wind that was still rattling the windows.

"Whoa there, Taylor. Let me get that for you. I'd hate for you to be swept off to Oz in this mess."

The words were friendly, but the voice sent ice through my veins. *It's him. It's finally him!* I rushed over as the two of them pushed the door closed. I wanted to memorize every last detail of this man so that I could broadcast it to as many minds as would be useful. It was hard to tell, with the misty veil of the Pale in my way, but I was pretty sure I could see a layer of makeup around his nose and eyes: perhaps trying to hide bruising from his recent encounter with Billie.

Rodger was dressed in a heavy black felt coat, blue jeans, and black leather gloves. His dark brown hair was of medium length and had been tossed into a messy jumble by the wind. His cold grey eyes were recessed under a set of thick eyebrows. I also noted the stubble of a beard that was at least a few days old. *Probably trying to cover that scar before it can give him away.*

"Whew! Thanks, Rodger. I haven't seen a storm like this in a while."

Just then, the lights flickered and the two locked eyes.

"Hopefully, the power holds. I've got a lot of cooking to do before the dinner rush tonight," Rodger sighed as he signed in on a volunteer sheet. *Rodger Roman. Gotcha!*

"We should be fine, we've got generators just in case," Taylor reassured him.

"That's great, but I think I'll get to work right away, just to be safe."

With that, Rodger made his way across the foyer and through a door labelled "Staff and volunteers only". I stuck with him throughout the day as he prepared the meals that would be handed out in the evening. He whistled as he worked, but like the smile I'd seen that day when I was looking for a job, it felt like a performance for others: a shiny veneer meant to disguise the ugliness beneath. There was no one else in the kitchen with him, but a large serving window was open between the kitchen and the dining area, which people scurried through every once in a while.

I watched everything that Rodger prepared, looking to see if he would include any ingredients that might have a deadlier kick to them than the peppers and spices that went into the chilli. My concentration was frequently interrupted by thoughts of Billie and what she might be up to. I knew that if he was here then she was probably safe, but I still worried about what might be happening in my absence. This was the longest I'd ever been away from her during the day, and it made me feel oddly lonely.

Your obsession with her is pitiful and your plan to avenge your pathetic end is laughable.

I was right. What did I expect to happen next? I wasn't going to suddenly gain the ability to reach through the void and stop this monster. I stopped focusing so much of my energy on what he was doing and started to work on the problems I could solve.

"I won't let him out of my sight. I'll follow him home. I'll poke around in his head and his house to see if I can find anything useful." There was no one except the voice inside my head to hear me, but it made me feel a little better to declare my plan of action out loud.

*

That night, I followed Rodger home instead of Billie. Except he didn't go home, but instead, went to some skeezy no-tell motel. Given the clothes I'd seen Rodger wearing, I figured this location was chosen more for its no-questions-asked kinda policy than due to a budget necessity. It also made me think twice about the too-clean car we'd taken from the shelter. I began to suspect that maybe it was a rental instead of his own car.

I'd expected Rodger to go straight to his room but, instead, he strolled into the lobby and up to the front counter. The mists of the Pale did nothing to disguise the worn carpet and water-stained ceiling of the tiny reception area. I imagined cockroaches scurrying about inside the hideously wallpapered walls. *There isn't enough detergent or bleach in the world capable of convincing me to sleep in this place.* Luckily, sleeping hadn't been a necessity for me in quite a while.

Rodger had to bang on a bell to get some service. The clerk slowly made his way out of a back room, clearly in no hurry to attend to his guest. His oily hair and zit-covered face made me think he might also work at some burger joint. He seemed to carry an aroma of fry grease in, with him. "Yeah?" was all he said when he came to the counter.

"I'd like some fresh towels. I forgot to take the do-not-disturb sign off my door today, so the cleaning crew missed my room."

I'm sure Rodger was lying about this. I doubt he was the kind of person who forgot anything. More than likely, he just didn't want anyone poking around in there when he was gone. There was also the fact that we hadn't been to his room yet, so he couldn't know for sure that it had been missed.

The clerk sighed and shuffled over to the computer. "What room is it?"

"Room 209, Geofferson Smith."

So, it's Geofferson now, is it? As if it wasn't going to be hard enough implanting a single name into dreams. Now I have to start a whole bloody list of aliases — aliases that couldn't be more generic than if he'd chosen John Doe! I guess I'll have to come up with my own name for him until I can figure out his real one.

The clerk handed "Geofferson" some towels from a storage room behind the counter, then schlumped his way back to the room he'd originally appeared from. Rodger — I'd decided to just stick with the first name I'd heard — and I cut across the parking lot to a set of concrete stairs that led to the second floor.

Once inside, he flicked on the light, and I wasn't too surprised by how tidy it all was. Mind, I didn't say clean: everything in the room had the same worn and grubby look as it had in the lobby. But the bed was perfectly made, the used towels hung neatly on the bar, and there weren't any clothing or toiletries anywhere in sight. The room looked as though it hadn't been used at all. *Maybe I should have called him Howard since he seems to be so obsessed with cleanliness.* Although, I was pretty sure it was more likely due to a concern with leaving behind some sort of evidence, than it was OCD. *You don't wrack up the kill list that*

Billie's put together without being careful. Which had me wondering how desperate he was, leaving behind such a mess at Jesse's place.

Rodger set the fresh towels in the bathroom, then went back to sit on the bed. He turned on the TV but didn't bother watching it. He was scrolling through his phone when a knock came at the door. As Rodger didn't seem surprised by this, I assumed he had been expecting someone. Just as I was getting my hopes up, thinking this could be a lead, a delivery driver handed him a bag of takeout and left.

Rodger spread some napkins on a small round table next to the door beneath a window that faced out into the parking lot. He carefully ate while staring out the window. Unlike Billie, he didn't have a cat to talk to, so it was turning out to be a rather silent evening. I had no way of gauging what was going through his mind or what might be coming next. I found myself wondering what Billie was up to. I could picture Taco curled up beside her on the couch while she continued reading the book we'd started together.

Keep your head in the game, Alex.

My inner voice was right. I couldn't let my mind wander. I had a job to do. I found myself wishing we were anywhere other than this cheap motel room. There was nothing personal here, nothing I could learn or discover.

After finishing his dinner, which had been some fish dish that did not smell particularly appetizing, Rodger carefully placed all the containers, utensils, and napkins back into the bag they'd come in, but placed the bag under the table instead of throwing it in the garbage bin next to the T.V. He then pulled out something that smelled like an alcohol wipe and cleaned the surface of the table. *I was right. He doesn't seem to want to leave behind anything that may tie him to this room.*

Next, Rodger replaced all of the dirty towels in the bathroom with clean ones. He piled the dirty towels next to the bag of takeout garbage, then grabbed the T.V. remote. Instead of settling into a comfortable spot on the bed, he continued to stand as he flipped through the channels. Stopping on a pay-per-view fight, he pressed the buttons on the remote to have it billed to his room, then turned the volume up enough that it was just under an annoy-your-neighbour level. He then grabbed the garbage and towels, pulling the curtains shut as he left the room.

Following closely behind, I hopped in Rodger's car as he was tossing his haul in the back seat. He drove around for a bit, but eventually pulled into a dimly lit parking lot. He left the car running as he quickly tossed both the towels and the trash into a dumpster, then immediately got back in the car.

The suspicious behaviour continued when he pulled around to the back of a gas station that had closed for the night. Here, he shut off the car and went to the rear to remove something from the trunk. Grabbing a duffle bag, he left the trunk open and casually walked into a porta-potty.

There's only one way out of there. Thankful that there was no need for me to follow him quite that closely, I waited by the car. *Is he so paranoid that he refuses to even use the bathroom at the motel?*

I soon got an answer to my question when Rodger emerged looking almost exactly as I remembered him the night of my murder. He wore a faded tan toque pulled down over his eyes. His army-green jacket was oversized and covered in stains, and his large cargo pants hung low over a pair of beat-up construction boots. The fingers of his black knitted gloves had a few holes in them, and a thick knitted scarf covered most of his lower face. The weather wasn't cold enough yet to justify this many layers, but no one ever gives much thought to the fashion choices of the homeless.

On some level, I should have been prepared for seeing him this way. After all, the whole reason I was following him was because I suspected the monster that lurked beneath that refined exterior. But being confronted with this version of him brought back the reality of what had happened. It was almost as if I was dying in that alley, all over again. It took me a minute to get a hold of myself and snap back to the present.

Dressed to become invisible in his urban camouflage, Rodger threw the duffle bag back into the trunk, then locked the car and moved out towards the sidewalk. I knew at once that I was following a hunter to his blind.

The air is cool and my breath adds to the morning fog as I exhale a long sigh. It feels like we've been here for hours, but the sun hasn't actually moved much. *This is boring*. I don't dare speak these words aloud. My father has been looking forward to this trip for weeks.

Resting my chin on my hand and my elbow on the edge of the opening we're watching through, I'm suddenly elbowed in the ribs.

"Pay attention, Alex. You're not going to spot any game if you're busy daydreaming."

"Sorry." I try to focus, but nothing is happening. I don't even want to be here. I know that my dad meant for this to be a nice day, just the two of us, but I don't get why anyone would want to do this. It's cold, it's boring, and where is the pride in killing something that never even knew you were there, never even remotely had a chance at defending itself?

Is that it? Is this guy simply just tired of killing innocent animals and has decided to step up his game?

I continued to follow Rodger for a few blocks. He eventually settled in at the doorway of a hardware store that had been locked up for the night. He pulled a ratty disposable coffee cup from his pocket and began shaking it back and forth in front of his crossed legs. His head was bent in the usual submissive position, but his eyes were sharp, continuously roaming.

He continued this charade for several hours. The majority of people carefully ignored his presence. A few tossed some change in his cup, but he never showed any sign that there was more to his plan than taking advantage of those who had taken pity on him. Eventually, another man in rags shuffled by and, based on the odours radiating from him, he was legitimately in need.

Rodger spotted the man and, for the first time that night, looked up. His interest made me anxious. I was still powerless to prevent him from committing any more murders and now I'd gotten myself a front-row seat to the horror show I knew was coming.

"Spare any change, brother?"

The homeless man looked a little surprised by this question. He glanced around to see if Rodger had been speaking to someone else, but the three of us were completely alone on the street.

"You're kidding right?" The man seemed to find some humour in this. He didn't look upset.

"No, my friend. I'm desperate. I'll take anything you can spare."

The smile faded from the man's face and was replaced by a look of understanding and sympathy. He patted his pockets and pulled out a tinfoil package. Slowly, almost reluctantly, he unwrapped the foil and revealed the remaining half of a sandwich. With a sigh, he held it out to Rodger. "Someone has to look out for us," he said as he stretched his hand forward. "I'm sorry I don't have more to offer you."

I could see what this sacrifice was costing the man. I had little doubt that he was telling the truth. *What the hell is wrong with Rodger? Does he get off on taking everything possible from his victims, not just their life?*

"Thank ya kindly, brother." Rodger reached forward and took the scanty meal from the man, clasping both of his dirty gloved hands over the man's as he accepted the offering. *This is it. He's gotten his excuse for getting close to him.* Even though I'd been dead for quite some time now, I could still feel my pulse racing as I tried to prepare myself for what was about to happen.

Rodger held the man's hand for a moment, then let it go. He tipped the sandwich towards the man in a sign of gratitude and wrapped it back up. The homeless man gave him a last smile, then continued on down the sidewalk.

What the hell? Why did he let him go? Not that I wanted anyone to die tonight, but I don't get it. Is it possible I was wrong about him? No. I would never forget that voice, that final voice I'd heard. And then there was all of his strange behaviour. I'd just seen him eat a full meal and ditch his expensive clothes, just so that he could sit out here and rob some poor guy of his last scrap of food. No, I wasn't wrong, but clearly, I was missing something.

Rodger continued to sit in the doorway for a little while longer until an alarm on his watch sounded and he gathered up his things to leave.

The journey back was quiet and methodical, much like our trip out had been. He disposed of the uneaten sandwich in a trashcan on his way back to the car. He changed in the porta-potty, then drove to another unattended dumpster and ditched his hobo gear. *I wonder where he gets all of his disguises. Maybe he steals them from donation bins? He's certainly not above taking from the needy.*

Once he got back to the motel, he turned off the T.V. and got ready for bed. I stood over him as he lay on his back preparing to sleep. While I waited for him to drift off, I tried to formulate a plan of attack.

"I'm not exactly skilled at this whole dream-walking thing. How am I supposed to get anything useful out of him?" I asked myself.

Or you could just give him a taste of his own medicine. You could be creative, Alex. I bet you could conjure up some truly terrifying nightmares.

This idea was appealing, but I had to stay focused on the end game. As enjoyable as torture may be, a poor night's rest would be small and inconsequential in comparison to what he deserved. And it wouldn't help me protect Billie or prevent anyone else from losing their life by his hands.

"No, I have to stay focused," I told myself. "There's been nothing personal to learn about him here. I need to see if I can get anything usable, like his *real* name."

But how are you going to know what's real in a dream? And how would you even get information like that?

Surprisingly, I hated to admit that *I* was right. It wasn't like people tended to narrate their life story when they were asleep. But then, inspiration struck! I might be able to get some information, while also satisfying some of my more vindictive impulses.

I waited until Rodger seemed deeply asleep. I wasn't exactly thrilled at the idea of being in such close proximity to him, let alone inside his deranged mind. I didn't want to dunk my head into his more times than was absolutely necessary. Eventually, once I saw his eyes twitching from side to side, I got up the nerve and dove in.

9

I'm not exactly sure what I'd been expecting. Maybe the cries of his victims while he stood, gloating over them, as the life slowly drained from their bodies? The scene before me would probably have been the last thing I'd have predicted.

It was a bright, crisp winter day. Not far ahead of me was a frozen pond surrounded by cattails and tall, dead grass. I could almost smell the ice as the breeze whipped through with a cold bite to it. The small pond barely had enough room for the goal posts and two skaters suspended on its surface. One man was gliding in figure-eights off to the right while the other adjusted his goalie pads and banged his stick on the poles. "Come on already! Take your shot. You know you're not getting past me, so why delay the inevitable?"

Then the goalie let out a laugh as the skater, who looked like a younger, air-brushed version of Rodger, came to a halt in a quick snowplow maneuver that sent flakes of ice flying towards the net. The goalie's face was obscured by his mask, but this reaction seemed to amuse him because he let out another chuckle.

I decided to let this play out for a bit in the hopes that I'd get something useful, like Rodger's actual name. At the very least, I needed to learn more… hell! *Anything…* about this cold-blooded killer. I had so little to go on and the encounter with the generous homeless guy had somewhat shaken my confidence.

You just know you're going to fail at this, like you've failed at everything else. Stop procrastinating.

"I am not." I scowled, and tried my best to concentrate on the dream that was unfolding.

Rodger went back to circling the small pond. He seemed to be trying to catch the goalie off-guard. He eventually took the shot, which was easily deflected.

"Come on, man. Give me a challenge," the goalie jokingly complained.

Rodger had a mischievous smile as an entire line of pucks appeared on the ice before him. Without a word, he began rapidly firing them off one after the other. Each rocketing puck resulted in a dull thud as it hit the goalie's pads and veered off away from the net.

Now completely out of ammunition, Rodger stood his stick straight up and rested his gloved hands on top of it. "You know, Bro, you just might make it to the big leagues, yet."

"Fingers tossed."

"It's "fingers crossed" you dummy," Rodger said with a laugh.

"Yeah, but you can't cross your fingers with these things on," the goalie replied while holding up his padded hands. "Besides, when you think about it, tossing your fingers has just as much of a chance to bring you good luck as crossing them would."

"You're such a dork."

As Rodger continued to smile at the other man's logic, the scene started to shift. I'd had enough of waiting around so I quickly tried to take control of where we were headed. I knew from experience that I needed to concentrate, so I closed my eyes and tried to focus.

Once again, I drew inspiration from the movies. Having never actually been in an interrogation room, I tried to picture the details I could remember from the fictional ones I'd seen. When I opened my eyes, Rodger and I were alone in a room made of grey cinderblocks. In the centre of the room was an old, beat-up black-top table. On the side of the table where Rodger stood, I placed a cold stainless-steel chair and to the right, I made one of those two-way mirror windows. I'd learned from my sessions with Billie that there was no way for me to get an actual interrogator into the dream, so I knew I'd have to use alternative methods of communication.

Rodger stood staring at the wall opposite him. His eyes narrowed as blood began to drip down the cinder blocks.

Once I knew that I had his attention, I used the blood to write.

CONFESS!

A puzzled look fell across Rodger's face. Before he had a chance to fully process, I filled the room with flames and tried to remember the searing pain of burning flesh in the hopes that I could somehow transfer that feeling to him.

That was a mistake, Alex.

```
A hand holds my small leg as I try to twist and
turn away from the pain I know is coming. I can't
tear my eyes away — they follow the smouldering
end of the cigarette as it makes its way towards
my exposed ankle.
```

I forced myself to snap out of it. I couldn't afford to get distracted and choosing something that was real nearly caused me to lose control of the dream. Already, the flames had begun to die. Rodger had turned around, possibly looking for an exit. Using blood once again, I wrote another message on this new wall.

CONFESS to their MURDERS!

Rodger backed up and turned towards the mirrored glass. He squinted his eyes as if trying to see through it. I rapidly began filling the room with water, hoping he was more afraid of drowning than he'd been of being burned alive. Seeing the danger he was in, Rodger grabbed the chair and began smashing at the glass with it.

"Oh no you don't."

I hastily filled in the mirror with more cinderblocks. The water had risen to Rodger's waist. He looked up at the ceiling tiles and quickly planted the chair back on the floor before climbing on top of it and then the table. His outstretched fingers weren't quite able to reach.

His gaze darted back and forth between the rising water and whatever safety he seemed to perceive in the ceiling. I bathed the tiles above him in blood.

KILLER of INNOCENTS!

I concentrated on raising the water high enough that he couldn't touch the table but not so high that he could reach the ceiling. I replaced my previous message.

CONFESS!

Rodger's mouth was gaping, struggling to pull in as much air as possible.

This isn't working. Maybe the threat of a much slower death will give him the chance to reflect on what he's done.

I transported Rodger out of the interrogation room and into a clear plexiglass coffin. I changed the setting to an old cemetery with a large creaking oak tree looming over a shallow dug grave.

The night was clear, and the moon was bright enough to provide plenty of light for him to see by. I struggled to remember the names of some of the victims from Billie's list and wrote them in flames across the night sky, one after another. With each name, I pictured a shovel full of dirt being tossed into the grave. I imagined how the thump of it landing on the glass would be amplified in that small space. I wanted it to fill his ears and drive him mad like the relentless beating of "The Tell-Tale Heart".

Rodger's eyes, focused and determined, looked out into the black depths of the sky as his fists pounded the glass. I began mentally piling the dirt over his head in an attempt to generate some claustrophobia. My plan was to let him stew in there until he begged for freedom, but I never got the chance to see if it worked. As soon as the nightmare I'd created was blocked from his vision by the dirt, the dream started to shift, and I lost control over it.

The setting became an indistinct blur and the rhythmic thud of the dirt morphed into more of a slap. Slowly, a garage door took shape, followed by a driveway and a house covered in beige siding. A kid, maybe ten-years-old, was repeatedly taking slapshots at the garage with a tennis ball.

More of the environment continued to form around us. Another kid, maybe a few years younger, ran out the front door of the house with an eager grin on his face and a hockey stick in his hand. The two chased the ball, sloppily trying to keep it away from each other. When the older one, who I was guessing was a miniature version of my murderer, made a wild swing, he hooked the ball up and onto the roof. As my eyes followed the path of the ball, I noticed that just below the roofline of the garage there was one of those pretentious signs scrolling the address in a fancy script, as if someone didn't already know the street they were on.

Forty-Nine Genten Avenue

I'd just spotted this when the dream began to dissolve around me. Rodger rolled over and I was back in his grubby motel room. I glanced at the bedside clock.

"If I'm lucky, I'll still have time to get this to Billie."

It wasn't much but I had to hope that this address could finally lead us somewhere. With my futuristic lightspeed travel, I was in Billie's bedroom almost as soon as I'd considered trying to plant the address in her head. I quickly checked to see if she was in the middle of a dream, but I wasn't that lucky. While I waited and hoped she'd have another dream before her alarm went off, I tried to figure out how I would tell her. The results of my attempted messages to her thus far had been pretty pathetic.

Fortunately, Billie eventually fell into a dream state. I hated to interrupt because it seemed that, for once, she was actually having a good dream.

A young Billie was seated on a blanket that was spread across a lush green patch of grass. Overhead, cherry trees released a gentle trickle of blossom petals that fell as slowly as if the scene were part of a snow globe. Billie's parents were crouched next to the blanket and were digging an assortment of containers and packages out of a picnic basket. Behind Billie was a babbling little stream that had a quaint wooden bridge arching over it. Birds were chirping overhead, but there was another sound that seemed out of place with the setting.

I turned to see what it was and realized the picture I'd formed of our location was incorrect. I'd imagined us in the middle of some enchanted forest or a secluded meadow but, in fact, we were in a park right in the middle of a busy city. Across from the happy family were skyscrapers and a street packed with traffic, and the buzz of a crowded urban landscape. The sound that had distracted me came from a peddler trying to hawk his wares. He didn't seem to be speaking English and none of the signs on the buildings were in English, either.

I turned back to Billie and her family. Spread before them was a buffet of a wide variety of foods, definitely more than would have fit in the basket. My guess was that Billie's mind had enhanced that wicker hamper with some Marry Poppins-like magic. I wondered if the feast before her was a collection of all of her favourite foods.

I was reluctant to tear Billie from this happy place. Perhaps it was even a memory of an actual day that she treasured? But I knew from experience how brief her dream stage was and this was literally life or death. I tried to console myself with the fact that at least I wouldn't be forcing her into another nightmare.

I'd decided that the best way to share what I'd learned would be to try to recreate it as best as I could. The park began to fade as I constructed the bland house and the dark little driveway. I could picture how scratchy and uncomfortable the pavement would be under Billie's bare legs in comparison to the soft blanket atop the pillowy lawn she'd been sitting on, before.

Billie stood and turned to face the house, aging into her current self as she did so. I recreated the flowing font of the address above the garage but tried to make it larger and darker than I remembered. Although the entire scene might provide some clues, I wanted this to stick out the most in the hopes that Billie might remember it.

Suddenly realizing that I needed her to know why this was important, I spray painted Home of the New Page Killer across the garage door with a giant arrow pointing up to the address.

Before I could come up with another way to help cement this information into her memory, the scene began to fade and I was back in Billie's room, kneeling on the floor with her bed wrapped around me up to my shoulders. I sat there for a minute and marvelled at the calmness on Billie's face. It had been so long since I'd been able to enjoy the peaceful oblivion of unconsciousness.

I continued to sit there for a little while, just enjoying the quiet rhythm of Billie's breathing, when an idea suddenly hit me.

"I could go there and see if I can find any clues!"

That's assuming it's a real place and that it has any actual connection to Rodger.

"It doesn't hurt to try and it's better than sitting around doing nothing," I argued with myself.

I hurried out to the kitchen to check the clock on Billie's oven. I still had some time to at least check out the spot and get back to the motel to keep tailing Rodger, but not much.

Like before, with my first trip to the amphitheatre, I closed my eyes and tried to form a clear picture in my head. I added as many details as I could remember and then I pictured myself travelling along invisible wires right to the base of the driveway.

When I opened my eyes, I was still standing in Billie's kitchen.

"Why didn't that work?"

Because you're an idiot. You've never been there, and you don't even know if it exists.

I didn't want to admit that the negative asshat in my head was right. Instead, I decided to try a real place I'd never been to before. Maybe if this worked, I could at least figure out if the house really existed or not.

Closing my eyes again, I pictured the ivory and beige stone walls, the six towers, the portcullis, and the traitor's gate. I tried to imagine myself standing directly on the lawn of the innermost ward facing the White Tower. Hesitantly, I cracked my right eye open. Instead of finding myself as a wide-eyed tourist in the Tower of London, I was just a moron staring at a refrigerator.

Obviously, my ability to zap myself different places wasn't as magical as I'd thought it was.

That's because it isn't magic, you dunce.

The more I thought about it, the more I had to admit that the disparaging me was right. The places I'd gone were ones I'd been to before. When I travelled, I pictured the wires along the route I would take to get there and then sent my body like a signal shooting along them. I couldn't get to this mystery house or the Tower because I didn't know where to lay the wires.

Once again, I was going to have to wait for Billie to wake up and hope that she'd remember something. Rodger's dream hadn't specified the exact location, and it's not like I could just look up all the cities that had streets with that name. If it was somewhere close by, I could try finding my way there, but I couldn't just wander around aimlessly hoping to stumble across it.

Glancing at the clock one more time, I noticed it was just after six and decided to head back to the motel so that I could continue to monitor Rodger. Before I left, I took one last look in at Billie. She was sleeping still but would be getting up in about an hour. I found myself a little disappointed at the idea that I wouldn't be joining her on our usual trip to work.

Don't become some mopey-eyed dope now. There are obviously more important things going on than hanging out with your new little friend.

"I know! Obviously, I know that trailing Rodger is more important. Can't you just let me have a single minute without your snide comments?"

My outburst seemed to quiet my brain for the moment. Without another look over at Billie I popped back to Rodger's room and what I found triggered an extremely long stream of profanity.

10

The bed was empty and already made. Worried, I ran to the bathroom, not caring what I might walk in on as long as I found Rodger inside. He wasn't. As I rushed to the parking lot, panic began lacing its steely grasp around my ribs, squeezing all of the air I didn't actually need from my lungs. It was about an hour until dawn and the motel lot wasn't well-lit. I ran as I checked each car individually, just so I could be sure, but Rodger's car wasn't anywhere to be found. The pressure on my chest became unbearable as my mind raced with the consequences of losing him. *He could be anywhere. He could be stalking his next victim. HE COULD BE ON HIS WAY TO BILLIE!*

With that thought, my panic had exploded to new extremes, but my subconscious seemed to have taken over. The second I'd thought of Billie, I was back in her kitchen. Once I realized where I was, I flew into action. I began with a quick sweep of the apartment to ensure that everything was as I'd left it. Then, I began a systematic search of the outside of the building and the surrounding streets as the sun began to rise.

While my body robotically searched, my mind continued its relentless stream of negativity. *You're fast, but you can't be everywhere at once. What if he's in the exact spot you're not checking? While you're busy patrolling the street, he could be in the alley cutting Billie's break line, or piping carbon monoxide into her room while she sleeps.*

A rational person might have been capable of arguing that I hadn't seen any evidence that Rodger knew where Billie lived, yet, but fear is usually stronger than logic, and I found myself constantly drawn back to Billie's room to make sure she was still there, still safe.

If he's lurking in the shadows, you can't do anything about it anyway. You're useless!

As much as I hated to admit it, there wasn't anything I *could* do if he showed up while Billie lay there, completely defenceless and unaware.

"I'll wake her up! Then at least she can fight off anything that might be coming for her."

I plunged my head into hers and could make out the faint tendrils of a dream that seemed to be dissolving. My anxiety began to skyrocket out of control as I felt my chance slipping away. All I could think about was the irrational horror of him lurking outside, already putting a plan into place that would result in Billie being permanently silenced.

Suddenly, Billie bolted upright in her bed. Her eyes darted around the room, she threw off the covers, then ran to her window. She scanned the alley but didn't seem to see anything. She let her hand rest on the windowsill as she turned her body back towards her bed. I wondered if she'd gotten light-headed from getting up so quickly.

Billie scrunched up her face, looking unhappy at whatever she was thinking about. Slowly, she began to make her way around the bed to the doorway. She was never a heavy walker, but she seemed to be taking the time to make as little noise as possible. Cautiously, she poked her head out and listened. After a minute or two, she glanced back towards where Taco was curiously watching the proceedings from on top of Billie's dresser. Silently, I urged her to get 911 ready on her phone, but when I looked around her room, I didn't see it anywhere.

The apartment was so quiet that I could make out the hum of the refrigerator from where we stood. The silence didn't seem to satisfy Billie as she kept her back to the wall and noiselessly slipped into the washroom. I couldn't tear myself from her side to scout ahead. *It should be clear, but what if there's something that the mists of the Pale had kept hidden from me?*

The shower curtain was pulled back, so I knew that no one was hiding in there. I figured Billie would move on to the kitchen next, but instead, she grabbed the bottle of liquid soap from the vanity and squeezed out a couple of pumps onto the tips of her fingers. She returned the bottle to the counter, then spread the soap so that the end of each finger was covered. I was so worried that I couldn't dredge up the mental energy to wonder what the hell she was doing.

The soap seemed to be all the preparation Billie needed. Just as quietly as before, she made her way out into the hall, moving silently towards the kitchen. She did a sweep of the rest of the apartment, then let out a little sigh of relief. "What's wrong with me?" she asked herself.

Taco had come out to investigate something even more important, the food bowl. Finding it empty, Taco began wrapping around Billie's ankles and purring. Billie let out a little laugh. "You trying to sweet-talk me into giving you some breakfast? Let me rinse these off and then I'll see what I can do for you," she said as she wiggled her fingers at Taco. Taco sniffed them, then made a face that clearly indicated that they did not smell appealing.

"In case of home invasion, you want to use a weapon that your attacker can't take and use against you. Soap directly to the eyes can blind someone long enough for you to get away," she informed Taco in a voice that sounded like she was repeating a lesson she'd heard many times.

Billie made her way to the washroom, peering back into the other rooms as she passed them, almost as if she wasn't fully convinced that the apartment was secure.

"I must have really scared her," I mused to myself. I started to feel bad about it but quickly remembered that a scared and alert Billie was safer than a drowsy Billie.

Knowing her morning routine pretty well by this point, I decided to do some more patrolling outside until it was time for us to head to work. I couldn't let myself get distracted. I needed to focus entirely on searching for the predator that could be hiding around every corner. Once Billie was surrounded by other people, tucked safely away in her cubicle, *then* I could try to figure out what my next move should be.

*

When Billie and I arrived at her office I wasn't in a hurry to leave. I needed to see if I could pick up Rodger's trail at all, but I also wanted to see if she'd remembered anything about the house I'd tried to show her the night before. There'd been no singing on the drive in this morning and Billie still looked a little rattled. When she walked in empty-handed, Jesse seemed to sense something was up.

"Billie Mauer, I can't believe you dared to enter this cubicle without a caffeinated offering for your personal hero or, at the very least, for yourself."

"Personal hero, eh? I didn't realize da Vinci had risen from the dead and was coming to our office today."

"What's so special about a painter?"

"Look him up. It'd do you some good to read something, hell, anything!"

"Ouch, that hurts. Never forget, Billie, words have great power. And with great power comes…"

"Don't even bother finishing that sentence," Billie half-heartedly chuckled as she flopped into her chair. "I'm sorry if I hurt your feelings, Jesse. I'm a bit on edge this morning."

"Rough night?"

"A lot of rough nights lately. I guess I'm just tired."

I didn't think my nightly visits had been affecting her that much. I started to feel guilty, but quickly remembered that, what was surely a minor annoyance for her, was literally a matter of grave importance.

Without saying anything else, Billie spun around to face her computer and got to work. I eagerly watched for any sign that she'd look up the address I'd given her but, of course, I wasn't that lucky.

As Billie got to work, I tried to figure out my next move. I decided to do another sweep of the motel in case Rodger had merely gone out for an early breakfast, but I certainly wasn't holding my breath. When I got there, the door to his room was wide open. The cart of cleaning supplies parked in front of it told me that he wouldn't be inside.

The next stop on my tour of dead-ends was the shelter. I checked the volunteer sign-in sheet, but his name wasn't there. I did a quick search of the building, but he was nowhere to be found.

As the day wore on, I found myself trapped in an endless loop of anxiety-driven pacing between the motel, the shelter, and Billie's office. I also made continual searches of the parking lot and shops around the area to make sure he wasn't lurking somewhere close by. I was so consumed with fear that I couldn't concentrate long enough to form my next plan of attack. By the time Billie's workday had ended, I was no closer to a solution and my stress levels had only increased with each moment that Rodger was free to roam around. I was positive he wasn't wasting a second of his time.

He probably already has his next victim chosen and an airtight plan for dealing with Billie. What have you done, other than keep her from getting a decent night's sleep?

"You know, you could contribute something constructive to this conversation for once. If you're so clever, what do you think I should do, eh?" I had little hope that my pathetic plan to trick that negative side of myself into being useful would help, but it did.

Easy, I would stop putting all my eggs in one basket, so to speak.

As I saw the plan laid out by my snarky subconscious, I had to kick myself for not thinking of it sooner. I'd gotten fixated on Billie and completely forgotten about my other options. But as soon as I knew what I needed to do, it felt impossible to take action, at least until tomorrow when I could count on Billie being surrounded by other people, again.

"You know, this idea would have been a lot more useful to me this morning. Now I've wasted the entire day."

Whose fault is that? I'm not the idiot who keeps following her around like some helpless little puppy.

"I am not."

Now you sound like an insolent child. Come now, Alex, you're better than this. Caring about her is making you soft, making you weak.

"I don't care about her. She's just the best chance I have at catching this guy."

Sure, keep telling yourself that — literally. Ha!

"You think you're *so* witty."

As I worked to come up with a crushing insult, I remembered that I was having this entire conversation with myself. Then I began to worry that the increasing separateness of this negative inner voice was proof that the Pale really was beginning to take its toll.

I tried to push those thoughts aside and concentrated on what I *could* control. For tonight, I would stay with Billie and try yet another new tactic once she was asleep. Then, tomorrow, I would explore some of my other options and hopefully, *finally*, make some headway.

*

While Billie cooked some pasta for dinner and listened to music, I tried to formulate a new strategy for communicating with her. The song that was playing suddenly reminded me of one of the early dreams I'd created for her. The harsh notes of the slasher music I'd been able to orchestrate filled my memory and gave me an idea.

That night, while Billie slept and I waited for a dream to begin, I finetuned the logistics of how I thought this would work. By the time a dream started, I felt like I had a solid strategy.

A bleak and dreary sky began to form overhead with heavy ominous clouds that released intermittent bolts of lightning. The ground was covered in smooth concrete, saturated with water for as far as the eye could see. Behind Billie, a large obsidian pyramid loomed. It had a doorway carved into the face that was closest to us.

Everything was monochromatic and almost completely devoid of colour. Even Billie's clothes were sombre: faded black jeans, a grey tank top, and her signature plaid shirt was now a dark grey button-down.

The wind began to swirl, whipping Billie's hair in her face as she struggled to keep it out of her eyes. I was about to take control of the dream when I heard a strange thumping in the distance. Both Billie and I turned towards the sound and there, on the horizon, was an army of some sort, moving towards us. At first, they were hard to make out. The drumming of their march grew louder, and I began to slowly discern the individuals in the horde that was drawing ever nearer.

There in front of us, with a dead and vacant look in their eyes, was an army of Kermit the Frogs. Their felt was the faded and washed-out colour of grass that had been scorched by the sun. Their arms were suspended in front of them as if they were a pack of mindless Americanized movie zombies. Thunder boomed in the background as the impossibly heavy stomp of their light puppet feet continued to advance towards us.

Billie looked around, then ran towards the opening in the pyramid for shelter. When she reached the entry, it was blocked by a monolithic boulder. She turned back towards the mob and, as she did so, the forward lines dropped to the ground and began scuttling towards us in a disturbing crabwalk. It reminded me of elementary gym class, but was much more sinister looking than I'd remembered.

The clomp of those webbed feet fell into a rhythm I couldn't drown out. Billie pounded on the boulder as she continually looked back at the pack drawing ever closer.

I tried to take control of the dream, but it wasn't working. I don't know if Billie was too focused or if I wasn't focused enough, but no matter what I pictured, I wasn't able to take us away from there.

"I guess I'll have to work with what I've got," I said to myself.

Using the steady beat of the muppet soldiers, I added in some guitar chords. They were hard to hear over the raging wind, but I was able to make them out.

"Now for the real test."

I'd been able to play instrumental music before, so this was nothing new. What I needed to know now was if I could add vocals. In answer to this question, I heard what I'd been hoping for. The words came just slightly louder than a whisper, but they were there.

♫ "Let's go!" ♪

Despite the creepy scene before me, a huge grin spread across my face. I tried to use the momentum of my success to take the terror factor of the dream down a notch. As Freddy Mercury's voice slowly grew stronger, I forced the menacing frogs' march to shift. First, I took control of their feet and made them match the beat. Then I imagined that I had control of the rods that would have worked their arms and choreographed a synchronized dance number that would be the envy of any K-Pop band.

♪ "Another one bites the dust." ♫

The lyrics were growing stronger, and I could finally make them out. The wind had died down, and Billie had turned to watch the strange performance I was directing, a look of confusion replacing the one of dread that'd been there a moment before. I had to admit, what I'd created wasn't that much less disturbing than the original nightmare, but I saw a smile creeping up at the corner of Billie's mouth as she watched these once terrifying amphibians vogue and chassé in their ranks.

I don't know why that song popped into my head. I'd planned to try playing one that'd been on while Billie was cooking, but I wasn't complaining. It had worked!

Now that the panic was gone from Billie's eyes, I tried once again to take full control of the dream. I concentrated on the scenery first. Buildings and lamp posts sprouted up from the ground, and the sky darkened to the hazy blackness of night in the city. Beside Billie, I placed a cop car with the roof-mounted emergency lights flashing. I kept the siren off since it would be counterproductive to what I hoped to accomplish next. I needed to draw her attention towards the car, but I also needed her to be able to hear, clearly.

Setting the scene was the easy part. I held my breath and closed my eyes as I put my full concentration into the next crucial piece.

The two-way radio in the police cruiser crackled, then a voice spoke. My voice.

"Hello, Billie. Can you hear me?". There was another crackle as I pictured letting go of the button I would have held while I spoke.

Billie looked confused as she moved towards the car, sticking her head in the open driver's side window. Now that I knew she could hear me, I tried to get an answer from her. This wouldn't work very well if the conversation stayed completely one-sided.

"Billie, you're in danger and I need you to listen to me. Please tell me you can hear me." I could clearly see that she could hear me, but I didn't want to spook her and let her know that. I needed to keep her here in this dream and upping the creep factor by sounding like a horror movie stalker wouldn't exactly help.

Billie pulled her head out of the window, opened the door, and sat down in the driver's seat. I watched as she searched the dashboard. Finding what she must have been looking for, she grabbed the handset for the radio and brought it towards her mouth.

"Who is this?", she asked.

I couldn't believe this was working! I started pumping my fist in excitement but quickly got control over myself so that I could answer her.

"Who I am doesn't matter. What matters is that he knows who you are. He's coming for you." I was purposely being cryptic to start with. I wanted her full attention on what I had to tell her, and I hoped that if there was some mystery to it, she might somehow keep puzzling it over when she woke up.

"Who is coming for me?'. Billie's voice was calm, but I caught the snap of her head as her gaze began searching the area around her.

"I think you know who. He's noticed you searching for him, and now, he's coming for you." I watched as Billie struggled to figure out what I meant. "He's already found you once. It won't be long before he finds you again."

Billie checked her surroundings again, then sat for a moment thinking. I'd hoped to see a sudden understanding wash across her face as the proverbial lightbulb clicked on, but I had no such luck. Instead, Billie's brows lowered, and her mouth went hard.

"Look, I'm not interested in playing any games. Either you have something to tell me, or you don't."

I think you've got her attention. Don't piss her off so much she takes back control of the dream. I listened to my own advice and got to the point.

Just then, a loud buzzing sound broke into the dream — a sound I didn't create. Billie heard it too, as it went off a second time. Suddenly, I was there sitting with my head in Billie's pillow. I tried looking around to see what was going on, but it was too dark in the room. Billie flicked on a light and I heard the buzzing sound again. Someone was calling and her phone was set to vibrate. I cursed as I stood up and started to pace.

"I was finally getting somewhere. Who the hell is calling at this time of night, anyway?"

I tried to listen in on the call. Billie had answered but hadn't spoken, since. After another minute of listening to whoever was on the other end of the line, Billie hung up with a sigh and shook her head.

"Thanks a lot, Jesse." she grumbled as she tossed the phone back on the night table. Billie rubbed her hands across her face and fell back on the pillow. She lay there with the light still on staring up at the ceiling.

I continued my pacing as I waited for Billie to turn out the light and go back to sleep so that we could pick up where we left off. All of a sudden, she bolted upright and grabbed her phone again. Her frenzied typing drew me over so that I could see what she was doing.

Billie had pulled up her spreadsheet of victims on her phone.

"YES!" I shouted as I began jumping up and down with pure joy and punching at the air. "Yes, yes, yes, yes, yes, yes, yes!"

I was suddenly a lot less annoyed about Billie being jerked out of the dream.

11

That night seemed endless, and I got the impression that Billie felt the same way. She tossed and turned for hours, frequently picking up her phone to check the time. She never fell into a deep enough sleep for me to try speaking to her again, but I was energized by the success I'd already seen. I anxiously waited for morning to arrive so that I could see what Billie would do with this information.

As the night wore on and her tossing got less frequent, I worried that by the time the sun rose she'd lose the urgent energy that had possessed her when she'd first made the connection. My euphoria at the success during the night had slowly turned back into a constant stream of angst-riddled doubts.

What if she brushes it off as just another dream? What would she even do differently now that she thinks her attacker is the killer? What is he doing while I clumsily try to get him caught?

"Just shut up! There's nothing I can do about any of that, so just be quiet and let me figure this out."

Shockingly, the negative voice in my head fell silent. No witty comeback. No snide remarks. With the extra room this left in my brain, I remembered the plans I'd already made for the coming day and tried to figure out how I'd fit them in with what I hoped would be a productive day of investigation on Billie's end.

"As fast as I am now, I still can't be in two places at once."
That's when an idea hit me. I'd spent all of my life handling things
on my own, but if I was going to catch that monster, I had to
finally admit that I needed help. I popped into the kitchen to make
sure that I still had some time before Billie would be leaving for
work. I'd be fine if I hurried but then I thought of all the other
times I'd quickly gotten what I needed and disappeared.

"This time will be different. I've even got a gift for her." A
smile crept across my face as I thought about how, for once, I had
something to give instead of just taking.

*

I checked at both the house and the hospital, but Ava wasn't at
either one. I tried to remember how long it had been since I'd seen
her. As I searched, I also began to worry.

"What if she's disappeared? She's been in the Pale longer
than I have, but I hadn't noticed any signs that she was fading or
starting to lose it."

*Like you would have noticed. All you do is look out for
number one.*

As much as I hated to admit that this might be partially my
fault, the negativity monster in my head was right. Use or get used
was a mindset that had taken care of me while I was alive, but
things were different now. I could be different.

While I paced outside the emergency room entrance, lost in
my thoughts, a sweet singsong greeting broke through my inner
monologuing.

"Alex! What a nice surprise." Somehow, I could hear the
smile in Ava's voice before I'd even turned to see it spread across
her face. I'd forgotten that she would still need to walk everywhere,
and I'd probably just missed her while she'd been enroute from her
family's place.

"Hey Ava, you're just the ghost I was looking for." I tried to joke with her, but it came out awkward since we'd never really had that kind of relationship before. Of course, being Ava, she was nice enough not to call out how weird I was being.

"What's up?"

"I have a favour to ask but I'll need to catch you up on a few things first."

"What can I do?"

That was it. That was all she wanted to know after I'd continually ditched her: "How can she help?" I had trouble believing that anyone as kind and good as Ava could possibly exist, but maybe people like her were there to balance out some cosmic equation that had to account for people like Rodger. I knew at that moment that I'd have to do what I could to try and shift myself closer to her end of the spectrum before I got sucked down into his.

I glanced at the giant combination digital clock and thermometer in front of a dental office across the street. I still had some time before Billie would be leaving.

"First, I have something for you. Actually, two somethings, but we'll start with one."

Ava looked a little confused, but she also looked excited about the prospect of something new in this void where not much changes. I explained to her the things I'd learned about travel in the Pale and even demonstrated for her by vanishing before her eyes. I'd only beamed myself across the street so that I could see her reaction. She hadn't spotted me yet and I laughed to myself as she spun around to look for me.

As I popped back into existence in front of her, she jumped back in surprise.

"How did you do that!" Her eyes were alight with wonder and her mouth hung slightly open in shock.

I couldn't help but enjoy the look on her face. As I let out a little laugh, her expression quickly changed to one of pure joy. I didn't understand what she could be so happy about, but she quickly answered my unasked question.

"I don't think I've ever heard you laugh before, Alex." Some of the previous wonder returned and I suspected she was trying to figure out what had happened to change my attitude so drastically.

I decided to attempt another joke, "I guess my atoms must have gotten reassembled incorrectly. I'll try not to let it happen again." The corners of my mouth were turned up to let her know I was kidding, but I still felt weird trying to tease her. Maybe it was because a part of me hoped the jokes would help to distract her from the fact that I'd essentially been using her the entire time we'd known each other.

Before my mood could sour too much, I gave myself a mental shake and tried to focus on the task at hand.

"Now it's your turn, Ava. Let's see what you've got."

Her eyes widened. "You've got to be kidding me."

"I'm completely serious. Try shooting yourself over to the office across the street." I gestured to the same place where I had appeared when I was watching her reaction earlier.

Ava's eyes followed my hand and, for the first time ever, I saw a crack in her relentlessly calm exterior. I placed my hand on her shoulder in an attempt to reassure her.

"Don't worry, you've got this."

Ava took a deep breath and squeezed her eyes shut. After a moment or two, she tentatively cracked one eye open to peak at her surroundings. Her bottom lip stuck out in an almost imperceptible pout as she noticed she was still exactly where she'd started.

"Give it another try. Only, this time, try not to think about anything except what you would look at if you were already across the street."

She closed her eyes again, scrunching up her face with what I assumed was determined concentration. When she took another hesitant look, she was still standing right across from me.

"I'm sorry, Alex. It doesn't seem to be working."

I tried not to let the rapidly passing time, or my frustration at myself for thinking this would actually work, harshen my tone.

"It's ok, Ava. We're not giving up yet. Maybe my way isn't the right way for you. When I say, "magic light-speed travel", what's the first thing that pops into your head?"

Her lips pursed as she thought about this for a moment, then a spark of inspiration lit her face.

"Narnia!"

I'd read the books when I was younger, but I wasn't exactly sure how an alternate universe was going to help us.

Without further explanation, Ava reached out into the air and twisted her fist like she was turning a handle. She then brought her hands together in front of her and pushed them apart again as she stepped forward and disappeared.

Having never seen things from this side of the equation, I imagined that I looked as dumbfounded as Ava had a few minutes ago. Knowing where I'd told Ava to go, I turned to look at the clock across the street. Just as I did, I could see Ava climbing out of the clock with her hands parted, as if she were holding open some curtains as she walked through.

I ran across the street to meet her and the smile on her face was a reward I'd never expected. It was kind of nice to know that

I'd done something to make *someone else* happy, especially someone like Ava, who deserved all the happiness she could get.

"That was amazing, Ava! How did you do it?"

She giggled as she said, "I just climbed into a wardrobe and pushed some old fur coats aside."

I wanted to give her a minute to celebrate her success, but I was running short on time. Another glance at the clock told me I was cutting things a little too close.

"Can you wait here for a minute? I just need to check on something and then I'll be right back."

Ava smiled up at me as she said, "Sure. That will give me a chance to practice some more."

"Ok, don't go far or I won't be able to find you when I get back."

"Aye, aye, captain," Ava giggled as she gave me a mock salute.

I waved as I beamed myself back to Billie's apartment. She wasn't there. When I quickly checked the alley out back, I saw that her car was gone too. It was still a few minutes before she usually left for work .She should have been here. Before a rising panic could take over, I zapped myself to her office, but she wasn't there either.

I hurried down the stairs towards the parking lot to see if her car was there, but almost ran straight through her as she came out of the café. She was carrying what must have been the largest caffeinated drink they had. She was probably exhausted from her less-than-restful night.

I escorted her up to her cubicle and found myself torn. I was dying to see what research she would try to get done before her co-workers poured in, but I'd also left Ava hanging. Billie was moving pretty slowly, so I decided to take the risk and pop back over to Ava.

When I arrived back at the hospital, I spotted a pair of red sneakers disappearing into thin air. Frantically, I looked around for where they would rematerialize with the kindest pre-teen on the planet attached. Ava hopped down a few meters away from where she'd been a minute ago and I rushed over.

"How well do you know the city?" I practically barked at her with no preamble or greeting.

She spun around a little surprised. "You're back! I think I'm getting the hang of this."

I forced a smile for her, but I suspect it came out more as a grimace.

"That's great, Ava, but I have somewhere I need to be. Would you mind coming with me so that I can catch you up on what's been going on?"

"Has there been a break in the case?" Her eyes widened and she reached out a comforting hand towards my arm.

"Yeah. How well do you know the city?"

"A bit I guess. I haven't really done any exploring since I got to the Pale, and the majority of places I was going before I got here, were doctor's offices."

I flipped myself back over to the street with Spectrum Publishing's building on it to check for a doctor's office. I didn't see any nearby, so I popped back over to the hospital.

"That's going to take some getting used to," Ava giggled.

"Sorry, I was trying to figure out a quick way to get us where we need to be. You don't happen to be a vegan café connoisseur, do you?"

"No. I never understood the appeal of drinking coffee when it always made everyone's breath so bad. I don't even think I ever heard the word vegan when I was alive."

This was the first clue I'd gotten as to how long Ava had been here. She'd never told me what year she'd died, but I'd also never asked. When I wasn't in the middle of a life-or-death situation, I'd have to get more details from her so that I could start to piece together how the Pale worked. With the increasingly distinct inner voice forming inside my head, I was conscious of the fact that a serial killer wasn't the only thing I had to worry about right now.

I shook my head as I tried to get focused again. I caught the clock out of the corner of my eye, and it gave me an idea.

"How about rollerblading?"

Ava looked a little confused about my train of thought but answered me right away. "No, but before I got sick, I used to figure skate. Does that help?"

"Yes!"

I quickly explained to Ava that she couldn't use the wardrobe to get to places she hadn't been to before, but that didn't mean that we were stuck hoofing it. She seemed to readily accept the concept of gliding our way across the city, maybe finding this easier to believe than the shortcut I'd already shown her.

As we skated our way along the streets, I couldn't help but enjoy the glee on Ava's face. It was nice to see someone, who spent so much time helping others, take a minute to enjoy herself.

She's not free to just enjoy herself though, is she? She's busy on her way to help you, again. The only reason you even told her about any of this is because it helps you.

I did my best to ignore Nega-me, although there was some truth to the barbs that were being slung my way. While we rushed

132

over to Billie's office, I tried to catch Ava up on some of what we had discovered. Since I was just giving her a quick summary, I didn't cover anything other than what Rodger had been up to. I was still hoping to surprise Ava with a second gift later on when things calmed down a little.

When we reached the café, I took the stairs beside it two at a time in my rush to see if Billie had found anything yet. I was already in her cubicle when Ava finally made it to the top of the stairs.

"Over here," I shouted as I waved Ava over with one hand while I kept my eyes trained on the computer screen. Other employees were starting to filter in, and I was worried that our time for investigation was coming to a close.

Frustratingly, there was nothing new on Billie's computer. Just the same list of victims that she'd looked at countless times last night. I continued to watch Billie's screen as I filled Ava in on what I needed her to do. I knew I was being rude, not even bothering to make eye contact while I explained, but I didn't want to risk missing any clues Billie might dig up. Once again, I found myself wishing that she spent a little more time talking to herself.

Ava accepted her mission and took off to get started while I continued to obsessively hover over Billie's shoulder. With any luck, I was going to have a very busy evening ahead of me and the more information I had, the busier it was going to be.

As Ava disappeared, Jesse came shuffling in looking a little hung over.

"Thanks for the butt dial last night, Jesse." Billie's tone clearly illustrated the level of gratitude she felt, but there was a mischievous smirk she struggled to keep concealed. I, on the other hand, was incredibly grateful.

Jesse practically whispered his reply, probably because he was nursing a wicked headache. "Based on the carry-on sized luggage under your eyes, and the trough of caffeine on your desk, I'd guess you're feeling just as well rested and ready for an exciting day of office work as I am."

Billie laughed. "Not quite. How was the campaign last night? It certainly sounded like you were enjoying yourself." Despite the sleepless night and the other, much more important, things she had on her mind, she seemed genuinely interested in whether or not Jesse had had a good time. As they chatted, I noticed the screen on Billie's phone was lit up. It looked like she'd been taking notes on the killings. Most of what she had were questions, but I was glad to see that she'd outlined some avenues of investigation too. I was hungry to dig in and hoped for a productive day of sleuthing.

12

As it turned out, we weren't spending long at the office. Billie had an assignment to take shots of the city that might *actually* inspire people to visit this mediocre municipality. I had my doubts that she'd find anything worth her time, but I was glad that I'd decided to stay with Billie instead of trading tasks with Ava. If she was leaving the relative safety of the cubicle, I wanted to be there to see if she made any progress on the case.

Or you just can't bear to leave her side because you're pathetic.

"I left her this morning to get Ava's help. I left her to follow Rodger. Get some new material."

Nega-me wasn't so easily deterred. *Congratulations, you managed to tear yourself away for a measly couple of hours and you were a nervous wreck the entire time.*

"I was hardly a nervous wreck. Billie is where the leads are and that's my best chance at getting revenge. I think you're just jealous that I've stopped listening to your useless petty barbs."

Without another word, I am transported back to that truck. The hands around my throat made more powerful by rage. I desperately gasp for air but not enough is getting through to my lungs.

"I'll kill you, you little shit!"

My one hand gives up clawing at the ones
wrapped around my neck and, instead, begins to
search for anything else that might help to set me
free.

"Do you have any idea what you've done?"

I'm not getting enough oxygen for my brain
to make sense of what my fingers are brushing
against. I try grabbing anything they touch but my
free hand is still empty.

I give my head a shake and take in quick lungfuls of the air I don't actually need. I'm bent over with my hands on my knees when I'm finally released from the memory.

Never forget how pitiful your existence was. All you ever had was me. You'd do well to remember that the next time you decide you don't need my advice.

The voice in my head went silent, almost as if it had retreated and slammed a door on the way out.

"What? Are you hoping to punish me with the silent treatment?" As terrifying as that memory was, I'd never bowed to bullies before, and I wasn't about to start now. I braced myself as I prepared for another attack in retaliation for my retort, but there was nothing.

I decided not to push my luck and dropped it. I needed to pay attention to Billie before I lost her. The sooner Rodger was stopped, the sooner I could escape this translucent void. Nega-me seemed to be getting more powerful and I wasn't planning on sticking around long enough to see what it would do, next.

My battle with the dark side had only lasted a few minutes and, luckily, Billie was just passing the reception desk. The guy there stopped her as she turned towards the door to leave.

"Hey, Billie. There was a delivery for you this morning."

"Thanks, Casey. I was just on my way out. Do you mind if I grab it when I get back?"

"Actually, it's kind of big and taking up some of the legroom under the desk. Do you have a minute to take it now?"

Casey rolled his wheelchair back to reveal a box that pretty much filled the rest of the space under the desk. Billie looked a little confused, then seemed to make a mental connection.

"Sorry about that. I thought I had ordered this to be delivered to my apartment, not the office. I'll take it down with me now."

Billie dragged the box out from under Casey's desk, opened the door to the stairs, then awkwardly tried to maneuver the box toward her while holding the door open with her foot.

Casey laughed a little at the sight. "You need a hand with that?"

Billie hefted the box up and pushed through the door with her butt. "Nope, I'm good. Thanks, Casey. See you later." Given the size of the box, I wondered if Billie would be able to make it down the narrow staircase without the ability to see, but it turned out that whatever was inside was much lighter than it looked. Billie rested the package on top of her head as she descended carefully.

When we reached the parking lot, Billie threw the box in the back seat with an unceremonious toss. Obviously, whatever it was, it wasn't delicate.

*

We spent the next couple of hours taking shots of the city. I was surprised at how beautiful Billie was able to make it look. I began to think that she saw a very different world through her eyes.

"I wonder how she would see me?"

The question popped out of my mouth without permission. It was a stupid question. She, and every other Vitae out there, would never see any of the inhabitants of the Pale, again. This fact had never really bothered me that much before. It wasn't like I'd left behind a treasure trove of loved ones and cherished memories. But the more time I spent with Billie, the more I wondered what things might have been like if I'd met someone like her, or even Ava, when I was still alive.

I didn't have too long to brood over what might have been. We were pulling up to a location that I assumed had nothing to do with improving tourism in the area.

As Billie parked the car a few buildings down from the New Page Centre, I was filled with nervous energy. We must have been there to follow up on some of the questions she'd typed out this morning. Unfortunately, I had no idea where Rodger was, and Billie could be headed straight towards him. I was torn between scouting ahead and the fear that he'd somehow snatch her while I was gone. Ultimately, I decided to stay with Billie, since it wasn't like I could warn her if he *was* lurking around a corner, anyway.

Somehow, the stress started to get the better of me. My chest was tight, and the bright sunny day suddenly didn't seem to provide enough light. The already hazy appearance of the Pale looked dim and drained of colour, like when a dark cloud unexpectedly blocks the sun on an otherwise beautiful day. The drastic change in lighting must have been harder on my eyes than I thought as I was getting dizzy, and having trouble focusing on anything.

The closer Billie got to the centre, the worse this weird panic attack seemed to get. I was having trouble concentrating and I'd fallen behind. When I realized Billie was already inside, I hurriedly stumbled forward, my limbs feeling completely drained of all energy.

I passed through the door and as I got closer to Billie, all of the symptoms began to ease up. By the time we reached the front counter, I'd regained control over my body and my breathing. My vision was still a little blurry, but it was no longer drained of colour. Things hadn't gotten as bad as the last time, when I'd nearly blacked out, but I couldn't find it in me to be relieved. Instead, I was concerned about what appeared to be a steady increase in attacks. I'd gone months in the Pale with no indication that I was on the verge of fading or going insane and now, it seemed, both were increasingly becoming a possibility.

I tried to shake it off and focus on the one thing I could control: trying to get a murdering P.o.S. off the streets for good.

Billie was talking to the clerk behind the counter. It wasn't the woman I'd seen chatting with Rodger. This clerk was a man, probably in his mid-thirties, with long blonde hair pulled back into a ponytail and tattoos climbing up his neck from beneath his denim button-up shirt.

Like with everyone else, Billie seemed to not only know him but was already on friendly terms with him.

"Thanks, Nicky. I was hoping to find out if anyone else hadn't shown up in a while."

"No problem, Billie. You know the drill. I can't give you any confidential information, but I also can't stop you from generously taking time to hang out with our members, especially those who love to chat." Nicky gave Billie a little wink. She smiled as she dropped her gaze to the volunteer sign-in sheet. As she held her pen poised over the page, she subtly bit her lip.

"Hey, Nicky. I think I forgot my hat the last time I was here. Would you mind taking a quick look in the back to see if it's around?"

"Sure thing. What does it look like?"

"It's a grey knitted toque. No pom-poms or anything though." Billie made a gesture and a face, as if it was obvious that she would never be caught dead wearing a pom-pom.

Nicky laughed, then hooked his thumb to point behind him. "I'll be right back. Let me see what I can find."

I suspected that Billie hadn't actually lost a hat. The second he was through the door she had her phone out. Billie quickly snapped a picture of the sign-in page, then flipped to the ones behind it, taking shots of each before turning to the next.

The lost and found pile must have been pretty small. Nicky was back before Billie'd gotten halfway through the stack of pages, but I hoped it was enough for her to have gotten a shot of Rodger's duplicitous moniker. I had no way of knowing if it was his real name or not, but I certainly hoped it could lead somewhere.

"Sorry, Billie. There were no toques, pom-pommed or otherwise."

Billie discreetly tucked her phone back into her messenger bag. "Thanks for checking. I'll be in the computer lab helping with resumés if you need me."

With that, Billie turned and headed for the stairwell. The boards of the old wooden steps creaked as she made her way to the second floor. We entered the first door on the left side of the hall, and I was reminded of the first time I'd seen this dusty excuse for a lab. I preferred the spot at the library to these ancient dinosaurs disguised as computers, but so did everyone else. Regardless, I'd quickly learned that it was faster to wait for some research student to finish writing their dissertation at the library than it was to wait for one of these relics to boot up.

Despite the barely functional devices, the room was fairly packed. Billie spent the next two hours rotating around the room and helping anyone who asked. I think I would have preferred having my fingernails individually ripped out over being subjected to the amount of small talk that Billie endured, but it was part of why she was here, and she never seemed bored or impatient with anyone she spoke to.

While she worked the room, I decided to do the same. I found a couple of conversations to eavesdrop on and saw more videos on power poses and interview hacks than I would have cared to, but by the time Billie was checking the clock on her phone, I'd found nothing useful.

We began to make our way back downstairs and this time I ran a quick sweep of our route to see if we were likely to stumble across Rodger on our way to the car. The coast was clear, and we got back to the bug without any incident.

I expected her to head back to the office but, instead, we went in the opposite direction. When Billie pulled up in front of the police station, I wondered what she'd learned at the centre while I was busy being useless.

When we approached the counter, the officer barely glanced up from the screen in front of her. "Please state the nature of your visit today." It seemed this robotic request was all the acknowledgment we were going to get as she continued typing away on her keyboard.

"Hi," Billie said, "I'm here to see if there's been any progress on the attack I reported last week." I noticed that Billie hadn't called it a mugging, and I hoped that she'd believed what I said about it being connected to the killings.

Without so much as making eye contact, the officer responded just as mechanically as before, "Do you have a case number?" Billie provided the number and the officer stopped typing, presumably long enough to review the file. "There's nothing to report at this time."

"Can I speak to the officer who's working the case?"

"According to the file, there were no witnesses, no cameras in the area, and nothing was actually taken. Unless you are able to provide any new information, there is no case to work."

I could tell Billie was getting frustrated, but I couldn't tell if it was with the lack of progress or just the complete absence of any empathy on behalf of the tired-looking officer.

"Is Detective Cuff available? I'd like to speak to him."

Without responding, the officer clacked away on her keys again. She stayed silent for so long, I thought that she'd forgotten Billie was even there. Billie shifted her weight from side to side and seemed about the say something when the officer finally replied. "He'll be down in a minute. Go take a seat in the waiting area." And with that, she looked past Billie and called out "Next."

Billie and I hung out in the waiting room for the next hour. She wasn't idle while we bided our time. As I watched over her shoulder, I saw Billie flip back and forth between the pictures of the volunteer sign-in sheets and her spreadsheet. She seemed to be logging the history of each volunteer, probably looking for a connection between the dates that the different victims had been murdered.

While we waited, Billie recorded every name she'd grabbed a picture of. Unfortunately, she hadn't been able to snap enough pages to take her back to before the killings started. I was curious if a certain volunteer would *coincidentally* show up around the same time as the first victim on her sheet. Or, if perhaps there was an even longer list of victims that Billie hadn't heard of, but could discover if she managed to narrow down when Rodger began volunteering. After all, *I* wasn't on her list.

I'd been so focused on what Billie was doing, I'd forgotten to keep an eye out for helpful inhabitants of the Pale roaming about. I realized I'd missed my opportunity to scope out some spooks to learn from, when I spotted a man in khakis and a blue dress shirt as he strode over towards us. On my plane of existence, he was not. A very audible sigh leaked from lips hidden beneath his dark, bushy mustache. The badge hanging from a chain around the man's neck hinted he was probably a detective. I didn't recognize him from the night of Billie's attack, but maybe he'd been assigned to investigate afterward.

"Hello, Billie. What can I do for you today?" He seemed resigned to getting this conversation over with.

Billie's face was serious. There was no hint of the friendly smiles she'd used on Nicky. "I wanted to talk about the murders, Detective Cuff, and see if there's been any progress in identifying a suspect."

Cuff shook his head as if this had been the response he was expecting but hoped he wouldn't hear. "Billie, I've already told you that we have no reason to believe that these deaths are connected. There are no patterns to the victims, the locations, or the timeline."

There was almost a growl to Billie's voice as she responded. "Except for the fact that every single one of them has visited the New Page Centre."

"That's more of an indicator that those people are in a higher-risk group, than proof of a serial killer."

"I think you mean "more vulnerable". Someone is taking advantage of the fact that the majority of people don't give a crap what happens to these victims."

"You may be right, but with no other evidence, there's no case here."

"What about Shay Walsh? No one's seen her in a few days. Could you check to see if she's here, at all? I know that she's helped herself to the food she couldn't afford, in the past."

Cuff sighed and waved for Billie to follow him. We wound our way up some stairs to a tidy little desk in the back corner of a room filled with cops. After a quick search on the computer, Cuff replied with, "Sorry, Billie. There's no one here by that name."

"What about Jane Does? Do you have any of them?"

Cuff hammered away on his keyboard, a frown forming as his thick eyebrows pinched together, shading his eyes. "We have two. One in holding and one in the morgue."

Billie took a deep breath. "Can I see if I'm able to identify them?"

Cuff brought up images of two women. It was obvious from the pictures who was here temporarily, and who would be relocating to very permanent accommodations in the near future. He rotated his screen so that Billie could take a look. Billie's gaze seemed to go straight for the corpse. Sympathy filled Billie's eyes as she quietly identified the body. "That's Shay. How did she die?"

Cuff looked sorry for Billie as he slowly turned the screen back to face him. He brought up the details on the dead woman. "She was found on a park bench, Thursday morning. Cause of death seems to have been an overdose a few hours before she was found."

The sorrow on Billie's face was immediately replaced with indignation. "She's been clean for over two years now. There's no way she was ever going to poison herself with that stuff again. She was even working towards getting visitation with her kids."

"Addiction is a very hard burden to bear, Billie. Each new day is another battle to fight with your demons. It looks like Shay may have lost a battle, Thursday morning, not realizing it would cost her the war." I was surprised to hear so much compassion from someone who spent his days sifting through the filth of our city. Billie didn't seem to listen to a word he'd said. "I think the centre has contact information for her sister. Her family will want to know what happened." Billie stood, quickly. "Thank you for taking the time to speak with me today, Detective Cuff."

He gave her a nod. "We'll make sure her family is notified."

With that, Billie turned to leave the station. As she walked, she pulled up the spreadsheet on her phone and added Shay Walsh to the list of victims.

*

By the time Billie plopped her bag down next to her desk, there wasn't much time left in her typical workday. She uploaded the pictures she'd taken of the city, sent some emails, and then gathered up her things to leave. Everyone in the office seemed to be anxious for the weekend. A group of about five of them all made their way down to the parking lot, together. I wasn't really paying attention to their conversation, so I missed what they'd been talking about when someone said "Okay. See you tonight, Billie?"

Billie raised her hand to wave. "See you later."

As Jesse slowly shuffled towards his car, Billie grabbed his arm and detoured them back towards the café. "I think you might need one of those buckets of coffee if you're going to make it home."

Jesse nodded in agreement. After grabbing their orders, they both flopped into chairs at a table near the garage-style patio door. It was rolled up, despite the fact that it was late September. The café was half full of people who were all incredibly focused on the screens in front of them. Billie and Jesse seemed to be the only ones interacting with another human being.

While the two of them talked about their plans for the weekend, I people-watched. This café seemed to attract all kinds. There was a woman with flaming red hair that had been twisted into dreadlocks, a person in parachute pants and a man wearing a beret, thick-rimmed glasses, and a handlebar mustache with a scarf tucked all the way up to his chin.

Oh, Alex. Look at how sloppy you're getting.

The snide comment put me on alert. I glanced around the crowd again and couldn't believe my stupidity. I ran over to the living caricature of a Parisian to analyze him, more closely.

Congratulations, Alex. You finally noticed that the person hiding their face and chin should be a cause for concern.

The man's hat was pulled down low and his head was angled, with his chin practically touching his chest as he stared at the laptop in front of him. I couldn't get a good enough look at his face, so I tried to see what he was working on. His hands hovered over the keyboard, but they weren't typing. The screen displayed the homepage for some news site. He could have been skimming the articles or he could have been using it as a cover for listening in on the conversation happening a few feet away from him.

I stopped for a minute and tried to think. Yes, I could hear Billie and Jesse's conversation from over here, but what are the chances that Rodger would just happen to be in here, in disguise, at the exact same time they decide to come in for an after-work coffee, which I've never seen them do before?

Given everything that was going on, a little paranoia seemed warranted, but I needed to keep it from getting out of control; keep it from distracting me from what needed to be done. I paused and tried to take a more objective look. The man sitting in front of me had a smaller build than Rodger. Also, this guy wasn't exactly dressed to blend in.

I relaxed a little and went back over to Billie and Jesse's table. I tried to ignore the inescapable feeling that they were being watched. Although I needed to be vigilant, I couldn't let myself slip into the insanity that would await with suspecting every person Billie encountered.

As Billie returned their mugs to the counter, I went ahead to scope out the route to the car. I noted a dog walker, someone pushing a stroller, and a café patron engrossed in a book on the patio. Further down the sidewalk was a man set up with a cardboard sign and a paper cup. I took off to see if Rodger had snagged himself another outfit from his tickle trunk.

By the time I cleared the homeless person, Billie was already getting in her car. I hopped in, but only glued my feet to the car floor so I could stand up to survey the lot, and make sure we weren't being followed. After a few blocks, I finally began to loosen up, the seemingly unwarranted high alert at an end.

13

Billie stopped to run a few errands on the way home while I ran over the day in my head. As we pulled into the driveway behind Billie's building, I couldn't help but wonder if there was anything I could have done to prevent Shay's death. If the timing was accurate, she "overdosed" the morning I'd lost Rodger at the motel. Logically, I knew there was nothing I could have done, but I still felt this irrational guilt. I'd never met the woman. Yet I couldn't help wonder if I'd been able to figure things out sooner, could Rodger have been stopped before he took another victim? I knew that there was no actual proof that Rodger had killed Shay, but it fit the pattern, and I knew that he'd been out lurking somewhere during the early hours of the morning.

Billie was quiet, which wasn't unusual. Her eyebrows were scrunched together, and her lips were pressed so hard against each other that they were almost white. I could tell there was a lot going on inside that analytical brain of hers.

She tossed the large box she'd taken from the office on the floor as soon as she was through her apartment door. She seemed in no hurry to open it and moved on quickly to the kitchen. After feeding Taco and warming up some leftover Pad Thai for herself, she took her bowl into the living room. As Billie shovelled the steaming noodles into her mouth, she scrolled through different social media accounts. For some, this would be an idle way to kill some time. For Billie, it was research. She would flip back and forth between the list of volunteers on her spreadsheet, then try to locate matching accounts online. As she found some, she'd record their handles on the spreadsheet.

After a couple of hours of this, Billie's phone pinged with a message.

"c u in an hour 😝 👻 don't 4get to wear some white 😎"

I didn't catch who had sent the reminder before she turned the screen off.

"Crap." Billie threw down her phone and rushed to her bedroom.

Given the fact that she'd just been instructed to wear something she didn't currently have on, I waited in the living room. When Billie came out, she was wearing makeup, tight black jeans, a white halter top, and a peacock-blue, leather-looking jacket. Based on the contents of Billie's fridge, I assumed it wasn't actually leather. She rushed around for a minute, grabbed a few things from her messenger bag, then threw on her black combat boots. "I'll be out late, Taco. Don't wait up!" With that, she quickly locked her apartment and rushed down the back steps to her car.

As she drove, Billie's fingers drummed the steering wheel. Since there was no music on in the car, I couldn't tell if it was to some tune playing in her head, or nervous excitement at whatever was planned for tonight. Her eyes kept glancing towards the clock on the dash and I had the suspicion we were on the verge of being late.

When we pulled up in front of another apartment building, I assumed it wasn't the final destination, given Billie's outfit. There was a group of four people, all wearing some form of white, waiting on the sidewalk and looking like they'd already started the night's festivities a few hours ago. I watched as Billie plastered a smile on her face that I couldn't help but feel was forced. She hopped out of her car but stood there with the driver's side open, leaning over the roof towards the waiting group.

"Your chauffeur has arrived!"

A general shout of cheers and whistles filled the air as the group piled into the car. In the dark, it'd been hard to see much but as they crammed themselves in, I recognized a few of the people from Billie's office. One person, named Ash I think, wore a great big pin that said "Party Animal" and another that said, "Buy me a drink, it's my birthday!".

It was a very noisy drive as Jesse, somehow recovered from his previous night, sat in the passenger seat blaring music and repeatedly using an air horn app on his phone to be as loud as humanly possible. I had no idea how Billy was able to concentrate on the road. I was also not thrilled with having to give up my seat. I knew that I could have just sat there at the same time as Jesse, but I chose to "glue" myself to the small space between the two front seats instead. At least I couldn't actually feel the gear shifter that would have been bashing me in the knees.

We eventually pulled up in front of what smelled like a cereal factory. There were no streetlamps, and the night was too dark for me to get a decent look at our surroundings.

"This city really needs to invest in more safety lighting," I murmured as everyone piled out of the car.

Given how isolated this area was, I began to question my assumptions about where we were headed.

"All right, you sloppy drunks, we'll hoof it from here. When we're ready to go, I'll come back for the car and pick you up. But I think a brisk walk in the night air will do you some good, before we try to convince the servers that you're ready for more fun."

This declaration was met with some giggles and some groans, but Ash was already linking arms with the others and trying to encourage them to skip to their destination, recreating a rather famous scene from an equally famous movie.

Once we made it to our destination, I saw the reason for all the white clothing. It seemed the Vitae were about to do some blacklight bowling. The entire alley was lit with black lights and the music was blasting. The only areas with marginal visibility for me were the semi-lit spots at the bar and washrooms. The dim light did not, however, prevent me from catching more than one pair of eyes checking Billie out as she and her friends made their way through the crowd.

As the others grabbed shoes and a lane, Billie went to go grab some drinks. Even the bartender, who probably spent the majority of her shifts brushing off clumsy advances, was putting the moves on. "What can I get you? And whatever it is, it's on me." She said with a wink.

Billie smiled, politely. "Thanks, but I'm topping up an entire birthday party. I'll take four beers and a water please."

The bartender pretended she couldn't hear Billie over the music and gestured for her to come closer. Billie seemed to laugh to herself at the obvious ploy. She leaned slightly closer, then yelled her order again. While she waited, I watched her keep a somewhat protective eye on her friends. She looked more like a teacher supervising a field trip than someone who was there for a good time.

When the drinks came, Billie tried to pay but the bartender refused. Instead, she slipped, what I can only assume was her number, into the top of the open water bottle. Billie nodded thanks, then carefully made her way to an available section of handrail that doubled as a counter overlooking the lanes. Holding two full beers over her head got her group's attention and she was quickly joined by the others.

When Billie removed the paper from the mouth of her bottle of water, she turned back to see if the bartender was watching. It looked like she was busy with other customers, possibly even casting her line to see if she could snag some other fish. Having confirmed that she was not looking, Billie quickly took the number out of her drink and dropped it in a nearby trash bin.

The birthday group returned to their lane with Billie joining, in tow. After a few rounds and some embarrassing gutter balls, Billie started to relax. For someone who had spent the entire time I'd known her alone or avoiding people, it was nice to finally see her enjoying herself. The office crew even started up an impromptu dance party. While Billie danced, she looked completely at peace, like she was in her element. Her forced smiles from earlier had turned genuine and I was glad to see her happy.

After we'd been there for about an hour, a very visible, very solid couple joined the Vitae who filled the bowling alley. They hadn't spotted me yet and just seemed to be there to take in the music and enjoy the pulsating life around them. I'd met so few dead people that I decided I should probably take advantage of this opportunity to see if I could learn any new tricks. I decided to take a note from Billie and Ava's books and tried being friendly.

"Hey. Sorry to interrupt, but I don't see many of us around here." The couple hadn't heard me over the music, so I got a little closer. "Hey!" The two turned to me a little startled. "I'm Alex!"

The man closest to me was wearing dockers, a dress shirt, a sweater vest, and a bowtie: not exactly dressed for a night on the town, but neither was I in my hoodie. He extended his hand for me to shake. "I'm Munin and this is Andrea." He had an accent that hinted that he probably came from Scandinavia.

I turned towards Andrea, who was dressed a little more appropriately for the venue. He was wearing a black dress shirt with the top few buttons undone, and dark blue jeans. His onyx hair was slicked back, and his flawlessly tanned complexion made him look like he sold watches or underwear for a living. His appearance made me wonder, if any of us had been wearing white, whether the blacklights would have worked on our clothes.

Andrea hadn't stopped dancing during the introductions, but he nodded his head in acknowledgement of my wave. I turned back to Munin and shouted, "How long have you two been here?"

Munin smiled as he replied, "I'm assuming you don't mean at the bowling alley."

I smiled a little at this. "No, I guess I was trying to find a polite way to ask when you kicked the bucket."

"I died about six months ago and Andrea has been dancing his way through death for about three months now. He seems to think that if he refuses to believe he is dead, then he simply won't be. How any living person could survive the amount of partying he does, though, would be completely beyond me."

"Would you rather I lay quietly in my grave, waiting for some tunnel of light?" Andrea shouted over to us. He too had an accent, but his sounded Greek.

"No, My Love. I would not have you any other way." Munin blew him a kiss. Andrea winked, then turned to glide solo down one of the lanes.

While Andrea danced, Munin and I talked as I kept an eye on Billie and her friends. We didn't discuss how we'd gotten here, but we did talk about some of the things we'd seen since arriving.

It turned out that Andrea hadn't much resembled his current self while he was alive. When Munin found him, Andrea was a scared and confused new arrival that more closely resembled a wiry long-distance runner than the muscled Greek model he now appeared to be. According to Munin, the base features were still the same, but somehow, Andrea had increased his muscle mass, cleared up his skin, and even changed his outfit on a regular basis.

"What about you?" I asked, "Have you made any modifications?" Although it seemed useless, I was intrigued about what this ability to change your looks could mean deeper down, at the heart of the rules that governed the Pale.

"Aldrig — no. I am content with who I am. The only thing I wish is that I had met Andrea when we were alive. But at least I am lucky enough to have met him in this afterlife we've found ourselves in. It looks like you have not been quite so lucky." Munin gestured towards Billie and her friends. "Were you forced to leave someone behind?"

I didn't think I'd been so obvious in my watch over the rowdy birthday group, and I was a little surprised that Munin would equate my protective glances with the connection he shared with Andrea.

"No. There was no one left to mourn me." There was a hint of bitterness that had unintentionally crept into my voice. Munin waited for an explanation, but I gave none. He didn't pry for more information.

In the interest of reciprocity, I shared my speedy travel tip instead. My not-so-subtle change of subject put a bit of a damper on the conversation. Munin asked a few questions about my methods of getting around, but our exchange quickly dwindled. We stood there awkwardly for a few minutes before Munin pretended that Andrea was calling him over, and he disappeared into the crowd that was gathering by the bar.

I was relieved to be left alone and moved to join the birthday revelers. Never having been a dancer myself, and seeing as I couldn't bowl, I hung out and vicariously enjoyed the fun of others. After a few hours of drinking, dancing, and occasionally bowling, the group finally looked ready to head out. Ash, Jesse, and the other two who I couldn't remember the names of, huddled together for warmth on the sidewalk while Billie ran for her car. Their giggles could be heard for quite a ways as we wove deeper into the poorly-lit side streets where Billie had parked.

The quiet and isolation reminded me too much of the night Billie was attacked, and I grew anxious for her to hurry up and get to the safety of her car. The distance hadn't felt this far when we were making our way towards the bowling alley with the whole group. Now that we were alone out here, I didn't like how vulnerable it made Billie — not that she was some defenceless mark — but even a trained professional can get overwhelmed if they're outnumbered.

Picturing an ever-growing mob of thugs hanging out just around the next corner had me on high alert. I was relieved when we finally got to the car without any problems. Billie buckled up and started the engine, and I'd just begun to relax a little when a sudden knock on her window had me nearly jumping out of my skin. When I looked over there was a cardboard sign with a message scrawled across it in permanent marker pressed against the driver's side window, "Will wash windows for food". The knock must have startled Billie, too. She unclenched the fists that had formed in front of her chest, then rolled down the window a few centimetres.

"I don't need my windows washed, but if you take this to the all-night diner on Mapleview, they'll give you a hot meal on me." Billie passed him a business card for the diner after writing something on the back.

Given my experience with Rodger and his disguises, I was immediately on edge. I popped out of the car and tried to get a look at the person holding the sign. Like Rodger had been, the other night, this person was covered in layers of clothes that made it hard for me to tell anything about them. Their gloved fingers took the card and flipped it over to look at what Billie had written on the back. It was her name, but just her first name. Even that could be enough for Rodger to make some headway with figuring out where Billie lived. I still hadn't forgotten the suspicious break-in at Jesse's.

The homeless person gave a palsied nod and backed away from the car. As they stood up straighter, I tried to get a better look at their size. This person was too short to be Rodger, but the encounter still had me on edge. I quickly scouted the area to see if he was hiding in the shadows. Maybe he'd hired this person to try to grab Billie and take her somewhere more convenient for whatever he had planned.

My, my, my. Getting quite paranoid, aren't we?

I rolled my eyes at Nega-me, who had decided to make another appearance. I hoped that maybe if I ignored it, Nega-me would just shut up and go away.

When I didn't find anything, I beamed myself to the passenger seat of Billie's car as it pulled away from the curb. I couldn't relax enough to feel relieved that Rodger didn't seem to be anywhere in sight. The escape of the evening spent at the lanes had lulled me into a false sense of calm, temporarily losing focus on what was important. I'd let myself get distracted and I couldn't do that.

What does it matter? Even if it was Rodger, you wouldn't have been able to do anything other than watch as he silenced your precious Billie, forever.

I tried to ignore the jab, but it's always hard to fight against logic. None of the tricks I'd learned so far would help me to prevent anything from happening in the real world.

While Billie drove her friends home, I stewed. My only hope was that Ava had been successful in the mission I'd given her.

14

After seeing Billie safely home and in bed, I went to wait for Ava at her family's place. I'd have preferred to have been dream walking with Billie, trying to find out what her subconscious mind was making of all this, but taking Rodger down was going to require a multi-pronged approach. With any luck, Ava would be expanding my resource pool.

My paranoia made it impossible to just hang out in the backyard. I found myself pacing, then popping back to Billie's, then zapping back to continue my pacing. If I'd actually been capable of touching the ground, there'd probably have been a noticeable lack of grass along my path by the time Ava finally arrived.

"Hey, Alex. Sorry, I'm late. I got a little lost."

I tried to push my impatience aside and take some of the urgency out of my tone. I needed to remember that Ava was doing me a favour, like she always did. "Hey, Ava. How did it go?"

Her great big grin implied that not only was she happy with the results, but that she was proud of herself too. "I found someone who I think will work."

"That's great. Do you remember the way back to their house? I'd like to get started tonight, if I can."

"I think so. I tried to find something special about each street I took. Kinda like a mental breadcrumb trail to follow."

As anxious as I was to get going, I'd mentally promised Ava another gift, and that wasn't the only thing I owed her. It was time for me to give her the props she was due. "I don't know what I would do without you, Ava."

The earnestness of my tone seemed to surprise her a little. She reached a comforting hand towards me, but before she could say anything, I continued. "I really mean that. I would probably be a raving lunatic if I didn't have you here to keep me going. I know I haven't been there, at all, for you, and I'm sorry about that. I'm going to try to do better."

She grabbed my hand and gave it a little squeeze. Her gentle smile reminded me of the one my grandmother would give me. It was a look that was a mixture of pride, compassion, and a hint of condescension; like she was pleased that I finally learned something that I should've grasped much earlier.

Before she could feel obligated to deny that I'd been a selfish ass, I pulled her towards the house.

"Where are we going? I thought I was leading the way."

I laughed a little at the puzzled look on her face. "I want to show you something first. Where's your brother's room?"

"Why do we need to see my brother?" Ava had stopped in her tracks and held fast to my hand, jerking me to a stop. This was the first time she hadn't just gone along with whatever I'd asked her to do.

"Don't worry. You're going to like this."

She seemed somewhat reassured, but I noticed the way she moved to stand between me and the house. I hung back a little, letting her lead the way through a few walls until we ended up in a space-themed bedroom. A mobile of the planets hung over a small desk stacked with books. The walls were covered in a swirling galaxy. I wondered if it was some sort of wallpaper, or if someone had spent days painstakingly painting this for him. The ceiling even had hundreds of those little glow-in-the-dark stars stuck to it.

I looked down at the sleeping child who was lucky enough to be surrounded by so many people who cared about him, even those he didn't realize were there. Although I knew this was Ava's younger brother, I couldn't help but think that he looked close to the same age as her. Again, I found myself wondering how long she'd been here.

Before I could get distracted, I asked Ava to check to see if he was dreaming. I certainly wasn't about to go snooping around in her brother's head. Ava crouched so that she was on her knees beside the bed. After a moment, she turned back towards me, her face a little serious and hesitant. "He's dreaming. Are you going to tell me what this is all about?"

I was so excited to give her the good news, I couldn't help the giant grin that now exploded on my face. "I'm going to teach you how to talk to your brother."

Ava's eyes went wide in disbelief.

"What's he dreaming about right now?"

It took a minute for her to respond. After she seemed to finally absorb what I'd said, she smiled. "He's dreaming about swimming at the beach."

"Can you try putting a radio on shore or in a boat near him, and playing some music on it?"

"OK. I'll give it a try."

After a few minutes, I started to get restless. I was excited to give Ava this gift, but we still had other things we needed to be doing. I tried to remember that this was something that took me time to figure out how to do and that I needed to be patient. While I waited, I found myself wondering, *If I'd been wearing a watch when I died, would it still work here in the Pale?*

Eventually, Ava sat back up with a smile on her face. "It worked. Now what, Teach?"

I laughed a little at her teasing. "Now, try saying something through the radio. If it helps, you could try picturing that you're just playing a recording of something you've said."

"You're a genius!" Ava immediately dove back into her brother's face. Seeing her excitement made me realize that it would be cruel to ask Ava to leave the second I'd given her a way to speak to her family.

Your sentimentality is going to cost you. Your weak need to pay this child back is eating up precious time you could be using to futilely attempt to stop a monster that is more powerful than you ever will be again.

"Shut up!" I'd accidentally answered Nega-me out loud. Ava jumped up startled.

"Alex?"

I scrubbed my face with my hands as I tried to break the connection with my pessimistic self. "Sorry. I was talking to myself."

A look crossed Ava's face, but I didn't quite catch the meaning behind it. She gave one quick glance back towards her brother. "Let's go. We still have a mission to accomplish."

"No, it's all right. Were you able to talk to him?"

"Actually, I couldn't figure out what to say. There's been so much I want to tell him about, but I just couldn't find the right words. I'll try again later. In the meantime, let's hit the road."

I felt bad for cutting the moment short, but I really did want to get moving. I tried telling myself that Ava would probably prefer to give it a try in private, without me lurking behind her having a screaming match with myself.

We walked out through the wall into the side yard. Instead

of rollerblading there, Ava had another idea. An idea I really didn't like but, considering the ass I'd been — both recently and pretty much since I'd met her — I decided to play along, under one condition.

Ava clapped her hands and jumped up and down a little. "This is going to be so much fun, Alex."

"I'm glad you think so." My stomach began to churn like there was a mixer full of hot nacho cheese in there. "Fun" wouldn't be the word I would use. Words like "terrifying" or "hellish" were probably more appropriate.

Ava made a fist and raised it over her head. She turned her gaze skyward, then slowly rose off the ground. As she tucked her other arm into her chest, she picked up speed and flew around the roof of her house in a superhero pose. I could almost imagine a bright red cape, the same shade as her shoes, flapping about behind her. When she had done one lap she came back down and landed on the balls of her feet, as if someone had gently lowered her to the earth. The smile on her face lit up the darkness around us.

"Now you try!"

Taking a deep breath, I spread my arms out beside me like they were wings. Instead of a bird, I pictured an airplane with jets so that I wouldn't need to ridiculously flap around. Gently, I increased the imaginary power to the engines. When I finally got up the nerve to look down, I could see that I'd risen high enough to clear the garden gnome that was beside me. The mess in my stomach immediately threatened to turn from a slowly churning condiment into a full-blown fountain of spewed sauce. I dropped back to the ground with a jarring thump.

Ava clapped and giggled with excitement. "You did it!"

I took a few deep breaths in an attempt to clear the remaining wooziness I was feeling. I had promised Ava that we would do this, so there was no sense in delaying the inevitable. I tried not to make my tone too harsh as I said, "Come on. Let's get going."

Ava clapped some more and began to take her hero stance again.

"Remember though, we're sticking close to the ground."

"Got it. We wouldn't be able to see my breadcrumbs from high up anyway. I walked home because I figured you probably wouldn't want to try my way of getting around."

Glad to be getting back on track, I spread my arms again and tried to focus on where we were headed instead of the uncomfortable fact that my feet were no longer touching the safety of the lawn. As I turned to lay flat in the air, I tried to imagine that I was just spread across the top of a car. It didn't help much, but at least I could pretend there was something solid between me and the rock-hard surface I'd crash into if the laws of physics worked properly here. It didn't matter that I couldn't die or even get hurt if I fell. My brain *was not* ready to be rational about heights.

Instead of panicking, I tried to stay focused on memorizing our route. We made our way along the sidewalk at a pace that was slow enough for me to check street signs and learn the area we were heading to, but fast enough that we would ideally arrive at our destination before daybreak. I'd been hoping to get some dream sessions in tonight, but it wasn't looking very likely.

When we arrived at a generic-looking two-storey brick house, I still had one more task for Ava.

"Hey, I was wondering if you could keep an eye out for someone new who might show up. Her name is Shay Walsh."

"Sure thing, Alex. What does she look like?"

I hesitated as I tried to remember details from the photo of the corpse I'd seen. I hadn't really paid that much attention, other than the fact that she was clearly dead. I decided to feign ignorance.

"I haven't actually seen her before. I know she died recently of a drug overdose, and she has some kids. Sorry, I can't give you more to go on."

"That's okay. I try to watch out for all the newbies, so I'll let you know if I meet anyone like that."

"Thanks, Ava. What would I do without you?" Ava's only reply was a smile as she said goodbye and took off into the sunrise. Once she was gone, I tried to focus on what I needed to do, now. Breaking my rule, once again, I headed inside and immediately went up to the second floor. The dawn light filtering in through the windows provided enough visibility for me to determine the layout of my surroundings.

Directly to my right was an open washroom with closed doors on either side of it. Tentatively, I poked my head through each of the doors to try to determine which one was the master bedroom. The first turned out to be an office. Behind door number two, I found my target.

I knew I'd probably already lost my chance to dream-walk, but any information I could get, before I returned to keeping an eye on Billie, would save me time later tonight. Things like the layout of the room and the orientation of the sleepers would be helpful if I came back in the pitch dark. I counted the number of steps from the door to the foot of the dually occupied, queen-sized bed.

As I approached, I was momentarily peeved that I'd forgotten to ask Ava for any details as to which of these two people was the one I wanted. Enough light was peeking around the curtains for me to make out two bodies, but the one on the right was sleeping on their side with the covers pulled all the way up to their ear. I couldn't make out anything about them other than a mop of curly black hair.

The sleeper on the left was laying on their back. Fortunately, when I drew closer, my question as to which of these two I was here for, was answered when I spied a familiar bushy mustache.

I'd asked Ava to find me the home address of a cop, preferably a detective. I'd instructed her to choose one that seemed the most sympathetic to those less fortunate, and didn't seem like the type to just try to get through their caseload quickly. It appeared that both Ava and Billie had identified Detective Cuff as the person most likely to help us.

The *very* audible snoring coming from his side of the bed hinted that I may still get a chance to lay some groundwork before I needed to come back, tonight. I quickly dropped my face into the detective's head. Unfortunately, he wasn't in the middle of a dream. Frankly, I was surprised that either of the occupants of the bed were asleep, given all the noise he was making.

There being nothing else I could do or learn at that time, I decided to cut my losses and return to Billie's. I was interested to see what we'd be up to today and, if I was lucky, I still might have a chance to try planting that address, again.

15

When I got back to Billie's place, she was still pretty zonked out. I was getting so familiar with her sleeping patterns that I didn't even need to check to make sure she wasn't dreaming. Her body was still, her face relaxed, and her mouth hung open in an almost silent snore. But knowing what I would see didn't stop me from checking. As confident as I was growing in my ability to read Billie, there was too much at stake to get complacent. After confirming my hypothesis, I plopped myself down on the floor between her bed and the window. From there, I could still watch her face, gently lit by the few stray sunbeams that made their way into the room.

"If I can't sleep, this is a pretty good substitute."

Watching Billie as she quietly breathed in and out let me slip into a similarly peaceful meditation. I was able to clear everything else from my mind and just focus on her breath. I hadn't realized how much I needed this. My days had been getting pretty full, lately. Between keeping an eye on Billie, patrolling the New Page Centre, and trying to invade the dreams of multiple people, I was really starting to feel spread thin.

And with that thought came the end of my temporary respite. My brain began to whirl with all of the tasks I was juggling. Instead of enjoying the quiet break, I now found myself eager for Billie to get up so that we could get started with the day. I hoped that whatever we would be up to would bring us closer to stopping Rodger and his merciless slaughtering.

"No, not merciless." I couldn't justify that categorization after watching him in action the other night. "He'd let that man live, but why? Did he decide it was too risky? Was there someone else, a witness of some sort, that I hadn't noticed? Was he simply collecting information on his target so that he could plan another air-tight murder?"

Once again, I had more questions than answers. I needed more information.

My train of thought was interrupted when, earlier than I expected, (especially given the late hour we got in last night), Billie's alarm went off. She let out a groan as she fumbled for her phone. Once the alarm had been silenced, she lay there so long that I wondered if she'd gone back to sleep. Eventually, she let out a sigh and half rolled out of the bed. As soon as Billie was standing, Taco greeted her with some ankle bumps that nearly caused her to trip. While the two of them went into the washroom, I headed to the kitchen to wait for breakfast. While I waited, I noticed the large package Billie had received yesterday and wondered what was inside. I tried sticking my face in, but with no light in there: I couldn't see a thing.

After a bowl of fruit, a very dark tea, and a toasted crumpet oozing with peanut butter, Billie pushed the large box into the living room with her foot. However, my curiosity wouldn't be satiated yet. First, Billie began pulling a bunch of stuff out of the closet. This assortment of items seemed a little less random than last weekend when she'd taken Sam to the archery range, and now that I knew Billie a little better, I had a guess as to what we'd be doing.

A hatchet, bug spray, metal dishes, a first aid kit, and a pocketknife joined the pile accumulating next to the cardboard box. One of the last things to come out was a tent. Finally, Billie opened the box and pulled out a sleeping bag. This surprised me a little since I'd already seen one of those get pulled from the closet.

I'd been too focused on threats and hadn't been paying close attention to Billie and Jesse's conversation at the café the day before. I didn't know who the second bed roll was for, and I found myself getting a little envious. Of course, I was still going to be going camping, but it wouldn't be the same as getting to actually be there. I wouldn't be able to gaze up at the stars or try to spook Billie with a scary story around the campfire.

I shook my head in an attempt to dispel my pity party. If we were going camping, then there wasn't likely going to be much progress made on the case. I just hoped that all the outdoor activity would wear Billie out enough that I might finally get some decent dream sessions in. It had only been one night, but it felt like forever since I'd finally gotten the chance to talk to her. I had so much more I needed to say.

After packing up some food, and confirming with Kaz that they would come to check on Taco a few times, Billie loaded up her car. I had to admit, I was a little surprised at how relieved I was when we pulled in at Asra and Frankie's place. I'd been wondering if all of the rejected advances I'd witnessed were because she was involved with someone. For all I knew, they could've just been away since I bumped into her. Although that still could be the case, I was happy Sam was the one joining her on the trip.

That's pretty selfish. It's not like you have a chance with her.

"I know that. I'm just glad that she's spending more time with Sam."

Sure, you just keep telling yourself that.

"Do you have any idea how much of a selfish little brat you are?"

My arms are sore where angry fingers grip them, and my neck aches from the shaking I've just gotten. I know better than to answer questions like this.

"I refuse to let the opinion of such a vicious person matter."

♫*I am he as you are he as you are me, and we are all together.*♪

"I am nothing like that tyrant." The ferocity of my denial almost disproved my point. If there had been a physical representation of Nega-me that I could strangle, I would have been strongly tempted. I needed to focus. I had a job to do and an afterlife to survive. Each time my past resurfaced, it felt like I was losing a little piece of my sanity. I visualized a thick, heavy black curtain being dropped to hide Nega-me, backstage.

I sat there for a moment and tried to concentrate on the present. Fortunately, my little episode hadn't cost me much. I was still sitting in Billie's car. She'd gone inside, presumably to get Sam for the camping trip. Although I'd never been camping, I used to go for hikes in the forest with my grandmother. We'd look for birds, watch tadpoles wiggle around ponds, or just stand there and listen to the creaking of fallen boughs. While I waited for Billie and Sam, I tried to focus on those memories, instead.

By the time they got back to the car, I was calm and looking forward to being out in the woods again. I wondered what our campsite would look like and if there'd be a lake nearby. Considering we were in central Ontario, you could usually guarantee at least some small body of water would be close, if not within walking distance.

As Billie drove, she and Sam chatted a bit while music played quietly in the background. I could tell that she was trying hard to compensate for how things went the last time. I think that Sam noticed, too. He even chose to sit up front, forcing me to hang out in the back seat. I didn't mind. It felt like I was giving them some privacy and it gave me the chance to try to memorize the route we were taking. I still hadn't decided if I was going to risk going to Detective Cuff's house tonight. If I left and couldn't zap myself back because I didn't remember the way, I'd be out of contact with Billie for a few days. I could see myself getting worked up about something happening to Billie, unable to focus on actually accomplishing anything until they got back. I didn't have to decide now, but I could at least prepare for the possibility of heading back to the city, tonight.

Even though we were headed hours away from the last place I'd seen Rodger, I couldn't shake the feeling that he was lurking around the corner. Highway 11 was practically empty. Most cottagers were almost ready to close up for the season and the cooler weather forecasted for the weekend didn't seem to be enticing many to head north. I'd been keeping an eye on the cars around us in my limited field of vision. None of them stuck with us for too long. But that didn't mean that there wasn't a car hanging back, far enough that Billie wouldn't get spooked, but so far that I wouldn't be able to spot them.

My mental bubble of doom and gloom was suddenly burst when Billie let out an excited little noise and cranked up the song that was playing. As she drove, her fingers drummed on the steering wheel. Weezer's *Pork and Beans* was blasting through the speakers. She started singing along and I was struck, not by the beauty of her voice — she was a terrible singer — but by how free and happy she looked at that moment. She clearly knew she couldn't sing well, since she winced along with the off keys, but she continued to belt out the words for the pure pleasure of the song. I found myself admiring her comfort in her own skin and her refusal to let a lack of talent take the joy away from something that made her happy.

Sam, on the other hand, did not seem to be enjoying her confidence and spirit. He had his fingers jammed in both ears and was rolling his eyes. She poked him in the ribs which forced him to drop his hands in defence and let out an unauthorized giggle. He quickly tried to regain his look of annoyance, but couldn't do it. A smile broke across his face, and he joined in as they howled down the road like a couple of wolves baying at the moon.

After a pit stop for gas, a washroom break, and some junk food, Billie pulled into the provincial park where they'd be camping. Sam waited in the car while Billie went to check in. I wanted to know the layout of the area, so I studied the park map while she got the permit.

When we were back in the car, I figured we'd be going straight to the site, but instead, Billie pulled into a lot near one of the park stores. She told Sam to hop out and grab his bag, then proceeded to load everything else onto her back. As I was wondering if there wasn't any parking right at the site, Billie led the way to the dock around the far side of the store. Using a key that I assumed she'd gotten when checking in, Billie unlocked a canoe and flipped it over. I began to wonder just how secluded the site she picked would be. After tossing their stuff into the centre of the canoe, Billie turned to Sam with a huge grin.

"So, have you ever been in a canoe before?"

Sam's hesitant look at the small watercraft clearly indicated he wasn't as excited about this as Billie was. "No, I've never even been near a lake, before."

I couldn't help but think of the huge body of water located in the North end of Sam's hometown, the one I'd pretended to have drowned in, but figured he must not be much of an outdoors type.

"That's okay. It's not too hard and I'll sit in the back to do all the steering. But you'll have to help a little with the paddling up front."

Sam looked skeptical but didn't complain. After grabbing some lifejackets and paddles from a shed nearby, Billie demonstrated how to safely get in and out of the canoe. Next, she brought Sam to the dock and got him to practice paddling a bit before they got in. The practice did not seem to be improving Sam's confidence. Eventually, Billie decided to have Sam get in from shore. She then rolled up her pants and tossed her socks and boots into the canoe so that she could push it out enough to jump in the back. The boat rocked a little as she did this and Sam clung to the sides like a cat being held over a bathtub.

I strolled through the water and sat in their pile of gear. I had to admit, I was really looking forward to this. To my right, a pair of mallards skimmed through a field of lily pads. To my left, the fall leaves painted the shoreline with a kaleidoscope of colours. Overhead, the sun shone brightly, and I could make out the sound of Canadian geese flying above. Straight ahead, the lake opened up slightly, but not so wide that I couldn't still make out the shore on either side. I found myself wishing that I could see the view properly, without the haziness of the Pale and the limitation of only a few dozen meters in each direction.

I took in a deep breath and savoured the scent of pine needles, moss, and decaying leaves. It had been far too long since I'd lost myself in the wilderness: figuratively, that is. It was almost as if I could feel my entire being growing stronger. I looked over at Sam and couldn't help but laugh. He did not seem to be having the same experience I was. He'd relinquished his hold on the sides for an awkward grasp on his paddle. With each stroke, he managed to soak himself a little more. Billie tried to give tips from the back, but Sam seemed to be concentrating too hard to hear her.

Luckily, it wasn't long until we reached the shore. Billie coasted us to a stop alongside the sandy beach of an island. It didn't take long to unload the canoe. While Billie tried to teach Sam how to set up the tent, I did some recon on the rest of the island. It was fairly small with only a handful of camp sites. Each one was separated by large patches of forest in between, providing the impression that you were completely alone on the island. A family of five was set up on the opposite side from Billie and Sam's site, but I didn't see any evidence of other campers.

When I got back the tent was up, and Billie was in the process of making lunch. The aroma of chana masala and naan warming over the fire was making my mouth water. Although I was grateful for never needing to eat anymore, sometimes I really missed food. I could picture how the smoke from the campfire would make it taste even better.

After they were done eating and tidying up, Billie and Sam got ready to do some exploring of their own. I assumed that Billie had broken the news about the lack of running water earlier, because Sam didn't seem too surprised when Billie recommended he use the outhouse before they set out. While Billie checked the map and oriented herself, Sam practiced paddling while standing in the knee-deep water of the beach. The air had begun to cool, but it seemed that the water had retained some of its summer warmth. Based on the map Billie held, this looked like a smaller lake, and I imagined that helped to keep the water at a relatively tolerable temperature.

When they set out, Sam looked slightly less terrified, and I could see him finally able to look around at the beauty that surrounded him. The three of us spent the day canoeing, hiking, and to my joyful pleasure, bird-watching. I even took advantage of my invisibility to get closer to the birds than they ever would have let me if I'd been alive. I won't bore you with a Jules Verne-style esoteric listing of all the species we saw, but it was a glorious day for someone who was ornithologically inclined.

On our way back to the site, we paddled past the spot occupied by the family. The kids were splashing about in the water and invited Sam to come join them. Billie promised they'd be by shortly after they had a chance to refuel and grab a few things.

After topping up their canteens, grabbing a pack of tofu dogs, and a few other supplies, we were ready to head over. Being near the end of what was probably one of the most perfect days in my existence, I found myself wishing we could just stay out here, forever. It would be easier to forget the past if I knew that I had infinitely more days like this to look forward to.

16

The sites on the island seemed to be designed for isolation. They were few and far between. While Billie and Sam walked to visit their neighbours' spot, they quizzed each other on various things. They covered movies they'd seen, books they'd read, and places they'd visited.

"What's your favourite colour?" Sam asked while watching a moth flutter on the trail in front of them.

"I don't have one," was Billie's simple answer.

When Sam looked over at her, his face crumpled in confusion. She elaborated. "To me, the entire spectrum of colours is beautiful, and you need the combinations of them to appreciate each individual one. The lush green of the forest needs the deep brown of a tree trunk to contrast against. The stained-glass window of a blue jay's feathers or the eye of a peacock's tail would be pretty boring if they were restricted to just a single colour. Why lock yourself in for one experience when you can open yourself up to all of them?"

Sam was quiet for a few steps. Eventually, he smiled and said, "I guess you're right. My favourite colour today is different than what I would have said yesterday."

"Don't worry about putting too many labels on things. Just enjoy them."

It was then that we reached the campsite and the conversation turned to formal introductions. The three adults were gathered around the picnic table preparing some food, and the two kids were still splashing about in the water. The two men and the woman turned towards us when they heard Billie and Sam approaching through the forest. They were greeted with warm smiles.

"Hi, everyone. Thanks for inviting us over. I'm Billie and this is Sam."

Sam took a small step to the side, hiding slightly behind Billie's pack. The taller of the two men stepped forward and shook Billie's hand. Even though Billie was taller than average, his huge stature made her look quite small.

"Welcome! I am Lerato and this is Alemayehu and Kabelo. Lesedi and Wafaa are the fish we can't quite seem to lure out of the lake."

Billie smiled as she took her pack off of her back. She rummaged around, then pulled out a small bucket, a hand trowel, and a couple of magnifying glasses. Placing all of the items in the bucket, she crouched down and passed them to Sam. "Hey, Sam. Why don't you take these down to the beach and see if Lesedi and Wafaa want to build a sandcastle, or explore for bugs?"

After a moment of hesitation, Sam took the supplies and tentatively made his way to the shore. The splashing in the lake paused as he approached the water. Then there was a mad dash to see who could swim back to shore the fastest. It didn't take long until an entire ecosystem was under construction. The three industrious architects were in a hurry to get fortifications underway before they lost their light; the evening was closing in quickly with the storm clouds that had moved in.

While Billie hung back and socialized with Alemayehu, Lerato, and Kabelo, I figured it was a good time to also take advantage of the little light that was left to do another quick survey of the island. I still hadn't decided if I'd be attempting to travel tonight, and I wanted to familiarize myself with the island as much as possible so that, if necessary, I could try to navigate it in the dark. My exploration got slower as the sky turned to an oppressive murkiness. Although I hadn't been able to see the stars since arriving in the Pale, I knew they'd be completely hidden. Not a single beam of moonlight reached the island. My progress was slow as I needed to keep checking my route to make sure that I could still find my way back to both campsites. The blazing campfire I'd left behind did little to light my path, but it at least gave me a target to aim for each time I circled back.

At one point, I got turned around and came out on a beach with a single canoe, and assumed I'd somehow stumbled back on Billie's site. But when I climbed the embankment, all I found was a lone pack beneath the picnic table. I wondered if someone could have forgotten it when they checked out, but that wouldn't explain why there was still a canoe here. The bag didn't seem big enough to hold a tent, even one for a single person, and it was already dark enough that pitching a tent would be a challenge. The wind began to pick up and, even though I couldn't see the sky, I was sure a storm was heading our way. That eliminated the possibility that this person planned to just sleep under the stars. I began to search the area for signs of where they'd gone. Something about this entire situation was bothering me and I needed to figure out what was going on here.

Growls of frustration did nothing to extend my visibility, but that didn't stop me from emitting several as I blindly searched for the mystery camper. In addition to making zero progress locating this missing person, I had also gotten myself lost, which was quite an accomplishment, considering I was on an moderately-sized island. I was relieved when I finally spotted the warm glow of a campfire.

Now that I knew where I was, I quickly beamed myself back over to the group gathered around the flickering light. Everyone's attention was focused on Billie as she told them a ghost story. It only took me a few minutes before I realized she was reciting one by M. R. James. All three children had eyes as big as owls as they listened with a tight grip on their roasting sticks. Even the adults seemed more than mildly interested.

When Billie's turn was finished, Kabelo took over and told the tale of how the jackal got its stripe. This led to a few more stories, and before long, the chill in the air was stronger than the limited warmth emanating from the fire. Sam began to shiver and Billie offered him her jacket, but that left her without enough layers.

"I'll just run back to the site and grab my coat, Billie." Sam said as he handed the jacket back to her.

"Okay, but stick to the path and take a flashlight with you." Billie pulled a small battery-powered lantern from her bag and handed it to Sam. I decided to take advantage of this opportunity to scout with the assistance of a light, and joined Sam.

As Sam walked, he kept bouncing the lantern's beam between the narrow path he was following and the branches overhead. I could only assume he was hoping to catch a glimpse of some nocturnal animal. Unfortunately for him, his beam was pointed upward when he came to a root that had grown at the perfect height to trip an inattentive hiker. Sam only stumbled, but his shoelace had also caught and gotten untied. As he set down the lantern to tie his shoe, it tipped over, aiming off into the surrounding forest. The sudden illumination startled something and at the last second, I caught a hooded figure darting behind a tree. Quickly, I glanced back at Sam to see if he'd noticed the person lurking in the woods, but he was focused on his laces and didn't seem to have seen anything. My heart began to race as I tried to catch another glimpse of the person, and cursed the darkness and the mists of the Pale for hiding them so completely.

I stuck with Sam for a bit longer to see if his light would provide any more glimpses of this creep. I could only assume that this lone person sneaking about in the woods was the occupant of the hidden backpack and beached canoe I'd seen earlier.

When no one jumped out and attacked Sam, I left him and feebly began searching the forest again. The mystery hiker had been headed in the opposite direction, so I started by popping back to the campfire and checking the thin strip of the perimeter made visible by the firelight. As the wind shifted, it blew smoke in my path, further decreasing my visibility. The scent caught in the back of my throat and almost made me cough.

Ding, ding, ding, ding, ding. Let's see if you're smart enough to use that information.

"What are you talking about?" When Nega-me didn't answer, I paused for a second and tried to figure it out. "You want me to smoke the lurker out? How would I even do that?" The only response I received was an exasperated sigh followed by some exaggerated sniffing sounds. "Seriously? You want me to sniff around like some bloodhound?"

What I want *is for you to use your brain! Your sense of touch and sight are pretty much useless right now, but that isn't all that you have.*

Obviously, taste wasn't going to do anything for me either. I moved back onto the path that led to Billie's site and closed my eyes and tried to concentrate. I could still hear laughing and the pop of the wood as it burned, so I moved a few steps further into the woods. As I stood there struggling to focus, I wished that there was something like my light-speed travel that could help me now. For some reason, at that moment, a memory of Andrea dancing at the bowling alley surfaced in my mind's eye. "I wonder..."

This ought to be amusing.

Once again, I was grateful for the breadth of my autodidactic education. During my evolutionary biology phase, I'd devoured pretty much any book I could get my hands on related to animals. I'd found that adaptations, in particular, were especially interesting.

What I needed now was to take on some of the adaptations of the animal that not only had the best sense of smell but also happened to have one of the top senses of hearing. I only hoped that I didn't grow a trunk and big floppy ears in the process. Closing my eyes once again, I imagined that my senses were as strong as an elephant's. I tried to focus on the living world diluted by the immaterial world of the Pale. Slowly, deeper layers began to surface. Beneath the rustle of the leaves in the wind and the chatter of the Vitae, I could make out the gnawing of a rodent of some sort. I could smell the deep, earthy aromas of soil and decaying debris on the forest floor. I kept my eyes closed and continued to concentrate on the subtle notes of the forest as I moved along the path to Billie's site. When the fresh scent of pine needles was replaced with the noxious odour of insect repellant, my eyes snapped open.

Sam and his flashlight were nowhere in sight, so there was nothing to see. My nostrils flared as I tried to follow the origin of the bug spray exactly like the bloodhound I'd snidely dismissed earlier. A bolt of lightning in the distance provided enough light for me to see I was no longer on the path. Whoever had doused themselves, they had wandered off into the woods in this direction.

The delayed thunder that answered the earlier lightning told me that the storm was still a little ways off, but the slight breeze from earlier was ramping up. This made it harder to both listen to, and smell, the faint trail I was attempting to follow. As I moved about frantically, trying to pick up any clue that might put me back on the right path, I caught a whiff of smoke and thought that I'd managed to somehow get turned around and had made my way back to the campfire. One glance at my surroundings rectified that assumption. I was still deep in the dark recesses of the forest and there was no firelight anywhere in sight. I decided to follow this smoke since I was fairly certain the wind was blowing the wrong way for me to be picking up the group's fire.

Running against the wind that was picking up, I hoped to find that our lurker had returned to their site to cook some dinner. I needed to see who they were and try to figure out what the hell they were up to. I didn't have to go far before the limited misty perimeter of my vision shifted enough for me to locate the source of the smoke. My stomach dropped as the forest became illuminated once again.

There, in front of me, was a fire spreading through the dry underbrush. The intensifying winds fanned the flames, rapidly expanding their domain. Using the increased visibility, I quickly looked around and tried to orient myself. I was immensely grateful for my earlier scouting when I spotted a cow-shaped boulder. I was closest to Billie's site, so I popped there first to see if she'd returned since I'd last checked in. What I found was Sam, still rummaging through his bag in the tent. He'd gotten his coat but must have stayed to find something else. He didn't have much time until the fire would reach him. Poking my head through the tent, I could already make out the faint glow in the distance.

Never had I wished more strongly for some way of interacting with the world of the living. I had no mythical ghost powers to scare him out of the tent towards the water where he would be safer. I had no way of telling him to run. I was powerless. My mind scrambled to come up with something, *anything*, but my brain had nearly shut down in panic.

Billie was, once again, my only hope. Even though I knew it wouldn't work, I tried to believe that my success communicating with her in the dream world meant that I'd be able to finally get through to her now. I zapped back to the group's site and began shouting "FIRE!" at the top of my lungs.

The light of the flames hadn't reached this far yet and I doubted they would smell the smoke over that of their own bonfire. A new crack of lightning, followed by a much quicker response of thunder, warned that the storm was drawing nearer. The wind picked up but I had no delusions that rain would save the day before the flames had completely overtaken the island.

Fortunately, it did trigger an abrupt conclusion to the festivities. Billie was quickly gathering her things. Alemayehu offered to walk Billie back since she'd given her lantern to Sam, but she declined, pulling out another smaller flashlight to guide her way.

I was torn between a desperate need for Billie to get to Sam, and the selfish wish that she'd remain where it was safe. Her jacket tugged snuggly against the wind, Billie hurried along the path. Her gaze had been down, her chin tucked toward her chest to shield her from the whipping wind. She was over halfway there when the glow of the flames caught her attention. Her hurried steps faltered for a moment as she took in the destruction that was slowly closing in on her.

Immediately, Billie turned back to face the direction she'd come. It was still open, but she wasn't looking for a retreat. "FIRE!" She shouted, several times, as she opened the canteen in her hand and poured its remaining contents over herself. I had no idea if the family of campers would hear her over the winds, but I hoped that they hadn't already turned in for the night, oblivious to the danger hurtling towards them. As soon as she was doused, Billie pulled the buff around her neck up over her nose and mouth, then ran like an animal being hunted. The closer she got to their site, the more intense the flames were. I could feel the heat like a sunburn on my right side as we raced through the forest. Every few meters or so, Billie would shout Sam's name. With all of the landmarks I'd memorized earlier now ablaze, I was having trouble figuring out how much further we had to go or whether we were still even on the right trail. Then the wind shifted, blowing the smoke and heat directly towards us. At the same moment, Billie and I could hear Sam in the distance. He was calling for her but kept choking and coughing. We flew towards him as fast as Billie's feet could take her. We found Sam rubbing his eyes, still shouting for Billie. Without a word, Billie took her drenched buff and pulled it over Sam's head so that it covered his entire face. She tossed her pack to the ground and threw her wet jacket around Sam's shoulders, then pulled him up onto her back. I saw her turn to check the way we'd come, surely hoping it was still open, but an impenetrable wall of flames had formed behind us. The woods to our left were too dense. Their only hope was to continue along the path that led back to their own site.

I could see Billie straining to pull air into her lungs as the smoke grew denser around us. With the rapidly spreading flames, they couldn't take the time to crawl where the air was clearer. They had to get out. Now! I could see Billie's strength beginning to fail as the amount of oxygen she was able to take in decreased with each smoke-filled gasp. When she finally broke through the trees surrounding her site, I caught a glimpse of the tent consumed by flames. Billie didn't spare a second to glance at their belongings: she headed straight for the lake and didn't stop until they were both submerged up to their shoulders.

I saw Billie's grasp on Sam loosen and I expected her to turn to grab the canoe so that they could get to safety, but instead, she sank beneath the water's surface. Sam had pulled the buff down so he could see, his eyes glued to the terrifying landscape they'd just escaped. It took a moment for him to realize that she wasn't resurfacing.

“Billie?” Sam scanned the water and found the crown of her head just barely breaking the surface. “Billie!”

He grabbed at her and struggled to pull her closer to shore. He screamed her name as he tried to drag her to the beach. Just as he'd managed to get Billie laid out on the sand, legs still floating in the water, a spotlight lit the two of them up.

Sam shouted for help while he tilted Billie's head back to open up her airway. He leaned over and tried to force breaths into her, but I could see her cheeks fill with the air meant for her lungs. Her airway was blocked. Sam started doing chest compressions and I was incredibly grateful that he'd been raised by doctors.

The light from the rescue boat continued to shine on Sam as the park rangers made their way towards the beach. Tears streamed down his face as Sam continued to pump on Billie's chest. “Not you, too. *Please*! Not you too.”

I blinked a few times to clear my vision. Surely, I wasn't seeing what I thought I was. I stepped closer to be sure, then nearly stumbled backwards as my fears were confirmed. Right in front of me, Billie was slowly becoming solid.

17

I can't even begin to describe the panic that ran through me as I watched Billie gradually taking form, becoming easier to see by the second. You'd think I would have learned this lesson by now. Being dead myself, I'm sure you would've thought that I, more than most, would be painfully aware of the fact that it's delusional to believe that some people will just always be there. Take my grandmother, for example. I loved and appreciated her, but I also took her presence in my life for granted. It never occurred to me to picture a world without her. Without realizing it, I'd done the same to Billie. Even though I spent the entirety of each day trying to track down the man intent on killing her, I don't think I ever truly believed he'd actually get her. I'd come to rely on Billie's intelligence and determination to get her through any situation.

Thankfully, Billie had clearly learned the lesson I'd had to die to understand: that no one can ever really go it alone. I'd made the mistake of pushing everyone away, locking the good out with the bad. I could tell that Billie had been tempted to do the same. I'd seen the grief she'd struggled with and the craving to hide out in her own personal bubble; her hesitation at getting closer to Sam; the way she stayed on the periphery with her friends from work, never making any connections that would expose the pain that always came to the surface in her dreams.

But she was out there, and she was trying. She volunteered at the New Page Centre, planned time with Sam, and lent a hand in the bookstore. Billie's time with Sam was the only rare occasion when I could glimpse the wall starting to come down, and it seemed like she was making a conscious effort not to rebuild it each time she dropped him off.

As Billie lay on that beach, gradually solidifying before my eyes, all I could think about was how much I wanted her to live, but not for a second was it because I was thinking about my own selfish revenge: I wanted her to get the chance to do everything she'd ever dreamed of doing. She didn't deserve to have this be her ending.

Fortunately, I wasn't the only one desperate for Billie to live. Sam kept up the CPR until the rangers could get ashore and take over. Together, they'd managed to clear the water from Billie's lungs, but she was still suffering from smoke inhalation. With the return of her laboured breathing, Billie's form had slowly regained its misty quality. After the excruciatingly slow boat ride, followed by the trip in the ambulance, we'd arrived at a small local hospital. I now spent my time as the resident spook, just like Ava.

I'd barely left Billie's side during the days she'd lain defenceless and vulnerable in the intensive care unit. At this point, I couldn't trust that Rodger wouldn't show up dressed as a nurse and pump air into Billie's IV or quietly smother her while she was alone. Fortunately, I wasn't the only one who refused to go anywhere.

Asra and Frankie had come. They'd tried to take Sam home to rest but he'd forcefully rejected the idea, clinging to Billie's bed as Frankie tried to guide him towards the door. The only time he could be convinced to leave the room, was when the doctors kicked him out for tests or to discuss her condition with her aunts.

The haunted look from the beach never left his face. He kept vigil next to her bed, one hand gently clasped Billie's while the other clenched the blankets next to her with a death grip.

I was glad to know that there was someone there who could actually do something, but I still couldn't tear myself away. Each raspy breath taken through the oxygen mask strapped to Billie's face sounded painful. She'd been in and out of consciousness on her way here. Each time she'd come to enough to speak, she'd wanted to know if Sam was ok.

I wanted to check in with her, but we hadn't been able to dream walk together since arriving at the hospital. The drugs she was on had her completely knocked out. I was impatient to make sure I'd still be able to communicate with her and needed desperately to pass along what I'd learned about the forest fire.

For now, all any of us could do was wait.

*

When Billie did finally wake, she was alone in the room with Frankie. Asra had just taken Sam down to the cafeteria to help her get some tea and snacks while a nurse came in for a routine check. Shortly after the nurse left, Billie's eyes fluttered open. Her gaze landed on Frankie staring out the window. Of course, the first thing Billie did was repeat her usual question. "How's Sam?"

Frankie turned from the window and came to sit in the chair next to the bed. She didn't reach out a comforting hand or crack an affectionate smile, but I got the impression Billie didn't expect her to. "Sam's fine. He didn't have a scratch on him. Unfortunately, I can't say the same for you."

As if on cue, Billie was wracked with a coughing fit. She tried to take the oxygen mask off, but Frankie held it on while propping Billie up on more pillows so that she could sit a little more vertically. As soon as the coughing had stopped, Frankie slumped back in her chair, again. They sat in silence for a moment. After Billie had recovered a little, she continued their conversation.

"*Now* do you see why I can't take him?" It was hard to tell with the mask on, but I caught the hint of a cynical smile.

Frankie let out a long sigh, pinching the bridge of her nose. "Sam is alive *because* of you, not in spite of you, Billie."

"This isn't the first time he's almost gotten seriously hurt around me. The more time I spend with him, the closer he comes to ending up like Mom and Dad."

Silence hung in the air for a moment, the two of them each seemingly lost in memories. After a minute or two, Frankie spoke. "Don't make excuses, Billie. He's lost his family multiple times over and he should be with the only family he has left."

That took me by surprise. I couldn't imagine being responsible for a kid and I was shocked that Frankie expected Billie to suddenly become a surrogate single parent to Sam. Billie turned her eyes straight to Frankie's, anger and defiance sparking in them. "And I will be with him, but I'm not ready to be a parent, and I don't think I ever will be."

While Billie paused to draw in a raspy breath, Frankie opened her mouth to reply, but Billie held up her hand to show she wasn't done talking yet. "You and Asra can give him the stability he deserves. You know Mom and Dad's will as well as I do. They wanted Sam with you two by default. I was only supposed to take him if that's what I wanted."

This little speech cost Billie and resulted in another coughing fit.

Frankie got up and turned back towards the window. "We'll finish this discussion when you're better."

"This discussion *is* finished. I'll be Sam's sister, not his mother." Sam and Asra walked through the door, putting an end to the conversation. Sam's gaze went straight to Billie. She gave him a big smile from behind her mask, and that was all the encouragement he needed to run over and throw his arms around her. Billie seemed a little surprised by this sudden affection from him, but returned it with a fierce hug of her own.

Obviously lacking the etiquette necessary to let this be a nice moment, Frankie gave Billie a significant look. Billie's eyes narrowed, but she didn't release her hold until Sam was ready to let go. While Asra passed out their haul from the cafeteria and checked in with Billie, I took a minute to try to get my anger at Frankie under control. Her attempts to force Billie into a role she didn't want and wasn't prepared for, coupled with her arrogant assumption that she knew what was best, really pissed me off. I knew firsthand what happened when someone who never wanted to be a parent got stuck with a kid. Sure, some people pulled their shit together and did a good job, but others ... others should never have that kind of responsibility.

Now that Billie was conscious, there were things that needed to be done. I decided that this was a good opportunity to walk off some of my frustration while also doing a sweep of the hospital to see if there were any signs that Rodger was skulking about. On the few occasions I'd torn myself away from Billie's bedside, I'd learned that the park rangers had been able to get the family that Billie and Sam had met to safety. The mysterious lone camper's site apparently showed no evidence that anyone had been there, and their canoe had been returned to the main grounds. This person's limited appearance in the woods on the island seemed too suspicious to be a coincidence.

The majority of the island had burned, making it difficult to pinpoint the exact place the fire had started. Asra had gotten a few updates from the park, but I decided that once I was finished my search of the hospital, I would pop over and see what I could learn.

I'd planned to start with the island. Unfortunately, arson was not one of the many things I'd spent my time studying. Added to that was the fact that I had no way of actually interacting with the crime scene, or even an unimpeded view of it. I reluctantly admitted the futility of the exercise, cut my losses, and went to the park office. Although I'd hoped to catch some gossip amongst the rangers, I knew it was a long shot. Everyone seemed to have gone back to business as usual. Giving up on the whole thing as a bust, I beamed myself back to Billie's hospital room.

The whole trip had only taken about half an hour and when I returned Sam was catching Billie up on everything she'd missed while she was unconscious, which wasn't much. As he babbled on, I couldn't help but think about Billie's comment earlier. I began to wonder if the near-miss on the archery range was *actually* the result of a drunk or an attempt by Rodger to take Billie out.

Don't be stupid.

"What? It can't be a coincidence that within a week and a half of being attacked in the alley, Billie's been shot at with a bow and nearly burned alive while camping."

Use your brain, Alex. Rodger is careful, meticulous. If he had succeeded at the archery range, he would have killed her in plain view of a dozen witnesses with no means of escape. He's smarter than that, and so are you.

"Fine. But don't try to tell me you think the fire was an accident too."

We never saw anyone light the proverbial match...

Billie's cough snapped me out of the debate I was having with Nega-me. It also reminded me that, although I spent little of my time encountering other dead people, I *was* in a hospital. The chances of someone overhearing me arguing with myself were much greater, here, than back at home.

I'd been so focused on Billie's recovery that the fact that I was sitting in prime dead-people territory had completely slipped my notice. I debated the benefit of going exploring again. I hadn't noticed anyone on my previous search, but a new hospital meant that I could go looking for other inhabitants of the Pale. After a few minutes of deliberation, I decided it'd be a waste of time. Anyone here was probably too new and would only slow me down.

I still needed to pay Detective Cuff a visit and I needed to check in with Ava to see if she'd bumped into Shay, at all. It was probably going to be a few more hours until Billie was released, and now that she was awake, it would be harder for Rodger to get the drop on her. I had to trust that he'd keep his distance while she was surrounded by witnesses and I knew that, even in her weakened state, Billie would still be a force to be reckoned with.

Since I still had a while until I could reasonably expect Cuff to be climbing into bed, I decided to start by checking Ava's favourite hangouts. With my lightspeed travel, it didn't take me long to eliminate all of the usual spots. Frankly, if Ava wasn't at home, at the hospital, or travelling between the two, I didn't have any clue where she would be. I realized, yet again, that I'd taken more than I'd given where Ava was concerned.

Not having any clue as to where else I should look, I turned my sites towards the police station, to see if the detective was on duty. Surprisingly, that's also where I found Ava, and she wasn't alone. She was talking to a man with warm tawny skin, curly black hair and wide-set eyes. Spying my approach, Ava waved me over and introduced us. "Alex, this is detective Yara Naifeh. Detective, this is Alex,"

The detective smiled kindly at me, and I nodded my hello, then I turned towards Ava and waited for her to fill me in.

"I've been telling Yara about your murder and he's offered to help."

He spread his hands in a gesture of surrender. "It appears that, even dead, I can't seem to give up the job."

I did my best to seem appreciative while battling my introverted reluctance to add anyone else to my small circle of allies. "Thank you, Detective. We could use all the help we can get."

The three of us spent the next few hours going over everything I'd learned since arriving in the Pale. Ava was noticeably shaken when I got to the part about Billie and Sam's close call. When I'd finished, Yara rubbed his chin for a few minutes while he pondered the information I'd provided. "I hate to say this, but there is very little evidence to go on. Your friend's hypothesis that there is a serial killer on the loose is conjecture. All you really have is your own murder, and the description of a scar on Billie's mugger that is similar to one on your attacker. You yourself did not identify the two as the same man."

The man that had been squatting with his hand clenched around my ankle is suddenly on his feet, pushing me into a dimly lit alley. His eyes are no longer pleading. They've gone dead and cold. He doesn't even hesitate as he plunges a blade into my stomach, his hand pressed over my mouth to muffle my cry of pain.

Although Yara had a point, I knew down to my bones that Billie and I were on the right track.

My first instinct was to listen to Nega-me, but I was trying hard not to make the same mistakes I'd made in the past. Instead, I decided to use logic to argue with both of them. "I know how flawed it sounds when you break it down to cold data, but I've seen this monster up close. I've watched him shift from a humble beggar to a completely detached killer. If I'm wrong, you've got nothing to lose, and if I'm right, you could save lives. I can't do this alone and, the more help we have, the better our chances of stopping this guy."

Yara reached out his hand and placed it on my shoulder. "I'm not saying I won't help, Alex. I'm just saying this won't be easy."

I let out a sigh of relief. I knew I would do what needed to be done, even if I only had myself to rely on, but the longer it took to solve this, the more danger Billie would be in. Sensing that things had come to a head, Ava piped up. "So, Yara, what do we do now?"

After mulling things over for a bit, the detective finally replied. "Our best bet is to divide and conquer. Ava, you see if you can find this Shay person and get any details on what exactly happened when they died. So far, we only have Alex's experiences with the killer to go on. It would be good to get more information so that we could narrow down his MO."

"I've been looking for her, but I haven't had any luck so far. Do you have any suggestions?"

"Alex said that she had children. Perhaps you can try seeing if there's anyone hanging around the schools."

"I'm on it." Ava immediately climbed into her wardrobe and disappeared before I could point out that it was Sunday night, and she didn't need to rush off. I turned to Detective Naifeh. "I'd like to work on passing what we know to Detective Cuff, and keep trying to get through to Billie. We need someone in the real world who can actually do something about this creep."

"Agreed. I'll stay here and see what I can learn. I'll monitor open cases and work as a central point of contact. You and Ava can report anything you learn back to me, and I can distribute any information I'm able to get whenever you check in."

With our plan in place, there wasn't any sense in me sticking around the station. After zapping back to the hospital up north to check on Billie, I made my way to Cuff's place. While I waited for him to get home, I mentally ran through the day's events again.

Rodger's drastic escalation from murdering individual people to setting an island with innocent bystanders on fire made me nervous. The longer this went on, the more desperate he would get to silence Billie. We had a plan but, when I stepped back to look at it, I still felt powerless. In an attempt to keep my anxiety at bay, I concentrated on what I could do. And what I could do *now*, was dunk my face into a head that harboured the most robust mustache I'd ever seen.

18

I tried to wait patiently for Cuff to wander off to dreamland. It was already pretty late by the time he trudged through the door. I'd noticed that the person I'd seen in the bed with him before hadn't been here, waiting for him to return, nor had they come home with him, tonight.

The detective moved slowly, like he was on autopilot, as he went about his pre-bed routine. I couldn't help but notice that his former milky complexion had taken on an almost grey tinge. I hung out in the hallway while he changed. When I heard the squeak of bedsprings as he flopped onto his mattress, I didn't immediately enter but it wasn't long before the raucous sound of his snores told me that it was time to get to work.

I guessed that he'd been too tired to notice that the drapes were still partially open. The streetlight shone on the foot of the bed and the residual glow lit my path. I took my position and tried to prepare myself for whatever I might see. I'd grown accustomed to Billie's dreams, but I was still uncomfortable with invading a stranger's headspace. The things I saw were so personal and intimate that I couldn't help but feel like I was committing a serious violation of privacy, no matter how justifiable. Once I was in, it took me a moment to figure out what was happening. Cuff was on an enormous speedboat, like one you might see in some

high-speed aquatic chase scene in a movie. The sky was dark and
ominous, the water a cold steel grey. Waves rocked the boat at
dangerous angles, almost capsizing it. I suddenly noticed that
Cuff's boat wasn't the only craft out in the storm. Off the tip of the
bow, I could see another vessel. This one was riding the shoulder
of a massive wave. Water came arching overtop and crushed the
craft into splinters. Cuff called out but I couldn't hear anything
over the smashing of the water. I tried to take control, but the
dream had already started to shift, without me. Around us, the
rotted boards of a shack right out of some horror movie started to
form around us. A flashlight in Cuff's hand flickered making it
difficult to see and easy to imagine demons lurking in the shadows.
Slowly, he began to search the endless rooms forming around us.
Even though the hallway we were travelling down seemed to go on
forever, I suddenly had the feeling that the door on our right was
the final one left to check. As Cuff's hand reached out for the knob,
I couldn't help but try to stop him. Whatever was behind that door
shouldn't be let out.

Before his fingers could even graze the knob, the door burst
open and a mess of limbs and bones in all the wrong places came
crawling out. Its skin was a putrid grey that gleamed with an oily
sheen. Somehow, I knew that it was out for revenge. The hideous
form began crawling towards Cuff with unnerving speed, its
distorted body chasing him down the hallway. When it was only
about a meter away, it leapt into the air. Cuff turned and tried to
block it, but it took him down hard. As he struggled for his life
against the creature, it began to morph. The report of a gunshot
rang out and everything fell silent except for the sound of Cuff's
rapid panting. In his arms lay the body of a man, a gunshot wound
in his chest flowing with blood as the life slowly drained out of his
eyes.

I suddenly realized I was just as breathless as Cuff was. I took a minute and tried to calm myself enough to remember why I was here. I knew I needed to redirect our focus, but I was still on high alert for whatever else might be lurking in this house of nightmares. I closed my eyes and tried to come up with a less terrifying location. The best I could do was the police station. I tried to remember the room where his desk was and the items that had been strewn across it. When I opened my eyes, we were in a hazy room with beige floor tiles and dark walls in the distance. But Cuff remained focused on the dead man draped limply over his lap.

I tried again, cycling through my memories, looking for a place I could picture in detail. I finally settled on one of the libraries I'd frequented when I was alive. I started with the musty scent of books that had passed through hundreds of different hands. Next was the texture of the carpet which was somehow both smooth from years of being tread on, but also rough and scratchy. Then came the shelves and the comfy vinyl-coated chairs that made up the reading nook. There was the sound of pages being leafed through and the squeaky wheel of the returns cart, in the background.

Cuff was still oblivious to the change in scenery. I knew that I wasn't able to create people, but I'd hoped that I could take them away. I concentrated on replacing the dead body with a file folder. Inside, I placed a dossier of everything I knew about Rodger and his victims. It took a bit for Cuff to notice my substitution. He seemed to be blinking back some tears that had clouded his vision. Once I had his attention, I placed a phone in his pocket and made it ring. Cuff patted his jacket until he located the phone and answered it. "Hello?"

"Hello, Detective. Have you finished reading your case file yet?" I had no idea what to call the document I'd given him and hoped that my lack of time spent watching police procedurals wouldn't hinder what I was attempting to do.

Cuff hesitated and looked down at the folder. "No, I haven't."

"Well, let me sum things up for you. We're hunting a sick son of a duck and I need you on the case. We've been unable to determine his legal name, but we have confirmed that he's used the following aliases: Rodger Roman and Geofferson Smith. He tends to use disguises, but witnesses have reported a distinct scar along his jaw. Photos are in the folder."

I watched as Cuff flipped through the dossier. I'd tried to construct photos of each of the times I'd seen Rodger.

"You're to apprehend this man using any means necessary." I ended the call and watched to see what Cuff would do next. He looked around and noticed himself still seated awkwardly on the floor. Instead of getting up and moving to one of the chairs, the detective simply shifted into a cross-legged position and started spreading the documents around him on the carpet.

I knew from my experiences with Billie that if I wanted him to retain any of this, I needed him to wake immediately. Unfortunately, I had no idea how to force that to happen. Given the horrors I'd just experienced in the dream that Cuff's own brain had created, I was doubtful of my ability to startle him awake and I couldn't rely on a well-timed phone call. Ultimately, I settled for having the dream run on repeat. My hope was that sheer repetition would help to plant the facts in his brain. I'd also hoped to keep the dream running long enough that it would be the last one he had when his alarm did eventually jolt him from his sleep, but I wasn't that lucky. I wasn't sure if he'd gotten bored of my endless loop or if it was just the natural change in his sleep cycle, but I found myself back in his dimly lit bedroom long before he could reasonably be expected to get up.

While I waited to see if Cuff would end up dreaming again, I decided to check in on Billie. At first, I thought that I'd beamed myself into the wrong room. The occupant of this bed had copper-red hair and copious amounts of freckles. I ran out to the hall to get my bearings. After quickly confirming that I'd had the right room, I checked the rest of the beds on that floor in case she'd been moved. Apparently, I'd overestimated the amount of time the doctors would need to monitor Billie's condition before releasing her.

I had no idea how long ago Billie had been released or even whether or not she'd gone willingly. No. I couldn't think like that. If I let my imagination get out of control, I'd end up paralyzed with anxiety. "Think, Alex. Billie was with Sam and her aunts. She wasn't in any condition to drive herself. They're probably just on their way back." I clung to this barely reassuring pep talk I'd given myself and shot over to Billie's apartment. It was dark and there was no sign that anyone had been there. Next, I zapped over to Frankie and Asra's place. The driveway was empty, and a quick search of the house showed me that no one was there either. It was at this point that I had to decide how much more of a useless twit I was going to be. I could either spend my night searching the highway for their cars *or* I could actually be helpful and go back to Cuff's house and keep planting information in his dreams.

Knowing what I needed to do, I returned to the symphony of snores and tried to focus on being practical. Each time Cuff fell into a dream state, I played the same loop until I lost control. While I awaited my chance to try again, I popped over to Billie's.

200

She never returned home. Eventually, I found the four of them
pulling into the driveway at her aunts'' house. Frankie had driven
Billie's beetle and Asra had driven the rest of them in her sedan.

I watched them as they went into the house and unpacked
from their trip. Before they all turned in to try to grab a few hours
of sleep with what remained of the night, I overheard Asra call and
leave messages both at Sam's school and at Billie's work, letting
them know that neither would be in tomorrow.

Seeing them all safely settled, I returned to Cuff to finish
my now monotonous task of planting information.

*

The next morning, I left the detective as soon as his alarm went
off. I dropped in at the station to check in with Naifeh and ask him
to keep an eye on Cuff to see if he followed up on the leads I'd
spent the night giving him. Ava had been by earlier to report that
she'd had no luck finding Shay, so far, but that she'd be scoping out
schools, today. Normally, I would have followed Billie for the day
to see what she'd dig up, but I had the feeling she wouldn't be
doing any investigating of her own for a little while. Either way, I
didn't have much else I could do right now, so I was able to justify
spending my time scouting to see if Rodger was skulking
anywhere about. After checking the centre and confirming that he
wasn't on volunteer duty, I headed over to the house to keep an eye
out, there. After doing a thorough permitter survey, I headed
inside. The main floor was quiet, and I assumed that everyone was
still asleep. The scent of pancakes quickly informed me that I was
wrong.

The kitchen was in the back on the main floor, just past a
modest living room. The walls were a shade somewhere between
nutmeg and cherry and the cabinets were an azure blue. Older,
white enamel appliances were tucked into the right-hand corner

with a lemon-yellow counter dividing the eating area from the cooking space. My eyes were overwhelmed by so much colour in a single room, and I could only imagine how much more vibrant it would all be without the mists of the Pale toning it down. Billie was at the stove in a pair of track pants and a hoodie. They both looked a little big on her and I found myself wondering if they'd bothered to stop for supplies at Billie's on their way over. I already knew that none of the gear from the campsite had survived the fire and my guess was that Billie had had to borrow some clothes from Frankie. They were about the same height, but Frankie was a little more filled out. I had to assume that Billie's super healthy eating habits, combined with all of the crazy activities she enjoyed, didn't leave much food for her body to store for later. It sounded like Billie had music playing while she was cooking, but it must've been turned down to keep it from waking the others since I could only catch small bits of it.

♫ "Though we're apart, you're part of me still." ♪

It seemed that Billie was listening to "Blueberry Hill" while making blueberry pancakes. I wondered if she'd put that song on or if it had been an extremely unlikely coincidence. The song must've come to an end just as Sam entered the kitchen. Still clad in safari pyjamas, he rubbed the sleep from his eyes. "That smells good," he half-mumbled as he yawned.

Billie flipped a couple of pancakes onto a plate and set them down in front of Sam, followed by a bottle of maple syrup. "I think we've earned the right to a little sugar to start our day, don't you?"

Sam's eyes widened and he licked his lips as he poured out a generous amount of syrup. Billie grabbed a stack for herself and sat down to eat. It wasn't long until Asra and Frankie joined them. After breakfast was finished and things had been tidied up, Sam went out to kick a soccer ball around in the backyard, while the others nursed tea and coffee in the kitchen.

Frankie was the first to break the comfortable silence that had fallen in Sam's absence. "By the way, Billie, the park let me know that a damage charge has been applied to your bill. I pointed out how ridiculous it was for them to penalize you for any losses they suffered due to the fire, but they tried to claim this wasn't related to the fire." It was nice to hear the frustration in Frankie's voice directed in defence of Billie instead of at her, for once.

Billie had pulled out her phone, presumably to check how much the added fee was. "What could they possibly think that I broke?"

"Apparently, the canoe you rented had sizeable holes in the bottom. The genius I was speaking to said that you either "rode that thing over a rock bank or used it for axe-throwing practice." I tried arguing that the fire could easily have been responsible but there was no reasoning with them."

"That's impossible. We stayed in clear waters the entire time. I didn't want to take Sam on any rapids until he was more comfortable." I'd been with Billie the entire trip and I knew she was right. There was only one logical explanation for how the canoe had been wrecked. Clearly, Rodger wanted to ensure that any attempt to escape the fire by boat would result in a sinking ship, ideally leading to drowning. I could picture Billie and Sam alone in the middle of the dark lake, desperately paddling to get as much distance as possible between them and the fire, only to find that their strokes wouldn't be enough to save them. Even if they were able to swim or bob along in lifejackets, it wouldn't take long for hypothermia to set in. I'd been surprised that Lesedi and Wafaa had been swimming so late in the year, but the shallow waters around the beaches of the sites would have been warmer than the cold, drafty depths further out.

Once again, I was disgusted with how little regard Rodger had for the innocents that would be sacrificed in his quest to take out Billie. I didn't hang around to hear the rest of the conversation. Instead, I decided it was time to take up my manic patrolling.

*

I didn't let up on my lookout duty until the Sun began to set. The dim light combined with the perpetual fog of the Pale made it pointless. I decided to head back to the house. It seemed that Billie was going to be staying there for a few days while she continued to recover. Billie clearly wanted to be back at her apartment, but Asra had hidden her keys and wasn't taking no for an answer.

This new development didn't bother me much. Kaz was going to bring Taco by when they closed up the shop, and Rodger would be a lot less likely to know this address than he would the one for Billie's apartment. After figuring out the logistics of how to keep Taco and Sam's ferrets (appropriately named Havoc and Chaos) separated, everyone settled in for a calm night of movie-watching. Billie's cough had decreased but she now had an inhaler that she'd probably be relying on for quite some time. Although relatively minor compared to what they could have been, the cuts and burns Billie had suffered would likely scar. Each time I pictured how much worse things could have been for both her and Sam, I felt a small pit form in the bottom of my stomach, the dense mass at the centre of it creating an inescapable pull.

I still had a while until I planned to check in with Detective Yara and I needed to take my mind off of what could have been. So, in between periodic searches of the yard and the block around Billie's apartment, I hung out with Billie and her family. Billie and Frankie sat on opposite sides of the living room, their postures both tense. Billie seemed to be pointedly staring at the T.V., while Frankie kept shooting burning glares in her direction. The four of them watched a Hindi film about a man who became a superhero because he couldn't feel any pain. It would have been a lot easier to watch the movie if someone had done something about the song stuck on a loop somewhere else in the house.

♪ "From the moment I could talk, I was ordered to listen." ♫

The weird thing was, no one else seemed to notice. I went out for another quick patrol and, when I came back, the repeating song had stopped, but there seemed to be something wrong with the soundtrack on the movie now. The chorus to a song I'd heard earlier kept repeating while the credits rolled, but only the chorus. Since it wasn't in English, I had no idea what the lyrics were, but I had to admit that it was catchy. Again, I seemed to be the only person who noticed. Maybe they'd seen it before and were used to this glitch.

When I came back from my next circuit, a new movie was on. This one was a Korean film about a group of people who had to fight off zombies while being trapped on a train. I was enjoying myself but a glance at the clock told me it was time to go.

19

When I got to the station, I decided to start off by taking a second look at the floor Cuff worked on. I wanted to be able to create a detailed layout of the area for tonight's sessions and I was hoping that setting the dreams at work would help to trigger memories of them when he was actually there, in real life.

I remembered that Cuff's desk was in the back corner. The office was pretty much one big room. Cheap linoleum, battered metal desks topped with faded wood veneer, and more filing cabinets than I would have expected for the "paperless age" filled the majority of the space. There were fewer cops in here than last time: presumably, the day shift had ended a while ago. The room was quiet except for the occasional sound of typing and the whirl of slowly circulating ceiling fans. When I got to the back corner, I discovered that Cuff was still there. I hurried to snoop and take a look at what he was working on in the hopes that it was related to Rodger.

"I see you've taken my spot."

I nearly jumped out of my skin at Naifeh's unexpected comment. He came from somewhere behind me.

"Sorry, Alex. I did not mean to startle you."

I did my best to recover some composure and not seem like a total dork. "No problem. I just forget how quiet we are now. I'm not used to not having any warning when someone's coming."

The detective smiled politely and turned his gaze towards Cuff's screen. "Regretfully, I have not seen any sign that your visit to Jonathan was successful."

It took me a minute to figure out that Jonathan must have been Cuff's first name. Currently, he seemed to be filling out a report on a recent robbery. "Has Ava been by yet?", I asked.

"No, you arrived just as I was returning from checking the lobby to see if either of you were there. I would expect that she'll be here soon. Shall we take another look?" Naifeh gestured for me to lead the way. I could have zapped myself down there, but I figured that would be rude.

Sure enough, Ava was standing there waiting when we descended the stairs. Her face lit up when she saw us. Even while on a mission to stop a deranged serial killer, Ava found reasons to smile. "Alex, Yara, you're late."

"My apologies, young Ava. We were upstairs checking on the detective's progress." Naifeh's calm demeanour had started to remind me of someone who knew they had an eternity ahead of them and, therefore, saw no reason to rush. I wondered if Ava had explained the consequences of spending too much time in the Pale to him, yet.

I, on the other hand, felt like we were never moving fast enough. Once again, I tried to stifle my urge to hurry things along in the spirit of being polite. "How's your day been, Ava?" I bit down on my tongue to keep from adding any questions specific to our mission.

Ava's smile dropped a little. "I found Shay, but her story isn't what you thought it was, Alex."

Ava described how she had spent the day checking all of the schools in the city with no success. Then she had moved on to her backup plan of checking all of the parks with decent playground equipment. At her third park, Ava had spotted a woman on this side of the Pale and approached her. As luck would have it, she was Shay Walsh. Unfortunately, she'd suffered a relapse and had, in fact, OD'd.

Detective Naifeh was the first to speak up when Ava had finished. "I don't know if it's better to have died accidentally at your own hands, or to have your life taken from you by another, but I hope that she is able to find peace."

Selfishly, all I could think about was how this impacted our hunt for Rodger. I knew that I had Ava's support, but Naifeh had spent his career relying on hard facts and evidence, something I had little of — that I could prove. "Thanks for your help, both of you. I guess I'll have to keep working on Billie and Cuff if there's going to be any hope of ending this." As I was turning to head back upstairs, Ava stopped me. "Don't worry, Alex. We'll figure this out." Naifeh was noticeably silent. I tried to give Ava a reassuring smile, then went back to my task of set decoration memorization.

*

When Cuff finally left for the night, I headed back to see what Billie was up to. Sam appeared to be in bed, already, and the rest of the household was getting ready to follow. It had been four days since I'd last had a dream walk with Billie, but it felt like weeks. I knew that my priority had to be Cuff, since he was the only one with any authority to put an end to Rodger's reign of slaughter, but I also needed to let Billie know what I'd seen, the night of the fire.

Reluctantly, I turned my attention back to the man with nightmares that would send even a horror buff running. I don't think anyone would have faulted me for having preferred to stay where I was. I spent the next few hours playing a new dream on repeat for the detective. This time, he was located at his desk, complete with photos of his family and at least four different half-eaten bags of fast food. A constant stream of recordings of the surveillance I'd done on Rodger, combined with both mine and Billie's attacks, played on his computer screen. The walls of the office were covered in wanted posters that depicted each of the disguises I'd seen him use and the aliases I'd been able to confirm. It was exhausting constantly keeping enough focus to have so many details running in a continuous playback. When Cuff's sleep cycle had dropped me out of dreamland for the third time, I decided I could take a break and see what I could accomplish with Billie.

Asra and Frankie's place sported a finished basement that had been converted into Billie's space while she and Taco stayed there. I couldn't imagine the pull-out couch was very comfortable, given the fact it looked older than the pyramids, but Billie seemed to be fast asleep. The blue glow from a router or something on the ceiling provided enough light for me to make out most of the room, but it also gave Billie's skin a cold, dead quality that only reminded me of how close she'd come to joining me here. It sent a chill down my spine.

I hurried over to check if she was dreaming. Even though I could see her misty body in front of me, I still needed to reassure myself that she was ok. The first thing I noticed when I joined her dream was the overwhelming smell of smoke. I shouldn't have been surprised that Billie was reliving the nightmare that was that fire. The majority of her time asleep seemed to be dedicated to traumatic episodes from her life.

Sam was clutched in her arms, but he was still just a baby. The two of them were surrounded by flames in every direction with no way out.

I quickly worked to change the scene to something happier. I concentrated on clattering pins and the scent of old shoes combined with spilled beer. I opened my eyes and saw the reflected lights bouncing off of a shimmering disco ball. Billie now held empty air; baby Sam had disintegrated with the change in scenery. I tried to remember what song had been on when Billie and her friends were dancing. Slowly, it began to play. Since I couldn't populate any people, she was left to stare out over the empty lanes. Her back was to me, so I couldn't tell if she'd started to relax, yet. Without really thinking about it, I put a slow song on next, which was probably for the best. It would be kinda creepy being alone in a dark, black-lit bowling alley with club music blasting. The change in music seemed to work. I leaned forward and rested my arms on the shoe rental counter while I watched Billie pick up a ball. She tossed it down the lane and before I could rig the pins to ensure a strike, I heard the satisfying crash as they all clattered to the ground. I applauded her skill and she immediately spun around. She seemed to be looking in my direction. I must have accidentally made the applause audible to her. I wanted Billie to be able to go back to bowling for a bit without being freaked out that there was someone lurking, so I put on another calming song.

♫ "Stars shining bright above you." ♪

Billie smiled a little but still seemed to be looking directly at me. She began to move toward me and as I moved to get out from behind the counter, her eyes followed. It was at this point that I realized I'd never been *in* the dreams before. I'd always watched them from a bit of a distance, almost like I was at a theatre. I shouldn't have been able to lean on the counter at all. We continued to move toward each other, almost in a trance. I wasn't ready to believe that I was reading the situation correctly. Billie walked right up to me, bringing her hands together at the back of my neck, burying her fingers in my hair. I could feel the warmth of her, but goosebumps trickled down my spine. Slowly, I brought my hands up and stroked them from her wrists near my face, gradually running them down to her elbows. Her skin was impossibly soft and the sensory deprivation of living so long in the Pale made me greedy for the contact.

I'm not a dancer, by any stretch of the imagination, but we began to sway together to the music. I found myself staring into eyes that reminded me of the event horizon of a black hole and wondered if they looked this surprising in the real world. A halo of golden flecks surrounded her pupil, gradually giving way to an iron-grey backdrop. I didn't realize how close I'd gotten in my attempt to take in every detail. I could feel her breath on my lips and her hips pressed against mine. My hands took on a mind of their own and began tracing their way up her arms and across her shoulder blades, eventually trailing my fingers down the curve of her back.

Like a wanderer in the desert finally discovering water, I drank in each element. I closed my eyes to take in every last detail of the fabric and warmth beneath my fingertips and that's when I suddenly felt the press of her smooth, yielding lips on mine. If I thought I'd been thirsty before, I was downright burning now. This wasn't about want, it was pure *need*. I pulled her closer and felt electricity course through my veins. I was overwhelmed by every sensation; her scent, her taste, the little gasps that escaped her lips as I grabbed her waist.

It wasn't until her hands started to lift my shirt that I finally snapped out of it. As my head cleared a little, I realized how wrong this was. Billie had no idea that I was real. She just thought she was having a particularly amazing dream — if I do say so myself.

Now that I'd opened my eyes, I could see that the setting had changed. I wasn't sure which of us had done it. We were now in a log cabin, the only light coming from the blazing fireplace, beside us. The floor was covered in plush blankets and cushions. As much as it physically hurt to, I tried pulling myself away. Billie moved her lips to my neck and was tugging on the waist of my jeans. My whole body was on fire, making it hard to concentrate on a way to end this without hurting her feelings.

I moved my hands up to her jaw as I gently dragged myself back. Her eyes caught me again and we both stood there, our breathing a little heavy. After a moment, Billie tried to pick things up where we'd left off. I didn't think I'd have the strength to stop again so, like a coward, I fled from the dream.

My abrupt departure must have woken Billie. We were both back in the basement, gasping for air. She flicked on a lamp and ran her fingers through her hair. It was hard for me not to notice how she looked in her thin t-shirt and the place where the covers had slipped revealing her long, very bare, leg.

I could still feel the palpable need and urgency in her kiss. I had to turn my back to try to get myself under control. Behind me, Billie let out an audible groan as she flopped back onto the bed. Glancing over in her direction turned out to be a mistake. Her shirt had crept up and I was having trouble tearing myself away from the smooth planes of her now-exposed stomach. I could make out the hint of a scar there, but the damn Pale kept me from being able to see it clearly. My fingers itched to trace the scar, to see if I could distinguish its ridge from the rest of that creamy surface.

I closed my eyes and tried to picture anything that might help me clear my head a little. That's when I heard music begin to play. Opening my eyes, I looked to see if Billie was using her phone, but she was still splayed across the bed. As the song grew louder I was finally able to make out the lyrics.

♪ "And the night goes by so very slow. Oh I hope that it won't end though, alone" ♫

I couldn't help but laugh, I knew this one and the song seemed too perfect. That's when I remembered how appropriate the song that had played in the kitchen this morning had been, too. I hadn't heard any songs other than that at the time, but I also hadn't seen Billie shut anything off when it stopped playing. "If this is some new sign that I'm starting to lose it, it's a lot less terrifying than I would have expected."

I wondered if my brain was picking out a soundtrack for its descent into madness. I certainly preferred that over the constant barrage of insults being hurled by Nega-me.

Since that's the way you feel, I'm not going to bother explaining what's actually going on here.

I was still enjoying the high of Billie's dream and didn't want to engage in a conversation that was guaranteed to ruin it, so I tried the silent treatment. Unfortunately, being part of my subconscious, Nega-me knew exactly what to say to ensure that I couldn't ignore what'd been said.

"What do you mean 'what's actually going on here'?"

Wouldn't you like to know?

"Yeah, that's why I'm asking."

Too bad. You'll just have to figure this one out on your own.

As annoying as the conversation was, it had at least distracted me enough that I was able to think a little more clearly

again. Although I'd confirmed that I could still dream walk with
Billie, I'd neglected to actually convey any helpful information to
her. Unfortunately, there was nothing I could do now except wait
for her to go back to sleep. Being no stranger to the occasional
carnal nocturnal episode, I knew that I could be waiting a while.
To further clear my head, I decided to drop back in on the maestro
of nostril percussion.

20

After playing my new loop for Cuff a few more times, I went back
to the basement to try talking to Billie again, preferably from a safe
distance. Perhaps even with several layers of bulky winter clothing
and the odour of broccoli and microwaved fish in the background
for good measure.

As it turned out, Billie wasn't in the dream phase yet and I
had to wait around for a bit longer. I spent my time both
simultaneously planning what I needed to say and elaborately
crafting the least appealing locations I could think of. When it
finally looked like I'd be able to dive in, I selected the worst of my
creations.

Whisps of colour floated in the otherwise blank expanse, so
I knew that Billie hadn't had the chance to start building things
herself, yet. I quickly took control. The air filled with the scent of
animal dung and the grating tones of a calliope. Overhead hung a
red and white striped tent that covered a stage of dead grass ringed
by bleacher-style seating. Since Billie would be able to see me, I
tried changing into the most repulsive thing I could imagine.
Starting with my feet, I added ridiculously oversized yellow shoes,
then a patchwork onesie that was about five sizes too large. I added
a hula hoop sewn around the waist to accentuate that particular
feature. Last, I imagined a puffy rainbow wig that I could just
barely see the tips of at the edge of my peripheral vision.

I'd been sure to stay hidden behind the bleachers until I was ready. When I was fairly certain the outfit would hold, I stepped out and shot water from the flower on my lapel to get Billie's attention. When she turned, there was a brief look of confusion, then she smiled and started to move toward me.

"Wow, weird stuff works on you." I'd said it out loud and forgot that Billie could hear me. She stopped when she saw me backing away from her.

"You forgot your face," she said with a bit of a laugh.

I took that chuckle to mean that I wasn't standing there devoid of flesh, a mess of muscles and ligaments. Just to be sure, I reached up and rubbed my cheek. When my fingers came back clean, I realized what she'd meant. I'd forgotten face paint and a false nose. "That's ok," I stuttered "I'm done with my shift now."

I was babbling and blowing this second chance to cover the essentials. Being here, being able to be with her, even if it wasn't actual reality, was making it much harder to concentrate than I had counted on.

"So, were you practicing or something?", Billie prompted.

Out of nowhere, she somehow had gotten a stick of cotton candy and was tearing off pieces of it while she waited for me to respond.

"Something like that.", I muttered.

I decided this setup was too distracting and quickly cleared the scene. Since I needed to focus on getting my message across, I left us in an endless dark void. Billie still had her cotton candy, but I'd changed back into my normal outfit. She didn't seem to notice the transition and appeared to be waiting for me to elaborate. At least she wasn't trying to rip my clothes off this time.

Now, now, Alex. That's not fair. You know you were just as interested in disrobing as she was.

I hoped that Billie wasn't able to hear Nega-me and decided that I needed to get this over with as quickly as possible. "I need you to listen to me. Ok, Billie? I mean really listen."

Her snack disappeared and her face became serious. "What is it?"

"I know that you probably won't remember any of this, but I need you to try."

"What's wrong?" She started to draw closer and as much as I wanted to hold her again, I had to stay on task.

"My name's Alex. This is going to sound like something your brain just made up in a strange dream, but I promise you, everything I'm about to say is real." Billie nodded and I hurried to continue. "I was murdered by the same killer you've been tracking, the New Page Killer. I'm not on your spreadsheet, but if you look me up you might find something about a stabbing victim found in an alley at the end of this past spring."

Her mouth fell open a little and she reached out to touch my arm. "I'm so sorry." Tears formed in her eyes.

I hadn't meant to upset her, I'd only meant to give her something she could look up and hopefully use to validate the dream — *if* I was lucky enough that she actually remembered it.

"Don't worry about it. All that matters now is that the killer is after you. That mugger you destroyed a few nights ago was him, and I don't think he was looking to rob you. Same with the fire you and Sam escaped. Before it started, I saw someone hiding in the bushes near your site. By the time the rangers got to the island, there was no sign of anyone else, but I know it was the killer who did it. He started the fire, and he sabotaged your canoe in case you used it to try to get to safety."

I avoided using one specific name to refer to Rodger so that I wouldn't skew any research Billie might do. Next, I pulled out the same dossier I'd made for Cuff. She hadn't gotten a good look at his face, and I wanted it burned into her memory. Billie flipped through the folder while I spoke.

"This is everything I've been able to put together on him. It isn't much, since we don't exactly have the internet here, but it might help you to convince Detective Cuff if you can dig up any connections between this guy, and the dates of the murders."

Just as I was about to let her know that some of the victims might not be able to be included, based on what happened with Shay, Billie disappeared, and I was back in the basement. The dim blue light showed me that Billie's eyes were open but that she was holding herself incredibly still. Her whole body looked tense and ready to spring into action.

Then I heard what must have woken her and set her on high alert. There was a squeak on the staircase. The limited glow didn't reach to the stairs, and I wasn't able to make out anything in the darkness. At the sound of the second creak of the stair, I noticed Billie's hand slowly reaching for her phone. I looked around to see if there was anything close by that she might be able to use as a weapon, but there wasn't anything she could reach without getting off the bed and giving away the element of surprise.

My mind raced with all of the ugly events that could have unfolded while we were busy in the dream. Rodger would have started upstairs where the majority of people would expect to find the bedrooms. Would he have murdered the rest of Billie's family to eliminate liabilities?

Another groan from the stairs let us know that he was almost at the bottom. Billie had managed to grab her phone, but it wouldn't do her much good. She was trapped. The only way out of here was blocked. Her only hope was to hide. Apparently, Billie had the opposite idea. She flicked on the bedside lamp and swung her feet around, ready to face the problem head-on.

That was when we both saw Asra, her hands full of bedding. I let out the breath I'd been holding, and Billie jumped up to turn on some more lights.

"Sorry, Billie, I didn't mean to startle you. The light at the top of the stairs must have blown. Sam had an accident and I wanted to sneak these into the laundry."

"It's ok. I was just about to get up, anyway."

"Don't rush yourself. Remember, you need your rest."

"I'm fine, Asra. I've taken my share of hits and I'm still standing." Billie tried for a lopsided smile, but it didn't quite cover the sudden sadness in her eyes.

"You more than most I think, priy. Now go back to bed. I'll make you some breakfast when you get up."

*

Even after Asra had headed back upstairs, Billie didn't show any signs of going back to sleep. She'd left the side-table lamp on and was slumped against the pullout couch-back, her arms folded across her chest. All I could do was sit there and hope that she would show some sign that I'd gotten through, some hint that she'd remembered anything that I'd said.

Eventually, after a quick breakfast and about a hundred reassurances that she was feeling much better, Billie was able to talk Asra into relinquishing her keys. Billie still had a few more days before she was expected to be back at work, so I was hopeful that we were headed out to work on the case.

Billie's first stop was to drop off Taco and their supplies from the sleepover back at her apartment. A cursory glance showed that there was nothing out of the ordinary there. I ran a few quick patrols after making sure the apartment was clear, but I wanted to ensure I didn't miss anything that Billie might learn if she started more research.

We weren't at the apartment long. After grabbing a few things and tossing them into her messenger bag, Billie was back on the road again. When we pulled up in front of the centre, I caught my first glimpse of hope that she'd remembered something from the dream. Billie went straight to the reception desk where Taylor was on duty today. "Morning, Taylor. Is Nicky around?"

"No, sorry. He's off today. Is there anything I can help you with?"

"Maybe. I've been thinking about what a great job you all do of protecting member privacy here, and it got me thinking. It would probably be a good idea if we could extend that same level of care to the volunteers."

I noticed the subtle "we" Billie had worked in there, making herself part of the team. It didn't seem to have caught Taylor's attention; she just smiled, perhaps wrapped up in the excited energy Billie was putting out. "What did you have in mind?"

"I was thinking that I could digitize the volunteer sign-in sheet for you. Not only would it keep each person's information private, but it would also give you the chance to run analytics. You could see which times you get the most volunteers, which people help out more often, and let you see which services you might need to recruit more help for. If you added a field for contact information, it would even make it so that you could reach out if you ended up short-staffed, or wanted to let people know about upcoming events or fundraisers."

"That sounds amazing!"

Billie was a genius. Given the skills I'd already seen her demonstrate, I had no doubt that she'd be building in access for herself. Sure, there was a grey area here where, ethically speaking, she wasn't being a hundred percent honest, but lives were at stake, and it wasn't like she was going to use the information for anything sleazy.

"I've got the day off. If you want, I can get started on it right now for you."

Taylor was only too happy to hand over the stack of pages filled with the history of the recent volunteers. She even offered for Billie to use one of the better computers in the back office so that she could have more privacy than what would have been available in the lab upstairs.

I left Billie to work her magic while I searched the rest of the centre. I'd just cleared the gym when a familiar feeling of fatigue and light-headedness overtook me. The already muted colours of the Pale drained from my sight, leaving everything in a dull monochrome.

Maybe I'd pushed it too far the night before, infinitely looping that dream for Cuff and trying to cram in even more sessions with Billie.

"Are you all right?"

I looked around the empty room knowing that there hadn't been any Vitae present a second ago. Just behind my right shoulder was Broden, the somewhat distracted man I'd met on one of my previous visits to the centre. I held up my hand to indicate I was fine, and he backed away a little. After a moment, my head cleared enough for me to steady myself. "I'm fine, thanks."

I was pretty rude the last time I'd seen him. I realized that, if he spent a lot of his time here, it would probably be a good idea to play nice.

"You're Broden, right? I'm Alex. I'm sorry I didn't get a chance to introduce myself before. I was in a bit of a hurry." He nodded, then just kinda stood there, so I tried again.

"So, you come here often?"

My lame joke didn't earn a smile, but he did at least answer me. "I used to volunteer here, back when I was alive."

This didn't really answer my question, but it was a start.

"How come you're still hanging around? There are way nicer places to spend your afterlife, or whatever this is."

Broden's face drooped and, for a moment, I thought he was about to burst into tears.

"I want to do something for them. I need to find a way to save them."

This guy was either a very dedicated volunteer or he was suffering from a severe saviour complex. I wasn't exactly sure what to do here. Clearly, the guy was suffering. I did my best to channel Ava. "I'm sure you did a lot while you were alive. It would have been appreciated, even if no one ever said anything."

Broden began rubbing his temples. "You don't get it. I'm responsible for their suffering, I have to save them."

I started feeling dizzy again. The room grew darker as I fell to my knees. The air felt thick and stale, I couldn't take in enough of it to fill my lungs. The fact that I didn't *need* air didn't seem to matter. As I struggled to stay conscious, I saw dark tendrils of shadow emerge from Broden. They wrapped around him and then he was just gone.

Immediately, the air cleared, and the room brightened.

"Holy shit. Was he the one doing that?"

I thought back to all of the other times I'd felt drained and realized they'd all been when I was here. Either the centre contained some kind of evil vortex, or Broden's bummer vibe was strong enough to pull others into it. It made me wonder if that's how people went missing from the Pale. Did they just get so depressed that it slowly consumed them until there was nothing left?

The whole experience had left me shaken. I hurried back to the office where Billie was working. I needed to see that she was still all right. When I got there, Billie appeared to be wrapping up, but just as she was about to head out, she hesitated for a moment. She turned back to the desk and picked up the phone. I wasn't sure why she wouldn't just use her own until I heard the one-sided conversation.

"Hello. I was at one of the sites on the island that was caught in the fire."

She paused for a moment while the person on the other end said something.

"Yes, we're ok, thanks. I'm calling because everyone on the island had gotten together for dinner that day and we'd exchanged numbers. Unfortunately, my phone was one of the things I lost in the fire, and I was wondering if you'd be able to give me the contact information for the other campers. I'd like to check in on everyone and see how they're doing."

That explained why Billie didn't want to call them from the number that they would've had on file. She kept her phone on her at all times, protected by a case that looked like it could withstand an apocalypse. The smoke and water from the weekend hadn't even left a mark. Billie listened carefully and I knew by the look on her face that her scheme hadn't worked.

"No, I understand. That makes sense. Thank you anyway."

Even though the call hadn't resulted in Billie getting access to the number for the mystery camper, it at least told me that she'd retained something from our conversation the night before. It also reassured me that, if Rodger tried to get any of Billie's personal information from the park, he wasn't likely to succeed.

After teaching Taylor how to use the new digital sign-in method, Billie headed back to her apartment. She spent the rest of the afternoon updating her timeline of key events. After adding her attack and the fire into the spreadsheet, she cross-referenced anyone who had been volunteering during those times. This ultimately resulted in three lists, one for those who stopped volunteering when the first murders happened, one for those who started close to that time, and one for those who were signed in during Billie's attack and the fire. I was disappointed that Billie hadn't researched my murder, but it looked like she'd at least remembered some of what I'd told her.

Once the lists were compiled, we were back on the road again. As we pulled into the lot outside the police station, I caught sight of Detective Cuff heading towards a car. Billie seemed to have spotted him too and parked a few spots over. Billie hurried to get out of the car and called for Cuff as an added measure to ensure that he didn't leave before she could speak to him.

I got the distinct impression that he seriously considered pretending he hadn't heard her. However, he stopped and leaned on his open car door, waiting for Billie to state her business.

"Detective, thank you for waiting. I promise I'll make this quick."

He pinched the bridge of his nose and closed his eyes as if trying to find the strength to get through the conversation. "Look, Billie, I get it," his voice was quiet, almost sad, "I realize that your parents were killed by a junkie when they walked in on their clinic being robbed. It happened a whole continent away and you couldn't do anything to help them, so now you're seeing victims everywhere. I'm sorry, but without any evidence, or even a suspect, there's nothing I can do."

Even though Cuff's tone had been apologetic, Billie's face burned as if he'd been mocking her. Billie's reply showed her barely contained fury.

"Yes, my parents were killed. And yes, if that "junkie" had had access to proper addiction and mental health services, they might both still be alive, but that *has nothing* to do with what's happening now. How did you even find out about that? You've got the time to investigate me, but not to look into these murders?"

Even though I could tell the detective genuinely felt sorry for Billie, I could also tell that he was someone who'd been spread too thin. He didn't look any better than he had last night when he'd stumbled through his door, and I'd noticed that his bedmate hadn't ever made it back either. He made an effort to control his clearly rising temper.

"Yes, as a matter of fact, I did investigate you. Contrary to what you may think, I do actually take some pride in my job and when someone who is so adamant that serial killings are taking place repeatedly ambushes me, I take their complaint seriously. For all I knew, you were the one going around killing people and were upset that no one had made the connection yet, getting you the media attention you thought you deserved. It wouldn't be the first time some psycho decided to open communications with the police."

"Of all the ..."

Billie was flat-out yelling now, and they were starting to draw attention. Cuff quickly grabbed her arm and pulled her around so that the car door blocked them both from the rest of the lot. The sudden jerk had stopped Billie's outburst and she settled for a death stare instead. The detective raised his hands, indicating that things needed to calm down. When he resumed their discussion, he sounded downright exhausted. "Why do you care so much about this, Billie?"

Billie wasn't ready to concede this fight, but she managed to keep her voice down. "Because someone has to. I've been all around the world and I've seen a lot of different ways of living. There's no excuse, in a country with this many resources, for anyone to be sleeping in the streets or going without a meal, let alone being murdered without any hope of justice."

"I agree with you. But I can't just go off on a wild goose chase and neglect every other case file and person who needs my help."

Having vented her frustration, Billie visibly started to calm down a little. "I know. That's why I've brought you some leads."

She passed her phone to the detective, and he began scrolling through the research Billie had compiled. It seemed like he was ready to dismiss her, but then his eye caught on something on the screen.

"Send this to me and I'll take a look. But I'm not making any promises here, Billie. I'll take the time to review what you've dug up but that doesn't mean that it will necessarily go anywhere."

Billie let out a sigh of relief. "Thank you."

She took back her phone and the detective gave her his email address. As she turned away, I heard Billie let loose one last vent of her frustration. "Good luck, Inspector Lestrade."

"Hey, I heard that."

Billie turned back and they shared a small smile.

*

That night, I spent the majority of my time doing everything I could to convince Cuff to trust Billie. I even tried hitting him with a stress bomb, like I'd accidentally done to Billie, to snap him awake in the hopes that he'd be more likely to remember the dreams if they were fresh. Unfortunately, the detective was either immune or the levels of anxiety that had worked before with Billie, weren't something that I could manufacture. On the plus side, Cuff didn't seem to be able to see me, or at the very least, he didn't want to make out with me.

Ultimately, I had to settle for another round of monotonous looping. Each time Cuff slipped out of the dream stage, I'd pop over to Billie's to see if I could pass anything else along to her. I couldn't entirely tell if I was disappointed or relieved when each time I stopped by, she wasn't in the middle of a dream.

21

The next day was Billie's final one off of work and it looked like she was going to do about as much resting as she'd done the day before. Bright and early, she'd grabbed her messenger bag and was headed down the back staircase. As she came out of the dark hallway and into the blazing sunrise, I caught the hint of another song that had no explicable origin.

♫ "You gotta kick at the darkness till it bleeds daylight." ♪

I wasn't sure where the music was coming from. Nega-me seemed to think that my "new symptom of crazy" hypothesis was wrong, but I had to admit that whatever was generating the songs certainly knew how to pick them.

You are rather dense. Do you know that?

"*Excuse* me. I'm *so sorry* that discovering the origins of a phantom radio is low on my list of priorities right now."

I can't believe we're related. It's embarrassing.

I went back to ignoring the party pooper in my head. I couldn't help but feel optimistic this morning and I wasn't about to let that schmuck bring me down. Billie was safe, for the moment, I definitely hadn't lost my ability to communicate with her, and I was cautiously optimistic that Cuff was starting to get on board.

Unfortunately, my high didn't last long. Billie pulled up at the centre, which normally would have been only slightly worrying. Whenever she was there, there was always the chance that Rodger was somewhere nearby, but today happened to be a Wednesday. Based on the last time I'd actually managed to follow him, it seemed that Wednesday was Rodger's regular day to volunteer.

I tried to find some solace in the fact that it was a very public place, and that Billie would probably be fine while she was there. What I was more concerned about was when she left. Since she was back at her own place, it wouldn't be difficult to follow her and seize an opportunity when she was alone.

Now that the sign-in was digitized, I had no way of scanning to see who had already arrived today. The centre had only just opened, so there probably weren't too many volunteers who'd started yet. After escorting Billie to the main lobby, I did a rapid-fire search of all of the rooms. The majority were empty, and those that weren't didn't have anyone fitting Rodger's basic build. I didn't expect him to be using a disguise in a place where everyone already knew what he looked like, but I wasn't going to take any chances.

The search hadn't taken me long and, when I got back to the lobby, Billie and Taylor were just wrapping up the banal pleasantries that everyone feels forced to recite.

"So, since I had a little spare time today, I thought I would stop by and see if you needed an extra hand." I wasn't sure if Billie was on a specific mission today or if she was genuinely just here to help out. Taylor seemed relieved, regardless of the reason.

"You have no idea how good your timing is. We actually had a few people cancel on us at the last minute and we're a little shorthanded. Flu season, it gets us every year."

"Glad I can help. Where do you need me? I've mostly just worked in the computer lab, but I'm happy to do whatever needs to be done."

"We're down our lunch chef and our supply distributor. Lunch can still wait a little longer before someone needs to start on it, so why don't you head over to the supplies counter? Nicky's over there and can give you the rundown."

Taylor gave Billie directions and while she walked, I found myself hoping that cooking the meals was Rodger's regular job.

After a few twists and turns, Billie finally found the right spot. I spied Nicky across the room, but Billie's eyes were focused on the wall above him. "The Broden Rodger Roman Canteen" was painted in big bold letters across the wall behind the counter.

Nicky spotted Billie and waved to her. She waved back but hadn't taken her eyes off the sign. "Shouldn't that say 'The Broden *and* Rodger Roman Canteen'?"

Nicky looked confused and shook his head. "No, Broden was a volunteer here. He died pushing one of our members out of the path of an on-coming car. The room is dedicated to him."

"Oh, I didn't know about that. How awful."

"What made it even worse is that the man he'd saved ended up dying about a week later. I guess he'd pulled some food out of the trash that he shouldn't have. They found rat poison in his system."

"I'm so sorry to hear that."

After a moment's hesitation, Billie continued, "It's just that I was updating the sign-in process yesterday and I remembered coming across both of those names as separate volunteers. I thought maybe it was a family donation or something."

Nicky processed that for a moment before responding. "Huh. I never really thought about it. Rodger is Broden's brother, and I hadn't made the connection that they shared a name. Weird. Thanks, by the way, for the new setup. It should be really helpful."

Billie's reply was a little distracted. "No problem. Hey, I just remembered a quick call I have to make. I'll be back in a minute so you can show me what you'd like me to do."

With that, Billie ducked around the corner. I watched as she typed out a hurried message to Cuff. She'd made the same connection I had, without the benefit of an eery conversation with Broden. His overwhelming sense of responsibility for the people using the centre finally made sense. He must have known what Rodger was doing and it was destroying him.

It seemed like the worst possible way to pay tribute to Broden's memory, but maybe that was the point. I wondered if some deep-rooted jealousy was at the heart of why Rodger would dedicate so much time and energy to hurting those who his brother had tried to help. I wasn't even sure if Broden was actually his brother or not, but he must have cared enough about Broden to use his name for the fake identity he employed to hunt his victims.

I also wondered if it actually *was* accidental that that man had consumed the rat poison. He certainly seemed like a good candidate for Rodger's initial victim. I wondered how this coincided with Billie's list and whether or not this man had made it on there.

We'd also all but confirmed my theory that Rodger wasn't even our killer's real name. He would have needed a background check and a vulnerable sector screening before he would have been allowed to volunteer. I wondered if there was something on Rodger's record that would have prevented him from passing, making it easier to use Broden's paperwork with a slight alteration. While Billie was relatively safe at the centre, I decided to pop over to the police station to see if Cuff was already looking into this.

When I got there, the detective was nowhere in sight. Unable to locate him, I set out to see if Naifeh was still hanging around. Unfortunately, it seemed that all of my detectives had gone missing. All I could do was hope that they were out following a lead that would finally put an end to all of this. Having nothing else I could do right now, I went back to the centre.

*

Billie spent the rest of the day bouncing between a variety of jobs. She hadn't uncovered anything else, and Rodger hadn't made an appearance. Every once in a while, I'd catch her checking her phone, presumably waiting for a reply from Cuff.

The soundtrack to our day had changed too. The current song was one I didn't recognize, which didn't make any sense if I was the source of the music.

Finally, putting the pieces together, are you?

Since this still wasn't a top concern, I tried ignoring the comments from the cheap seats. Apparently, Nega-me had other ideas.

Billie almost dies, and all of a sudden, you're now directly in her dreams. You also magically start hearing earworms, ones that you only hear when you're around Billie, but you assume that your subconscious has sprung a DJ. I'm really quite disappointed in you.

With it all laid out like that, I was a little disappointed in myself too.

"So, you think this means something?" I tried to reason through it. "Earworms dominate your interior dialogue... and I can hear them. Do you think that means that Billie might be able to hear me? Like right now, while she's awake?"

You won't know until you try, will you?

If this actually worked, I might be able to do more than just helplessly watch from the sidelines. I could keep an eye on Billie's back and warn her if I spotted any danger. Maybe I could even get her to be my hands in the real world, so that we could investigate together.

I ran over to the delivery truck where Billie was currently unloading a shipment of donations. I called to her; my excitement barely contained. "Billie!"

She didn't give any indication that she'd heard me. No look over her shoulder, no scrunching of her face as she tried to catch something she hadn't quite heard. I tried again, a lot louder this time, "BILLIE!!!"

Nothing. "Maybe it's not a vocal thing. I'm hearing her background thoughts. Maybe I need to *think* at her instead of shouting at her."

There's a giant spider crawling up your arm. It seemed that Nega-me had decided to "help" with the mental message.

Billie still didn't give any reaction. Next, I tried occupying the same space as her head while attempting to send a message. I had more control over this one and kept it simple.

This is Alex. Say my name if you can hear me.

I let out a growl of frustration when nothing happened. Without realizing it, I'd made the mistake of getting my hopes up. Nega-me chimed in with a mocking rejoinder, *Say my name, say my name.* And then I heard something completely unexpected.

♪ "If no one is around you, say baby I love you." ♫

"No way. There is no way that that just worked."

It certainly seems to have done the trick.

To test this theory, I tried sending Billie a completely different song. *I know there's no one in the universe, as magical and wondrous as you.*

Her mental reply came immediately, ♫ "Turn around." ♪

I burst out laughing. I had no idea how, or even if, this could actually be useful, but it was something. It also meant that I was going to have to start putting some real thought into which songs might come in handy in an emergency, so that I could have them ready.

Luckily, I didn't need to come up with a musical prompt to look into Rodger's files at the centre. Sadly though, the staff did a better job of protecting their volunteers' information than they did the sign-in sheets. Billie tried several times to discreetly gain access to the office, but without any success. Frankly, I doubted the information in Rodger's file would have been legit, anyway. But there was always the hope that even fake contact info could have still provided some sort of clue.

While Billie finished up her day of volunteering, I tried to come up with a strategy for tonight. It was hard to know if I'd been making any progress with Cuff, and I didn't relish the thought of spending another evening plodding through the same dreams on repeat, again. But I also had to be sure I wasn't just coming up with excuses to spend my time with Billie instead. Other than trying to strengthen our methods of communication, there wasn't any immediate need for me to contact her. She'd already identified Rodger as a likely suspect, and I knew that warning her to stay away from the centre for her own safety would be useless: she'd been going there for who knows how long, suspecting a murderer was connected with the place.

Ultimately, I decided to split the difference like I had the night before. I dedicated my time to the detective, and when I couldn't work on him, I dropped in on Billie. Since there wasn't anything new that I could tell her, I figured I could at least make sure her nightmares were kept at bay.

The first time I stopped by Billie was still up. When I'd left to check on Cuff, she'd been scouring the internet for anything related to Broden. At that point, it had been hours with only the article about his death and a few mentions of his junior hockey career, so I figured I wasn't going to miss anything. It now seemed that Billie's persistence had paid off and she'd managed to track down some social media accounts linked to Broden. I watched as she skimmed through the posts, hopeful I'd see "Rodger's" face pop up. A tag with his real name would have been even more helpful. Alas, it wasn't going to be that easy. Billie had started to compile a list of the people who had liked or commented, but those would take time to sift through, individually. I didn't even know if Billie remembered the images of Rodger that I'd planted in her dreams. If nothing else, that at least gave me something useful to work on with her, whenever she finally managed to get to bed.

On my second trip back from the master of nasal acoustics, Billie was finally asleep. After about thirty minutes she dropped into a dream state and I was quick to join her. It seemed that Billie was in the middle of a classic test-day torment. The kind where you're in class and aren't even remotely prepared for the test you've just learned you have to take. I always found it weird how, even after you're no longer a student, these dreams seemed to have a way of creeping in.

Before it could get too far, I moved us to a tropical lagoon I'd once seen in some movie. It was fed by a modest waterfall and surrounded by lush greenery. The sun was warm, and the water looked very inviting. I found myself hoping that, when this was all over, maybe I could spend some time creating a little dreamland vacation for the two of us to enjoy.

But first, we needed to catch a killer. It didn't take long for me to remember the task at hand and get down to work. I turned down the volume of the falls and called out to Billie. "Hey. I'm Alex. Do you remember me?"

Billie's mouth quirked to the side. "Should I?"

Well, that stung a little. I certainly thought that our previous encounter had been memorable. I was tempted to take her back to the bowling alley to trigger a connection, but decided it would be better to focus on business. "We've met before, here, in your dreams I mean. I'm one of the New Page Killer's victims."

Suddenly, a cone of cotton candy appeared in Billie's hand and little beams of reflected light danced across her face. When she didn't say anything, I went on. "The man who's killing all of those innocent people is out to get you too."

She already knew this, but I didn't see the harm in re-enforcing this information. I hung a wanted poster with his face and aliases mid-air in the space to my left. The jungle behind Billie caught fire. She still hadn't spoken but I took her additions to the dream as a good sign.

"That was great work today, finding out about Broden. If we can figure out his brother's real name, we might actually have a chance at stopping this guy."

A car with a smashed windshield covered in blood and bits of hair and flesh appeared on my right. The dream was getting crowded and chaotic. The lagoon had started to shift and glitch. I didn't know how much time I had left. "This guy likes to use disguises, so *please* be careful."

I don't know if my last warning had gotten through. The dream had ended, and I was back in Billie's room. It would have to do, for now.

22

Billie's first day back at work was fairly routine. Some asked how she was feeling, while others just seemed interested in the gory details. Billie had a lot of work to catch up on and was glued to her desk for the majority of the day. Since I suspected that Rodger had figured out where Billie worked, and had likely overheard her weekend plans from the patio of the café downstairs, I spent the day sweeping the surrounding streets. The fire had shown how desperate he was, and I worried about what he might be willing to do next.

At the end of the day, when everyone was packing it in for the night, Billie decided to stay behind to get some more catching up done. I didn't like the idea of her hanging around the office alone but, as it turned out, she wasn't alone for long. Shortly after the majority of people had left, Jesse came panting back upstairs. "Billie, you've gotta see this. Everyone's tires have been slashed."

"Everyone's?" Billie had already started to get her jacket on and move towards the door.

"Yeah. I can't believe someone got away with this in broad daylight.

When we got outside, the parking lot looked normal. It wasn't until you got closer to the cars that you could see the damage. Each vehicle had a flat. When I jogged over to the sidewalk, I realized that anyone who crouched would be able to make their way from car to car without being seen. Their only real chance of being caught in the act would have been if someone came down for something. The lot itself was just for employees, so there wouldn't have been a lot of coming and going.

After inspecting the damage to her tire, Billie shouted over to Jesse. "Has anyone called the cops yet?"

"Ash did as soon as we saw what had happened. They're sending someone over and they told us to contact our insurance companies."

After everyone's statements had been taken, most of Billie's co-workers had decided to just leave their vehicles there for the night. Apparently someone had a friend that owned a shop and he'd offered to come by and replace people's tires tomorrow. Those who were interested, shared their info so that the proper tires would be brought over in the morning. By the time things were wrapping up it was getting dark, and someone was organizing a carpool. Billie declined the offer and went to work changing her tire herself. It didn't take long for her to get her spare on, but she did have to stop to take the occasional puff on her inhaler.

When she was finally finished, it was pitch black out, the only light coming from the streetlamps and the handful of businesses that were still open. I was anxious for Billie to hit the road but, instead, she headed back towards the office. At this point, there was no one else left in the building. Even the hum of the heating system had died out.

Billie walked back to her desk, but she didn't sit down. She just kind of leaned over the top of her chair to type on her keyboard. I hoped this meant that she didn't plan on being long. Just then, all of the lights went out. Billie grumbled and started waving her hands over her head without really looking away from the computer. I guessed she was used to some sort of motion sensor kicking in after business hours, but I didn't like it.

Shortly after the lights cut out, I heard a thump come from the back of the office but Billie didn't seem to have noticed it. The lights still hadn't turned back on and when I tried to investigate the noise, all I could make out were dark blobs. If I'd been able to bump into the furniture, I'm sure my shins would've been purple by the time I got to the other side of the room. I was about to head back over to Billie when, out of the corner of my eye, I thought I saw something move. Immediately I started broadcasting a warning song to Billie.

♫ "Up all night long, and there's something very wrong." ♪

I kept playing the lines over and over until I heard her repeat them back. I could've kicked myself for not telling her to pay attention when stuff like that popped into her head during last night's dream session. I was so focused on the mental noise I was making, that it took a minute for me to realize that I couldn't hear the sound of Billie typing anymore. As I hurried back to her desk, I tried to catch another glimpse of the form I'd seen. I hoped the silence meant that Billie had finished and was heading home, but I hadn't heard the rustle of her messenger bag being slung over her shoulder, or the jangle of her keys ready to lock up.

I threw another alert out to Billie as I went.

♪ "And now they coming, yeah, now they coming, out from the shadows." ♫

Just then, there was another thud, this time from one of the cubicles ahead of me. I raced back to Billie's desk. She seemed to have heard this new noise. I could see her slowly reaching into her bag while she tried to turn on the light on her phone. While her hand was still in the bag, I heard a muffled pop. When she pulled her hand back out, I could see she had the travel-sized spray deodorant and the sound had been the lid being worked off. Next, Billie tucked her phone into her shirt, the top-half sticking out so that she could see and keep her hand free at the same time.

As we listened, she transferred the deodorant to her left hand and picked up her keys off of the desk, carefully placing one key poking out each end of her fist. If Rodger was here, Billie was ready for a fight.

The sound of breaking glass drew both of our attention towards the door. Unfortunately, that was exactly what Rodger had been hoping for. While her gaze was turned, he launched out from behind a cubicle, knocking Billie down. Her cell phone went flying but by the light coming through the window, I could see them struggling on the ground. Rodger was dressed all in black. Even his hands were covered by dark latex-looking gloves. Billie's knee came up, but he was expecting it and was able to block her. Rodger kept her pinned, using the full weight of his body to hold her down. Her face was too close to his to use the spray. If she did, she'd end up getting just as much of it as he would. Rodger leveraged himself up a bit to try to free his right hand. Billie took the chance to jab one of her keys into his ribs, causing him to buckle over. He fell forward and used his shoulder to re-pin Billie while trying to protect his core. Billie's hand was still free, and she stabbed wildly at his back.

Rodger shifted and snatched Billie's wrists, pinning both of her arms to the floor while he tried to catch his breath. I watched as Billie planted her feet flat against the ground and then launched her hips into the air like she was trying to form a bridge with her body. Rodger immediately went sailing forward and Billie used his momentum to snap her arms down towards her sides, breaking his hold. Gravity took over and Rodger's head pounded into the floor.

Billie barely got her face turned before his torso came smashing down on top of her head.

Like a flash, Billie's arms were wrapped around Rodger, pulling herself as close to his body as possible. I didn't understand what she was doing until I saw him struggling to find enough space to get his arms between them and push her back down again. He also now needed to support their combined weight if he wanted to avoid doing another faceplant. While Rodger's arms were busy supporting them, Billie's arm shot around on top of his left one and pulled it, knocking the two of them into a roll to the side. She scrambled to get up, but now that Rodger was on his back, he didn't need to worry about using his hands to keep himself from falling over. He grabbed Billie's leg and pulled her flat onto her face. In no time at all, he had his fingers wrapped in Billie's hair. With a heave, he wrenched her head back, then slammed it into the floor. I watched, breathless, as she just lay there, not moving at all. As the seconds passed by, I lost all hope that Billie was just stunned or faking unconsciousness. Rodger used his foot to lift Billie's arm, then let it fall leaden to the ground before moving any closer. After he was satisfied that she was out, he removed some zip ties from his pocket. He bound her wrists behind her back, then secured her ankles. When he was done, he threw her over his shoulder like a sack of laundry.

I didn't know why he wasn't just killing her, but I was grateful for it. I tried to keep my panic at bay by reassuring myself that he wouldn't be able to just waltz out the front door with Billie and stroll down the sidewalk to his car. There were still a fair number of people out when I glanced through the window to see if help was on the way. I'd hoped that someone downstairs would have heard all of the noise, or that one of Billie's co-workers would return for some forgotten item.

There was no such luck and things got even worse when Rodger arrived at the back of the office. I'd assumed that he was just moving deeper into the shadows, maybe planning to wait until the streets were quieter, but when we rounded the corner into an alcove I'd never noticed before, my heart sank.

I'd been too wrapped up in everything that was going on to have ever wondered how Casey, a person who obviously couldn't use the stairs that Billie always came and went by, managed to get to the second floor each day. Rodger's gloved finger pushed the button for the elevator and while he waited, I suddenly understood why he had only cut the lights instead of just knocking out all of the power.

From the position of the elevator and the fact that it only had one set of doors, I knew that this was bad news for Billie. When we reached the ground floor, my fears were confirmed. The doors opened out onto a back alley, where a charcoal grey car was waiting.

After tossing Billie in the trunk, Rodger added one more zip tie, attaching Billie's wrists to her ankles so that she was forced to lay there in a painful-looking arc. He quickly slapped some tape over her mouth, then covered her with a false bottom made of the same scratchy fabric that lined the rest of the trunk. I climbed in next to Billie so she wouldn't be alone but left my head sticking out so that I could keep an eye on where we were headed. I didn't dare try to dream walk with Billie right now and risk losing the car if I came unglued. As useless as I was, I could at least try to track where we were headed. I didn't know what I could do with that information, but it was better than nothing.

There was no one other than Taco waiting up for Billie, and her co-workers probably wouldn't even realize she was missing until late into tomorrow. I could feel the panic seeping in as my mind raced to find some way to help. My only hope was that Cuff would turn in early tonight. If I could show him where Billie had been taken and scare him awake, there was an infinitesimally small chance he would spring into action and save the day. I knew it was impossible, but it was the only hope I had to hold onto.

*

We eventually arrived at a farm in the middle of nowhere. Rodger pulled the car straight into the barn, then closed a huge wooden door behind him. He grabbed a flashlight, then headed into a back room, leaving Billie in the trunk. While he was gone, I took two seconds to zap to Cuff's bedroom and found it empty. Not wasting any more time, I immediately returned to the barn. Since I couldn't control whatever Rodger was up to, I focused on trying to get Billie conscious. She was the only one who had any hope of getting her out of this without further damage. When I plunged my head into hers, I wasn't able to make a connection or craft any dreamscapes.

My only other resource was to try to annoy her awake with a barrage of earworms. I doubted it would work, but there was nothing else to try. I started with some screaming death metal at full blast, then launched into "The Hamster Dance Song", followed by bagpipes. I don't know if it was the Scottish torture sack that did it, or if Billie just came to on her own, but I could hear her starting to move around.

It wasn't much longer before Rodger came back and popped open the trunk. He shone the light on the false bottom but didn't reach in right away.

"If you're thinking of doing something foolish, you can forget it. You're in an isolated location where no one will hear you scream. There aren't any other people around for at least thirty minutes by car, and the only vehicle on the property has been disabled."

I was pretty sure this last part was a lie since I hadn't seen Rodger do anything to the car. After giving Billie a minute to absorb that information, he issued his instructions. "I'm going to lift the cover off of you and untie your hands from your feet. Your wrists and ankles will stay bound. If you try another stunt like what you pulled back in the office, our conversation is over. There will be no second chances. I think you know by now that I mean what I say when I tell you that I will not hesitate to kill you."

With that, Rodger lifted the mat covering Billie. She squinted into the beam of the flashlight blaring onto her face. I could read the silent rage that burned under the surface. It looked like Billie was barely containing the urge to headbutt Rodger the second he got close enough to cut her ties.

When her legs were detached from her wrists, she straightened them as much as the limited space in the trunk would allow. As Rodger reached down to grab her arm, she jerked it back out of his grip. "You think you can climb out on your own? Be my guest.'

Rodger backed away from the car and waited while Billie struggled to get upright. She started by rolling her shoulders until her top half was laying on her back with her knees still twisted to the side. She winced and I could imagine the strain this was putting on her arms. Next, she tried to jerk her knees over so that she ended up in a hovering crunch position. Finally, she got her legs twisted around underneath herself and sat up. From there she hunched herself over the lip of the trunk and did an excruciating-looking roll out onto the ground.

The exertion required for the maneuver had taken its toll on Billie, and I could see she was fighting to breathe. Rodger didn't lift a finger, he just watched her as she lay there, trying to get control. I doubted Billie still had her inhaler on her, and either way, her hands weren't free to use it. I watched her as she closed her eyes and seemed to concentrate on filling her belly, instead of her chest, with air. This looked like it helped, and after a few minutes, she slowly rolled over until she was in a position to get herself standing.

Her feet were still bound, so she wasn't going to be walking anywhere. Rodger slipped off to the side, keeping the light in Billie's eyes the entire time, and returned with a folding chair.

"Sit."

I knew Billie wouldn't want to follow any of his commands, but I hoped that she was smart enough to conserve her strength. It seemed like she'd already spent a lot of it rolling out of the trunk. After a moment's hesitation, she did as she was told and plopped down into the chair, her hands were left to hang out the opening at the back. I took a quick look to see if there were any jagged edges she could rub her ties against like in the movies, but it was too dark for me to see anything.

Regardless, it seemed that Rodger wasn't taking any chances. He pulled out more zip ties and fastened Billie's ankles to a leg of the chair, and her hands to a rod at the back of the chair. If she wanted to try hopping away, she now needed to do it while strapped down.

I figured that would be the end of the precautions, but Rodger wasn't finished. He tied a rope around the rod on the other side of the chair-back and looped this through the arm of the still-open trunk, effectively tying Billie to the car. After all of this was done, he left the light shining in Billie's eyes propped up on something and went back to the room he'd disappeared into, earlier.

I took this opportunity to quickly zap back to Cuff's place again. The detective still wasn't in bed and a quick search of his empty house showed that he wouldn't be any time soon. I returned to the barn and waited with Billie while Rodger prepared whatever it was he had in store for her. She kept glancing over her shoulder to get a look at where he had gone, but the car was blocking her view and it was impossible to see anything. Billie blinked angry tears from her eyes as they darted around the room. I took a quick lap outside the barn to see if there was anything useful I could pass along, but all I could see was pasture and dirt road. On my way back in, I passed through the room Rodger had scurried off to. I expected to find him sharpening implements of torture, or draping a room in plastic to make a nice, easy-to-clean killing floor. What I found was him eating a cold sandwich and drinking a bottle of water. It appeared he planned to use suspense and fear of the unknown to break Billie.

I still didn't know why he wanted her alive, but I was sure that she wouldn't be leaving this barn in that condition. She knew too much, and she'd seen his face. Things were starting to look so grim that my mind ran towards the worst-case scenarios. We might have to rely on any DNA Billie knocked out of him at the office as the only hope of having our murderer caught. I wondered if he planned to go back and clean up before the night was over.

When he'd finished his meal, Rodger grabbed an envelope from the counter he'd used as a table and headed back out. On his way past Billie, he grabbed the edge of the tape and ripped it from her mouth. I cringed as I imagined how much skin it must've taken with it. After visibly pushing back the pain, Billie spoke up. "Is this the part where you confess your entire plan and expect me to sympathize with you?"

Billie seemed to know as well as I did that she wasn't leaving here. And the longer she could keep him talking, the longer she would have to come up with some way of getting out of here. I'm sure some people would have tried to appeal to his humanity or beg for mercy, but Billie knew what he'd done, the innocent lives he'd taken. Any attempt to build a connection with him would've required him to actually be human, not the cold, callous monster that he was. There was no smile, no emotion whatsoever when he replied. "No. This is where you tell me what I want to know, or I pay *him* a visit." Rodger tossed a pile of photos onto the dirt floor and shone the flashlight on them so that Billie could see. They were all of Sam.

23

As I stared down at the photos of Sam, I couldn't help but notice that they were all from locations we'd visited during the camping trip. None of them were at the house or looked like he was at school. There was a glimmer of hope that Rodger was bluffing and had no idea how to get to Sam. Although I knew that Billie would never do anything to put him at risk, I hoped that she'd make the connection too and be somewhat reassured. As it was, she kept her face composed, giving nothing away. Rodger waited for some sort of reaction. When one didn't come, he finally explained what he wanted. "What have you learned so far?"

Billie was quick with her reply, "The Eiffel Tower can grow up to fifteen centimetres in the summer, it's illegal to own a lone guinea pig in Switzerland, and the unicorn is the national animal of Scotland."

Without another word, Rodger slapped Billie so hard I thought her head was going to spin all the way around. After taking a minute to recover, Billie practically growled her response through gritted teeth. "If that wasn't the answer you were looking for, then you'll have to be a little more specific."

My response was much more colourful, and Rodger should have considered himself quite lucky that he couldn't feel any of the things I was doing to him at that moment.

Without a single crack in his calm veneer, he moved on to his next question. "Let's forget what you know, for now. Who else have you told?"

"I tell a lot of people a lot of things. Maybe if I knew what you were referring to, I could come up with a list."

I knew Billie needed to stall for time, but I wasn't convinced that Rodger would tolerate her obstinance much longer. Her continuous prodding to get him to admit what he'd done wasn't helping, either. I doubted he would suddenly break down and repent once he'd confessed his crimes.

Rodger rubbed his knuckles. I couldn't tell if he was just posturing or if he was considering taking the beating to the next level. As useless as I knew it was, I moved to plant myself between him and Billie. Right at that second, I saw a faint light pass under the gap of the barn door. In a flash, I was outside, searching for the source. A moving light could mean only one thing: someone else had arrived. If Rodger had an accomplice, things would only be that much harder for Billie.

In the distance, I heard the crunch of tires on gravel. Following the sound, I shot up the driveway as it snaked around a pond. At the end closest to the road, I spotted headlights that had stopped just at the top of the driveway. When I poked my head in to take a look at the driver, I spared only a glance at him before returning to the barn. As soon as I arrived, I blasted a new song at Billie.

♫ "Just hold on, I'm comin'." ♪

Technically I was already here, and it wasn't me who was coming, but that wasn't important. What mattered was that Billie kept Rodger busy just a little while longer. Since Billie had already been stalling, I had no idea if she'd gotten my message or not, but she continued to make things slow and difficult for Rodger.

"Maybe you should start by telling me how I'm supposed to know you. I think I would've remembered meeting someone so pathetic that they could only get off on hurting others."

I could tell she'd struck a nerve with that one. The vein in Rodger's forehead looked like it was about to give birth to a xenomorph at any second. "I'm not some deviant bent on sexual gratification. I'm ridding the world of parasites… leeches who only take and never give back."

I thought back to the man who'd offered Rodger his last bite of food. *Is that why he hadn't killed him that night? He was operating under some twisted moral code that allowed those who still might be useful to survive?* That also explained why I hadn't made the cut. He'd judged me unworthy to live because I'd refused to hand over what little I had. I seethed at the thought that this man had such a flimsy excuse for taking lives. What gave him the right to judge?

Billie was obviously also outraged and not making the slightest attempt to hide it in the interest of self-preservation. "How dare you! Those people have just as much a right to live as you do! At least, Broden certainly thought so."

Rodger's face went slack. Billie's barb had struck deep. Outside, I caught the sound of running footsteps. Our visitor must have heard Billie shouting. I popped outside and saw that he'd drawn his weapon. He was moving off of the gravel and towards the quieter path available through the long grass. There were no windows for him to recon and I hadn't noticed a back door.

I left our potential saviour to figure out his next move on his own, there was nothing I could do to help him. When I got back inside, I saw that Billie had continued to poke the bear. "Broden would be disgusted by you and your sham morality. You're nothing but a sadist."

Rodger took a slow, deliberate step forward and loomed over Billie. Slowly, he pulled a knife from his pocket and twisted the blade on the tip of his finger. Billie kept eye contact the entire time. "Go ahead! Do you think cutting me up will prove me wrong? That will *definitely* show me that you're not just some pervert who gets off on pain.", she scoffed.

He hesitated and I knew that Billie had found his weakness. Rodger's vanity couldn't stand her thinking of him as some common lowlife. He was the hero of his story, the only one smart and strong enough to solve the problem plaguing his city.

As I watched Rodger trying to reconcile his desire to punish Billie with his need to maintain his delusions, I heard a creak above us. Rodger and Billie had heard it too, their eyes snapping up to search the darkness. Rodger moved back to grab the flashlight from where it had been propped. Before he could reach it, a completely different light trapped him in its beam.

"Stay right where you are, Ryker, and put your hands above your head."

Miraculously, Cuff had found some way into the loft. Although he had the high ground, he was going to have to find a way down that somehow allowed him to keep Rodger, or should I say "Ryker" in his sights. I obviously wasn't the only one who had figured this out.

Ryker dove to the side, out of Cuff's beam, and towards the cover provided by the car. Billie shuffled her chair and tipped it, landing hard on Ryker's legs. While this was happening, the detective's light bounced around the loft, presumably looking for a way down.

It was then that I heard a click come from the side of the car, I realized that Ryker hadn't been reaching for the flashlight. An instant later, a bullet whizzed towards the shafts of light peeking through the loft floor. Realizing he now had a target on his back, Cuff switched off his light.

I could see Ryker listening for movement up top, and Billie must've noticed it too. Suddenly, she started screaming her head off, making as much noise as possible. Ryker's legs were still pinned, and he now turned his attention to Billie as he worked to get her off of him. I winced as a swift kick to Billie's stomach temporarily put an end to her distraction technique and Ryker wiggled free. The vapours of the Pale combined with the darkness that enveloped the majority of the barn made it impossible for me to see where Cuff was now or if he was even still breathing.

When Billie had recovered her breath, she resumed her job of providing auditory cover by producing a frankly impressive stream of profanity that spanned several languages. Unfortunately, this drew attention that she was now a liability that Ryker could no longer afford. Billie went silent as he pulled back the hammer on his gun.

Before I knew what was happening, I found myself hurtling towards Ryker at the exact same moment that he let out a yell of pure anguish. Everything took on a strange slow-motion quality. I saw Ryker's face twist into a grimace of pain; I saw Cuff, his weapon drawn; I heard the air crackle with the sound of electricity, and I collided with my target.

Everything was darkness and pain, and then I was staring up at the wooden boards above me. I tried to make sense of what I was seeing, but all I could think about was finding my gun. It was then that I realized the boards overhead were solid and I could feel the grit of the floor under my back.

This isn't my body. The realization shot through me like the agonizing burn of a Carolina Reaper. Before I had a chance to consider what that might mean, I felt the smooth, warm gun I'd been searching for beneath my fingers. As my/Ryker's hand fastened around the grip, I snapped out of my shock. I watched him take aim, then I fought with all of my strength to redirect the gun.

I could feel Ryker's muscles shaking with the strain of resisting my commands, but slowly the barrel moved towards his temple. I had no idea what would happen to me if I could get him to pull that trigger, but I no longer cared. All that mattered now was putting this rabid dog down.

Just as it felt like I was going to win the battle, I was pulled back into one of my worst memories.

The truck comes to an abrupt halt. I know this is my fault and there's going to be hell to pay. Before I can jump out the door, rough hands wrap around my throat. Her hands are always so much stronger when she's angry.

I gasp for air as my fingers claw at the ones slowly crushing my windpipe, unable to loosen their hold.

"I'll kill you, you piece of shit!"

Still clawing with one hand, my other searches for anything that might help to set me free.

"Do you have any idea what you've done?!"

She doesn't let me answer and I'm not getting enough oxygen to make sense of the surfaces my fingers brush against. Blindly, I grab at anything I can keep clasped in my grip. Each time my hand comes away empty, my heart beats faster and I realize she might go too far, this time.

Finally, I grab something cool and smooth. I use the little strength I have left to raise it and bring it down on her head with as much force as I can muster. The shattering of glass is followed by the sweet release of air finally flowing into my lungs. My breathing is raspy as I choke down as much oxygen as possible. The fog in my brain clears enough for me to realize that I'm still in danger. I fumble for the handle and fall out the open door onto the dusty gravel road. I cough on the dirt that's flown into my mouth as I push myself upright.

I'm about to bolt into the field beside me when I realize the cab of the truck is quiet. Too quiet. Carefully, I peer around the corner of my open door. She's slumped forward and a river of blood is flowing from where the beer bottle made impact. I can't tell if she's breathing, and self-preservation takes over. My throat aches, but I turn and run as fast and as far as my legs and my strained lungs will take me. I never look back.

When the memory ended, I was back in the Pale, staring into the darkness of the barn, trying to decipher what had happened. I panted, unsure if the cause of my short breath had been my battle with Ryker or the demons from my past. I searched desperately for some sign that Billie and Cuff were all right. On the periphery of my visual bubble, I saw moonlight spill across the dirt floor. Someone had opened the barn door. Racing over, I could see Cuff sawing at Billie's restraints, Ryker handcuffed face down on the ground.

I let out a sigh of relief.

The rest of the night was a blur. Cuff had called for additional support and a forensics team after tossing Ryker into the back seat of his car. While they waited, the detective got a breakdown from Billie of what had happened before he arrived. Apparently, his timely appearance was complete luck. He'd discovered Ryker's true identity and was checking out the viability of the property for a warrant application. I guess he hadn't bargained on finding such probable cause. It wasn't long before an ambulance and a few more cop cars pulled in. Billie's wounds were examined, and a uniformed officer escorted her to the hospital. They still needed an official statement, and Cuff had requested that someone stay with her until Billie's family could be contacted.

I spent my time split between the investigation of Ryker's property and Billie's bedside at the hospital. Ava was on duty and offered to keep an eye on her whenever I wanted to pop out. By the morning, it seemed obvious that things would not be tied up with a neat little bow. No souvenirs from the victims could be found, although a cache of fake IDs, most likely used for car and hotel rentals, had been discovered. In the end, I didn't think we'd ever find out exactly how many of the people from Billie's list Ryker was responsible for killing.

Billie's family came once again to stay with her while she recovered. Asra had already warned Billie that she'd kidnap Taco, if that's what it took to keep her under their roof until Billie was fully healed this time. As I sat there, enjoying their banter, I couldn't help but feel a little hollow. I'd completed my mission, yet no ferryman had come for me; no triumvirate of gods weighed my heart against a feather. That last part was probably for the best. I couldn't be sure if I would have pulled that trigger if I hadn't been kicked out of Ryker's body, first. Ever since that day in the truck,

I'd sworn off using violence to solve my problems, but it had certainly seemed like the right solution when I was lying there; when I had been forced to choose between Ryker and Billie.

While I was contemplating the depths I would go to for this person who I'd only known the better part of two weeks, Ava came around to check on us.

"So, Ava, I think there might be some holes in your theory." I did my best to fake a stern expression and placed my hands on my hips. Ava laughed and tilted her head to the side. "What're you on about now?"

"The foe is vanquished, wrongs have been righted and yet, here I stand."

"Ah... that. Are you sure you've tied up *all* of your loose ends?" Ava's eye gleamed with more intelligence than I was entirely comfortable with.

"Well, there is that needlepoint I never got around to."

Ava ignored me and tried another prompt.

"So, there's *nothing else* you wish you'd done, wished you *knew*?"

My mother's hunched-over form, dripping in blood, appeared before my eyes. The possibility that I was a killer had haunted me for years. I'd run away, never once daring to find out what had become of her. I hadn't even called an ambulance out of fear that it would implicate me in her murder. It didn't matter that I'd struck out in self-defence, or that she'd abused me for as long as I could remember. What mattered was the choice I'd made that day, which had proved I was no better than she was.

Ava was right. I had to know. "Will you come with me?"

Ava reached out her hand for mine. "Of course, Alex."

*

The house was exactly the same as I remembered it. Every faded windowsill; every dead blade of grass. The screen door hung open and the hinges whined as the wind jostled it. The cracked driveway was empty, except for where the occasional weed had broken through the asphalt. I took a deep breath and Ava squeezed my hand. "You can do this, Alex."

Before I could lose my nerve, I headed up the stairs and through the peeling wooden door. The sound of some game show murmured in the background, and the air was heavy with the smell of cigarettes and stale beer. I steeled myself and moved further into the house.

I wasn't sure if she would even still live here if she'd managed to survive that day, but there she was, comatose on the old moth-eaten couch.

I crunched my eyes shut and fought the barrage of memories that came flooding in. I could feel myself shaking, hear my shallow gasps for air. Then I heard Ava's soothing voice and felt her hand on my back. "It's ok, Alex. Just breath. Try to focus on something good. There must have been some happy memories here." The scent of my grandmother's apple pie suddenly washed over me. The sound of crinkling paper and carols playing in the background.

"Come on, Alex. It's your turn to open one."
My chubby little fingers aren't strong enough to untie the bright red bow. My father laughs.
"Here, let me help you with that, monkey."
He isn't sick yet. No tubes hang from his nose or his wrist. We're all together and smiling like the families in the commercials.

I open my eyes and try to imagine that day, the way the lights shone from the tree and the never-ending sweets that we ate. But that memory wasn't enough to wipe clean all the years, since.

I'd had my life, the one I deserved, taken from me by that excuse for a human being currently passed out in her own filth. She lay there, peacefully oblivious to the damage she'd done. Well, not anymore. I was relieved that I hadn't killed her; that I didn't have her blood on my hands. But at the same time, I couldn't stand the thought of her continuing to exist.

I took a step forward and I could almost feel the rage rolling off of me. Ava tried to hold me back, but I shook her off. I may not have been able to make her pay in the real world, but I could at least give her a dose of her own medicine. I plunged my head into hers and prepared to dole out justice.

When the images around me took shape, I saw that I was in a room with shag carpet and floral wallpaper. I could hear the whimpers of a little girl. Looking around, I noticed an old wooden dresser, a night table, and a small twin-sized bed. The blanket was a muted yellow that reminded me of Dijon mustard.

I took a peek under the bed and found the girl curled up in the corner furthest away from the open edges of the bed. She clutched her knees to her chest as she tried not to make a sound. The door banged open, and my head shot around to see my grandfather. I hadn't known him, but I'd seen photos. His face seethed with a familiar hatred I'd seen before, on another face.

"If I have to drag you outta there, it's gonna be much worse for you, girl."

The girl under the bed, my mother, didn't move a muscle.

"Five, four, three..." With each count, he took a menacing step closer. By the time he hit one, he was already on his knees, reaching under the bed. "And don't even think about going crying to your momma. If you do, I'll be sure to show her the strap too."

As his hands wrapped around one of her ankles, my mother became a wild animal. Frenzied by fear she kicked and screamed and clawed at the carpet, trying desperately to keep hold of her refuge. I knew all too well how the rest of this scene would play out and, in that moment, I took pity on her. I changed the scene to one of an empty parking lot, then stood up and left her there.

Growing up, my grandmother had never spoken about my grandfather, and now I knew why. It made me wonder how far back this chain of pain and suffering went. I took one last look down at my mother's motionless form on that couch. "I don't forgive you, but at least I understand now. *I* was never the problem. You wanted me to believe that everything was my fault, but now I know you were damaged. If only you'd gotten help, instead of becoming the very monster that you feared."

I finally felt like I could leave the past behind. I'm sure it would come back to haunt me every once in a while, but Nega-me had been silent lately, and I was hopeful that the rest of the skeletons in my closet could now consider themselves buried.

I looked for Broden at the centre a few times. I wanted to let him know that it was finally over, to try to end his anguish. Ava seemed to be enjoying what a softy I'd become.

After yet another unsuccessful visit to the centre, I stopped by Ava's family's place. She wasn't out back, and I hadn't had a chance to find out how her attempts to speak to her brother were going. Figuring she might be inside, waiting for him to head off to bed, I risked going in to see if I could find her.

This was my first time in the house while the lights were on and I was struck by how much it felt like a home, a real home. The majority of her family was gathered around the kitchen table. The dining area was divided from the cooking area by a short counter that doubled as a breakfast bar. Ava's father was doing the dishes while the rest of the family was putting the finishing touches to their Halloween costumes. They all laughed and teased each other. It was like something out of a storybook.

The wall behind them was covered in family photos, none of them the stiff, posed type where it's obvious a professional took them. These were all snapshots of genuine happiness. As I looked through them, some a little out of focus, some taken at strange angles, I realized that I didn't see Ava in any of them. I wondered if it made them too sad to have reminders of her around, and then I got angry. Ava was the kindest, most generous and most thoughtful person I had ever met. She deserved those twinges of sorrow on their part, if it meant that she was still remembered; still thought about.

Disappointed, I went back out into the yard to wait for Ava. I'd broken my rule and gotten what I deserved. I didn't plan to stick things out entirely on my own anymore, but that didn't mean that I should forget everything I knew before, either.

Since Ava didn't seem to be showing up any time soon, I decided to work on expanding my fast travel network for a couple of hours. Now that I finally had free time, and hadn't heard the siren call of any bright lights, I'd been spending my time pushing the boundaries of my "telegraph grid" further and further out. After finishing with Canada, I was going to try to figure out the logistics of going overseas. I wasn't sure if knowing the way, say, to Lake Bled in Slovenia, meant that I could zap myself there again, or if I'd have to make sure there was a flight available, first. But I'd worry about that when I got to it. For now, I was enjoying travelling the vast forests, the deep waters, and the mountainous peaks of my home.

When I finally started to lose the light near the confusingly named Peter Pond Lake, I headed back to the city. Since Saskatchewan was two hours behind, it was already close to the time that Billie tended to turn in. Popping into the living room, I played one of my many theme songs to let her know I was there.

♫ "Only in dreams, we see what it means." ♪

While I waited, I plopped down on the couch to finish up the movie that Billie and Taco were enjoying. To be honest, Taco was enjoying being brushed — not the vocal stylings of acapella bands competing for a national championship.

As the three of us sat "together", I found myself quite satisfied with the halfway existence I'd found myself in. I didn't know how long I would be here, but I was determined to savour every moment of it.

About the Author

This debut novel highlights the unique first-person perspective technique this author has been developing through shorter works. Everything by J.McDonald is written in this style to enable the reader to choose the gender and overall appearance of the main character for themselves. This illustrates that surface appearance is not what matters. What *is* important are the thoughts, actions, experiences, and feelings of the person beneath.

J.McDonald has a B.A. Honours degree in English and an M.A. in Novel Writing.

For more on the author, please visit jmcdonaldworks.com. For pictures of the author's cats, and the occasional book recommendation, follow on Instagram @j.mcdonaldworks.

www.ingramcontent.com/pod-product-compliance
Lightning Source LLC
Chambersburg PA
CBHW061149210726
48294CB00006B/1627